THE MOMENT WE SHARED

KATHLEEN MARY O'BRIEN

KATHLEENMOBRIENBOOKS

A WORLD OF LOVE SERIES

Love stories set in the most memorable places in the world. Say yes to love—in the romantic south of France, on the breathtaking coast of Spain, amid the lush hills of Ireland . . . or wherever love will find you.

Love gives naught but itself and takes naught but from itself. ~ Khalil Gibran

CHAPTER ONE

$\mathcal{I}$t seemed romance was everywhere. In the quiet villages tucked into the cliffs along the *Côte Vermeille*, in the soft rustle of the vegetation on the hillsides above the sea, in the ripple of the waves as they gently rolled in to caress the sand, in the clusters of homes creviced into the hills around Collioure, France—romance was in their wine, the presentation of their food, and the pull of the French language, in fact, everything screamed romance. And it all reminded Sammy Driscoll that true love had been out of her reach for too long.

This was Sammy's first visit to France and she was confused— until this weekend her lack of a permanent relationship hadn't mattered to her. Her busy life in Barcelona didn't allow for romance and that had been fine with her. Even her involvement with Javier had been tentative, a convenient placeholder, a six-month tryst to fill the empty spaces in her life. And their liaison hadn't seemed to matter to him when he said goodbye to her as she boarded the train in

Barcelona two days ago. A farewell that felt final, and a farewell she'd initiated when she'd discovered he'd lied to her. When she returned to Barcelona after the wedding she wondered if he would be waiting to lure her back. Not that she really cared. His charm wouldn't work this time, and she chastised herself for believing him in the first place; she'd known from the beginning he was fickle and his proclivities had always been to walk away. She'd wasted months with him, thinking he might be the one to change her mind about love and relationships—then she discovered he was still married and that fact slammed the door on everything.

Sammy shook her head to clear her mind of Javier and to vanquish any melancholy that still resided since arriving in France. Barcelona, her home, was different; it pulsed with a vibrancy that made each day full of expectation and activity, so much so that it had replaced the need for domesticity and she rarely had to think about the absence of a stable or long-term partner. These romantic stirrings were new and they were not her anyway—she was bold, alive with energy and passion—and unapologetically so. She'd only come to France to support her cousin and his bride, and here she was mooning like a lovesick puppy. But, she reasoned, it wasn't hard with a couple like Ian and Cassie. Their union was serendipitous; a chance reconnection that Sammy was certain had contributed to her current romantic state of mind. A state she hoped to abandon as soon as the event-filled wedding weekend was over.

It was Saturday and the wedding ceremony had ended. Everyone was immersed in the élan of the reception in the crowded special event room of *Auberge Sur Le Mer*—a spectacular inn on the Mediterranean coast in southern France.

Sammy watched her cousin and his bride move through the room greeting guests: Ian, smashing in his tux, and Cassie, stunning in a fit-and-flare ivory gown, a bohemian dream with a butterfly embroidered train that when a breeze caught it looked like the butterflies were scattering in the wind. A gown perfect for this romantic spot, for this romantic night.

Ian and Cassie continued moving through the room accepting congratulations, but each time Sammy had tried to include her best wishes another couple pulled them away. So instead, she grabbed a glass of champagne from a passing waiter, sipped, and let the fizz tickle her nose, and the bubbles —as they slid down her throat—calm her earlier disquiet. She should be feeling the joy that weddings elicit and though she was happy for Ian she didn't know any of the other guests except Jim Picard, a good-looking, testosterone-fueled friend of Ian's who was currently surrounded by a group of besotted women. Chest out, he appeared confident and cocky by the apparent feline adoration. The women flitted around doing the bidding for his attention. They giggled or touched his hand, flipping their hair as they did. Seduction in their eyes, seduction their end game.

Sammy glanced around the room, looking for someone to talk to, but noticed everyone was clustered in groups or coupled up. Sammy rarely lacked confidence and usually had no problem carrying on conversations with strangers, but tonight for some reason she felt a bit out-of-sorts then berated herself, she needed to get a grip. She took another sip of champagne and to collect her thoughts she walked to the quieter side of the room where floor-to-ceiling windows overlooked the inn's patio, the pool area, and in the distance where the night sky met the sea, the Mediterranean sparkled from the brilliance of a full moon. Seeing the ocean relaxed her. She fell in love with the Mediterranean the first time she caught a glimpse of it on her inbound flight into Barcelona years ago. Since most of Ohio where Sammy grew up was landlocked, the sea had become her touchstone, a place that gave her serenity whenever life threw its weight around.

Well beyond the resort's property and off to the right where land jutted outwards, another village on the *Côte Vermeille* rested at the edge of the sea and flickering lights confirmed the existence of other lives where couples and families gathered. She sighed and stared out into the darkness briefly catching her reflection in the window. The person who stared back at her seemed like a stranger. She still hadn't gotten used to her short, cropped hair. She'd cut off her long brunette locks on a whim—a transitory interlude a few years ago when a desire to erase part of her past caught her by surprise. A moment of clarity that resulted in spiked hair, weight loss, and dark circles under her eyes.

Sammy rested her forehead against the cool glass window, letting the cold and stable surface help her find her footing. She watched as a brisk fall breeze teetered copper tiki torches lightly anchored to the edges of the inn's patio. A few couples lingered outside until the September wind caused them to huddle together, bracing themselves from its intrusion into their intimate moments. It ruffled the women's skimpy dresses and caused the men to turn up collars on their suit coats. Sammy watched as one of the men took off his coat and wrapped it around his companion, touching her hair, and lightly kissing her nose. The scene made her wistful and for a second she remembered a similar moment from her past and felt the deepening sadness it always caused, but she let it go. Still, she wondered, why did everything in France seem to make her yearn for romance; everything she saw, everything she experienced let her know that romance could be in repose just waiting for her. But she knew it wasn't to be—it had been once, but that was a life-time ago.

The conversation in the room suddenly quieted and everyone watched as Ian and Cassie said their goodbyes. Sammy caught Ian's eye and waved to him over the crowd. He blew her a kiss as he and Cassie left the reception. She adored both of them, but chided herself—love or marriage weren't things she was looking for now. She didn't really need the love of her life. At this time in her life, all she wanted was to be able to trust someone enough so that they hung around for more than a couple of weeks.

But then—did she really?

She laughed.

"What's so funny?"

She turned. Jim Picard stood next to her perusing her body with a glint in his eyes perhaps thinking she was ripe for seduction. She wasn't. Not that she didn't find Jim interesting in an annoying egotistical, condescending male way. She'd known and been hurt by too many men like him before. But she'd flirt with him. Why not? She needed to repair this long romance-filled weekend with some fun.

He asked her again, "What were you laughing about?"

"Nothing really. I'm happy for my cousin, and I'm loving that Cassie, but marriage." Sammy shook her head. "Not my thing."

"Not mine either," Jim said, and shouted out to the newly-weds as they left, "Don't do anything I wouldn't do." Then he turned back to Sammy and said, "You're looking mighty fine tonight."

As he had earlier in the day and since she'd arrived Thursday night, Jim tried to entice her with alcohol, his forgettable charm, or his bank account. Each time she'd gotten restless and ventured out of her room to explore the grounds of the inn or walk down to the beach, or every time she tried to find time to herself because everyone was coupled up, he was there. He was easy on the eyes, but she had heard all about him years ago from Ian and again more than once this weekend.

"Stay away from him, Sammy," Ian had said. "He's a nice enough guy, heck, he's my best friend, but I've seen him ruin relationships—his own and others."

For some reason, it was the 'and others' that now intrigued her.

Of course, she would take heed, but what harm could it be to have some fun with him. A change of pace might do her some good during this couple-filled celebration, and necessary it seemed, to vanquish longings for love. After all, Jim was a handsome guy with penetrating blue eyes and sporting a scruffy unshaven strong jawline; he was obviously fit and looked dapper in his tux. Plus, there was that jet he kept talking about parked not too far from here, less than an hour away. She wouldn't mind seeing more of France and, after all, he had offered. His reputation for being a ladies' man made her feel safe—until Javier, that type of man had never appealed to her. Jim seemed harmless and she suspected his macho exterior was a cover. She liked a man who was confident, didn't get too serious, could hold his own with a strong woman, and still have fun. Jim might fit the bill for what she needed after this weekend full of love and commitment. She shrugged off previous ruminations of romance. Damn weddings.

Jim touched her arm and reached for her empty glass. "Can I get you another?"

"Yes, but not champagne; a real drink. But not here. Somewhere more exciting." Her long evening walks around Collioure, which was a lovely village with its harbor setting and imposing castle, didn't exactly fill her adventurous soul and even Cassie's restaurant was too sedate for Sammy tonight.

Jim seemed to agree with her when he scratched his chin and said, "There's a shortage of nightlife in this town. Most places don't cut it."

"How about your earlier offer to show me around France in your jet? Ian and Cassie have left. You could take me to Paris for a nightcap."

"Now?"

"Why not? I've never been. Have you?" She'd grown weary of this crowd of people, this event, and was tired of feeling lovesick. Sammy stifled a yawn, looped her arm around Jim's and said, "Let's go before I fall asleep from boredom."

"Wait here. I need to find my driver".

* * *

AN HOUR AND HALF LATER, they landed at a small airport on the outskirts of Paris. While inflight, Jim had ordered a limo and as they got in, he instructed the driver to cruise around Paris before dropping them at the avenue *Champs-Élysées—*

where Jim said he'd heard there was a plethora of some of the best bars and clubs in Paris.

As the limo crept along the side streets at an unhurried pace, Sammy marveled at the spectacle of Paris at a time of the night when the rest of the world was asleep. And yet Paris was not; the City sparkled like no other city Sammy had ever seen. It was as if all the stars in the cloudless night sky rained down their light on the City, a city clearly lit for romance. And here she thought she'd left all of that behind at the wedding.

They meandered along a road that ran along the Seine. The river rippled and shimmered in the moonlight and when they crept slowly past the *Pont des Arts* pedestrian bridge that crossed the Seine, gaslights like tall candles stretched across the span illuminating couples strolling, arms tight around each other, stopping to kiss or leaning onto the railing of the bridge as they stared out in the distance where a peek of the top of Eiffel Tower glistened. Sammy sighed at its beauty and felt her emotions slowly soften to the place she didn't want it to go. She opened her window to clear her mind, but Jim seemed to sense a mood shift and put his arm around her.

No, that would not do, so she moved Jim's arm off her shoulder and nudged him to the other side of the car. Paris could have its romance, tonight she wanted excitement. "Enough of this; I'm ready for this night of fun to begin." She tapped the driver on the shoulder and said, "Onward James."

The limo dropped them in the heart of the Champs-Élysées and Jim offered his arm. "You asked for it so, take hold and better hang on, honey, this is going to be a busy night."

The first nightclub they entered was packed; the dance floor filled elbow-to-elbow with people twisting, turning, flaying arms out to their sides and over their heads—it was dark, chaotic, and the right vibe for what Sammy needed. The music was loud, fast, and a bass guitar boomed over the room drumming a beat that made Sammy's feet itch to dance. Spotlights hung from the ceilings and changed colors whenever the music tempo changed.

Jim leaned into her. "Drink, first?"

"Sure."

They made their way over to the bar but stopped short when they saw the line of people waiting to get a drink. They turned around to find a table, but all street-level tables were filled, and upstairs it was so crowded that people lined the balcony railing drinking, laughing, and pointing at other patrons. The energy tugged at Sammy and since it appeared it would take them too long to get a drink and there was nowhere to sit, she needed to dance—right now. She grabbed Jim and pulled him towards the dance floor.

He pulled back. "Hey, I need a drink before I dance," he shouted above the noise.

She dropped his hand and stared at him. "Are you going to be difficult? Look around you." She spread her arms out. "Does it look like we can get a drink any time soon?"

He glanced around the room. "All right, but look, I need one, so if the line doesn't thin out, we're leaving and going somewhere where I *can* get one."

They wedged themselves among the masses and danced. For the next hour, they never took a break and Jim seemed to have forgotten about needing that drink. He was lively, flirty, fun, and a darn good dancer. Sammy flirted back and had an equally good time. She only became irritated when during a slower dance she felt his fingers creep tighter around her waist and he pulled her closer. He started to nuzzle her neck and when his hand squeezed her backside, she pushed him away, smacked his hands, and said loudly, but with a smile, "Knock it off, bud."

Finally, after another hour or so, he abruptly stopped dancing, just stood in front of her, his face flushed, beads of perspiration dotted his forehead. When she kept dancing, he reached over and held her arms down so she had to stop and said, "Look I'm not dancing anymore until I get a drink. Let's find somewhere else."

"You're no fun," she chided him, but she needed one, too.

They left, but most of the bars they walked by were as crowded as the one they'd just left. Eventually, they found a bistro that served liquor, but after a few drinks, Sammy was bored and decided she'd had enough. "This place is dead. At least the other place had music. Let's head back to Collioure."

He shook his finger at her and said, "You give up too easily, girl. We've hours before this town closes up. Preference?"

"Dancing," Sammy said. "I need music." And she slid off the barstool, took a few steps, did a few ballet moves, then a quick tap dance.

He threw his head back and laughed. "You're an original all right. A bit offbeat, but I like it." He gulped his drink, slid off his chair, and said, "Let's bounce."

They visited other bars, a few clubs, talked to people they didn't know, they drank, and continued to dance. Sammy felt like herself again: vibrant, upbeat, and happy to be single. This was exactly what she needed: freedom, no commitment, just fun, no complications.

After several hours Jim said, "Hey, what you say we head

up to the *Arc de Triomphe*? It's only a few blocks up. I've never been." Jim reached for her hand. "You game?"

"I'm beat and I need to get back to pack. My train leaves," she said and looked at her phone, "oh, not for eleven hours." The evening had been the perfect diversion; the alcohol had lightened her, dimmed all of her previous longings for romance and Jim seemed to be behaving. "Sure, it seems we have time. So, as you say, let's bounce."

She ignored his outreached hand and felt so unencumbered that when they got outside, she ran, danced, and skipped on her way toward the top of the Champs-Élysées. This freedom of the night, the steadiness she gained in the past few hours after a day of confusion about romantic feelings, flooded her body with lightness so much so that memories of her childhood flooded back to a time when she'd realized she loved dancing more than anything in the world.

She was about eight and for years had been begging her parents to let her take ballet. They finally allowed her to take one class. "Only one Sammy, we are not going to waste time on dance, you need to concentrate on school," her father insisted. She was only eight for God's sake and her brothers had always been allowed to do whatever they wanted. But she promised her father: school first. The dance class was ten lessons and by the time she finished, she knew it was the only thing she would ever want to do. After that, her parents saw how much she loved it and as long as her grades were good they let her continue, so she took every type of dance class that was available whether it was ballet, tap, jazz, modern— any. Even at such a young age, she'd recognized the freedom dance gave her. All her childhood awkwardness and inhibitions fled. The control was hers. Anything she wanted her body to do, any music that was played, her body responded, she never fell, never tripped, just flowed like she was doing now. To prove it to herself, as she reached the end of the street, she did a pirouette and then *Grande Jeté*— a long horizontal jump, starting from one leg and landing on the other. From a distance, Jim cheered and Sammy bowed to his enthusiasm.

"You're pretty good at that, you should be onstage," Jim yelled.

Sammy shook her head at him in disbelief then laughed and said, "I am. Didn't Ian tell you?" She twirled and yelled back, "I'm on stage every night, and I love it."

Jim caught up with her, stood next to her, and said, "What do you mean?"

"It's my profession. I'm a dancer at a flamenco club."

He winked. "No pole dancing? Because I'd love to see that."

Typical male response. Disgusted, she rolled her eyes, shook her head, ignored him, and walked to the intersection. Across the street, spotlights encased in concrete around the bottom of the Arc de Triomphe lit up its façade, highlighting stone statues and carvings. The Arc and everything around it glistened, more proof that this beautiful city with its plethora of lights was made for the night sky.

Jim walked up next to her and said, "Pretty impressive, huh?"

"C'mon," she said and tugged at the sleeve of his coat. "Let's go over there."

They waited at the curb and watched as cars from twelve arterials converged into a ten-lane traffic circle. Traffic whizzed by, horns honked, the line of cars was endless, flashing by at speeds that seemed too fast for the road.

Jim shrugged and said, "It's too crazy. We can't get there. Let's bag this."

But Sammy was determined, so she pulled Jim with her as they walked across a crosswalk to the other side of the Champs-Élysées, kitty-corner from the Arc. They stood, trying to figure out a way to cross over.

"Let's go," Jim insisted.

"There's got to be a way to get over there," Sammy asserted. "Don't be a downer."

"But look," he said, pointing to the Arc, "there's no way."

"There's a tunnel over there," an unfamiliar voice behind them said. "You go through and it brings you up on the central island."

They both turned to thank him, but the man had already walked away.

"Hey, *Monsieur*." Sammy felt giddy and wanted to try out a bit of French. When he kept walking, she hollered, "*Merci, beaucoup, tu es très gentil.*"

Over his shoulder, the man yelled back, "*Vous es un idiot.*"

She looked at Jim and said, "Well, that was rude."

"You used the term for 'you' wrong. Tu is familiar vous is for everyone else."

"Tu, vous who cares." And she giggled.

Jim ruffled her hair and said, "I think you might be a bit drunk."

She felt playful and ruffled his hair and said, "Nope, feeling better than I did hours ago." She ran toward the entrance to the tunnel stopped, turned and yelled, "Well, maybe a little drunk."

Jim caught up with her and they went through the tunnel to the center island where the Arc rose above them. They walked around the perimeter gazing, mesmerized, and feeling dwarfed by its size.

Looking up, Sammy said, "We have an arched structure like this in Barcelona, but it's half this size." She stretched her arms out to her side and twirled around, laughing. "But . . . this . . . is . . . spectacular."

Jim reached out, grabbed her arm, and said, "Whoa, slow down there little filly, you'll fall over."

She almost burst out laughing. Little filly? Who was this guy?

Then he pulled her close and whispered in her ear. "So, there's one of these in Barcelona, eh? Well, I might have to see that. How about it? Would you show me around?"

When she didn't answer, he tried to kiss her. She pushed him away and he tried again. Well, there, he'd done it. Messed with her euphoria. She moved away from him. "Okay, I'm done. Let's go back."

He sighed. "Look, I'm sorry."

"I'm sure you are, but it's time for me to get back anyway. And it seems you don't stick to your promises of staying within boundaries."

"Ah, come on. You're overreacting. I thought you were flirting with me."

"That might be, but I told you not to expect anything. Let's go, please." She walked toward the exit with Jim following close behind her.

"Look, I said I'm sorry. It's something I'm working on. I promised my fiancée—"

She stopped, stunned, and turned around, facing him, she said, "You have a fiancée? Are you effing kidding me?"

He shrugged; eyes downcast.

"You're disgusting," she said and walked away.

He followed close behind her. "Wait. Damnit, wait. Don't be a bitch. I'm trying to be a better man. It's just . . . "

She walked faster. She couldn't even think. He was like every other guy. If there had been any residual feelings of romance, they dissolved and all she could think about was how sorry she felt for his fiancée and any other unsuspecting women who fell for a man without her eyes wide open. True, there were some good men out there, but Jim Picard certainly wasn't one of them.

They said very little to each other on the trip back, but when she got out of the car once they were back at the inn in Collioure, she motioned for him to roll down the window. "Go back to your fiancée, Jim. It seems that if you loved her enough to ask her to marry you, you should love her enough to be faithful. If not, you need to let her go." He started to say something, but she shook her head, turned, and walked into the inn.

* * *

HOURS LATER, packed, and eager to get home, Sammy boarded the train for Barcelona. Wanting solitude for her journey she walked through the train until she found a seat in a sparsely occupied car, put her overnight bag on the shelf above, dropped her purse on the aisle seat, and sat on the window seat ready to relax. She'd have several hours on the train to get rid of the headache that materialized while she was packing—hangover headache or lack of sleep either way she'd have time to rest and mentally ease back into her life; a life before she let romance take her captive and fill her with a longing she couldn't explain and before this fun evening had been spoiled by another egotistical male. She needed this travel time to reconnect and appreciate her life in Barcelona: a career as a dancer that she loved, friends who were loyal and enjoyed adventure as much as she did, a home that filled her, and a city she adored. She shelved this weekend of confusion and disappointment, stored it away until she was ready to figure out why she'd allowed thoughts and longings of love to confound her into thinking that's what she wanted again. She didn't. But that was for another day—for now, she'd let her anger at Jim and the weekend's melancholy regress to the back of her mind. All men, save for one, had disappointed her. She settled into her seat, leaned her head against the window, tucked her legs under her, and she'd just closed her eyes as the train moved out of the station when she felt someone tap her on the shoulder.

"Excuse me. Samantha? It's Samantha, isn't it?"

She stared at his face and it was all there. All there in crushing detail: the memory of the best and worst day of her life, a day that had branded and defined her existence these last few years. "Uh, yes, it is." She leaned forward in her seat to see him better and try to regain her composure.

"May, I?" He pointed to the seat next to her.

She moved her purse and said, "Yes, of course, doctor. But I'm sorry I don't remember your name."

"Roan. Roan Adair." He sat down, then flushed and seemed nervous. "I don't mean to intrude, but . . . how are you doing? I've thought about you a lot since that night."

"Oh, I'm fine really. You needn't have worried about me." She was flustered and trying to breathe through the grief that filled her throat and threatened to spill into her eyes. And she was trying so hard without success to push down the memory of her husband lying on the floor of the basilica still, lifeless, and with this doctor crouching over him, frantically trying to save his life.

"I'm sorry. I see I've upset you." He touched her arm and she instinctively pulled back. Not because of him, but because his touch was so connected with the life and death of her husband, her husband of just over two hours when the deadly aneurysm struck. The doctor rose to leave, his face visibly disturbed, and remorseful.

He looked so uncomfortable she insisted, "Wait, please sit." She cleared her throat and said, "I don't talk about that night much." She clasped her hands together and stared at them. "I don't talk about Peter much either." Then she looked at him. "You took me by surprise."

This wasn't the first time she'd faced someone who knew about Peter and what happened, but except for a few of her friends, it was the first time in a long time she'd faced someone who'd been there. Since then, she'd not been able to bring herself to go back to the mountains of *Monserrat*, the Abbey, the monastery, even the basilica where they'd been married—places she loved and places where she had once found so much peace. She hadn't been able to talk to Sister Mercedes whom she'd known since moving to Barcelona nearly a decade ago nor Father Thomas who had married them then presided over Peter's funeral.

"I understand. Truly, I can leave if you like," Dr. Adair said.

"No, no. I'm okay." She again motioned for him to sit and smiled, trying to make him see she was fine—of course, she wasn't. "So, what brings you to France?"

"Actually, I'm heading back to Barcelona from a quick

holiday in Marseilles. I don't know if you remember, I'm a doctor on one of the cruise lines that depart out of Barcelona. The ship I'm assigned to doesn't sail until Saturday but I need to get back to prepare."

"I remember very little about any conversation with anyone that night nor the days and weeks following." Again, she stared down at her hands, took a deep breath, turned, and tried smiling at him. "It's been three years now, you know. Or maybe you don't, but most of the details of that night have morphed together into an almost dreamlike memory." She sighed and said, "Sometimes I even allow myself to believe it never happened." Right now, she was desperate to erase the memory that seeing Dr. Adair had evoked so she frantically tried to focus on a subject that would give her control of the conversation. "A cruise doctor? Really? I didn't know doctors were assigned to cruises. But of course." She paused and continued, "I never thought much about it; I've never been on a cruise."

He cleared his throat. "I had a private practice in the states with a partner but left about four years ago. I'd heard about these types of posts from a patient and it came at a time when I'd been thinking of taking a sabbatical." He glanced at her. "Burn out. It can happen in my profession."

Then there seemed like nothing to say. He took off his glasses, rubbed his eyes, and attempted to clean them with a handkerchief from his pocket. The silence separated them like the dark cloud it was. But she needed to be kind; she could tell he was nervous. She struggled for something to say. "I dance. The flamenco. In Barcelona."

He nodded then seemed to sense her anxiety. "Well, look I should let you get back to your nap." He stood and reached out to shake her hand. "I'm happy to see you and that you're coping."

She took his hand, but she really didn't know what to say. Her standard 'it was nice seeing you' after casual encounters wasn't appropriate this time, so she reached for the only thing she could think of. "Well, thank you for checking on me, Dr. Adair. It's kind of you."

He nodded, gave her a brief smile, and walked toward the entrance to the other train cars, rocking back and forth and touching seat tops for balance as he went.

She leaned her head back, gripped the armrests, closed her eyes, and strained to will the tears away; to vanquish the images and emotion the doctor had unearthed after years of attempted suppression and denial. Peter had been her love, her only love, her never to be found again love. And then he was gone. No honeymoon, no move back to the states like they'd planned, no white picket fence, no travels, no anniversaries, no dogs, no kids, nothing but a bleak emptiness that had never been filled. She'd tried filling that vacuum with friends, dance, and activity. She'd been determined to fill each day with some new adventure, anything to keep her mind and body occupied. Whether it was skiing, backpacking, or hiking the Pyrenees; biking the *Tour de France* route through Andorra, or walking the *Camino de Santiago* through Spain into Portugal, or, well, anything to keep her busy. And it had worked to fill the moments, but never completely the days and certainly not the nights. When a year had gone by after Peter's death and she was still struggling to keep her sanity and move on with her life, she'd made a vow to never to love again, to try to be happy with the help of friends, to allow adventures to fill the time and empty spaces—but without love. Sex—yes, companionship—yes, but love—no—love meant heartache.

Damn the doctor. He'd opened that closed door.

Determined to block out her brief conversation with him, she closed her eyes again and only woke when they were pulling into Barcelona.

CHAPTER TWO

*S*ammy stretched, still a bit disoriented and groggy from her nap that had been filled with images of Peter and snippets of the life they could have shared. It was always the same when she dreamt about him; she'd wake up thinking he was still alive like right now he was home waiting for her to return from her trip.

But he wasn't.

As the train slowed into the station, Sammy looked out the window. The rail terminal was busy, people milled around waiting for the next train or walked pulling their luggage behind them; people waved, laughed, kissed each other either bidding goodbye or saying hello. Active, alive, a thirst for life —this was so Barcelona and she felt the excitement this city always gave her. She couldn't wait to get off the train, get home, and plunge into her life again.

The train rolled to a complete stop and Sammy stood to gather her luggage, but when she bent down to grab her purse off the seat, she caught a glimpse of Javier through the train's window frantically pacing along the platform; she watched him stop a few cars up from hers, peer into the windows of the train then turn and head further away from her. But she knew he would come back this way soon. He didn't give up easily, he was a headstrong Latin man who demanded what he wanted and until last week she'd given in to him because it was what she had needed. Seeing him, especially after her encounter with the doctor, was something she wouldn't allow.

She approached the exit door of her train car, glanced back toward her seat and saw Javier still walking the other way. Relieved, she tightened her grip on the suitcase and began to maneuver it across the narrow space between her train car and the vestibule. She glanced into the forward car and saw the doctor walking toward her, entering from his. She started to turn to go the other way when Dr. Adair saw her.

He tilted his head and said, "Ah, here we are again."

"Yes, here we are." She had no choice now so she moved forward and struggled to lift her bag over the threshold between her train car and the exit-way. It wobbled and started to teeter.

The doctor grabbed it as it started to fall and said, "Here, let me help." He let go of his bags, lifted her bag and carried it down the stairs to the station platform, helped her down, then went back and retrieved his. Out of the corner of her eye, Sammy saw Javier begin to make his way toward her.

She turned her back, hoping he hadn't seen her. The doctor exited the train car and stood next to her, and said, "Samantha?"

"Yes, Dr. Adair."

"Do you need a ride home or do you have a car here?"

"Thank you, but I'll grab a taxi." She started to walk away, but he continued to talk.

"I'd be happy to give you a lift. I keep a car in Barcelona in case I need it. It's parked here at the station."

She feared Javier was near and decided to be safe, so she said, "That would be wonderful. And you can call me, Sammy. Everyone does."

And as Javier got closer, she tucked her free hand into the doctor's arm and walked beside him. She heard Javier call her name then as they walked away, he hollered, "Sammy, wait! I'm divorcing her, my love. We will be together soon."

His voice reverberated off the concrete walls of the station, echoing through the train tunnel; clearly the doctor heard everything. He glanced at her and she said, "Long story, but I need to get out of here."

THEY FOUND the doctor's car, a late model BMW that, though immaculate, looked like it had seen better days. The passenger door was a different color than the rest of the car, and there was a small dent on top of the trunk.

"Sorry about the car. The cruise line doesn't pay like private practice. My wife joked that she looked better after all the miles I put on her than this car." He laughed and explained, "But the engine is only a click over forty-thousand miles; it's in tip-top shape and it gets me where I need to go." He lifted their bags into the back seat.

"It's fine Dr. Adair. I appreciate the ride."

He walked around and opened the passenger side door for

her and said, "Tell you what. I'll call you Sammy if you call me Roan. Deal?"

Calling him by his first name suggested a familiarity that made her uneasy given that the day her husband died was the first time they'd met. And after today she had no plans on seeing him for any reason. The memory he unintentionally educed was much too painful. Any future interaction or friendship with him was out of the question, but she didn't want to be rude. She paused before getting in the car, looked up at him, and said, "Sure. Roan, it is then." She slid into her seat, dropped her purse on the floor, reached across the console, and opened his door for him.

"Why, thank you." He seemed surprised, smiled at her as he settled in his seat, and started the engine.

Opening the door for the doctor was a reflex; a habit she'd developed for Peter after the first time he'd done it for her. She remembered how he'd laughed at her astonishment and chided her, 'Sammy dear, hasn't anyone ever done that for you?' He'd always called her Sammy dear, no matter where they were or who they were with. She'd loved that about him. She'd loved everything about him.

"Occasionally my wife would do that for me, too," the doctor said then took off his glasses and tossed them into the console. "Can't drive with these. Farsighted."

Once they exited the parking garage, she asked him, "How does your wife like Barcelona? Or does she travel on the ship with you?"

He shifted in his seat, turned to check traffic coming on the highway before merging, and said, "She liked it okay. There were other things she didn't. She's no longer my wife and much like yours, that's a long story." He ran a hand through his sandy-colored hair, which she noticed, looked like the tips had been dipped in bleach or like he'd spent some recent time in the sun. She waited for more information about his wife, but his jaw was tight and his body language told her he did not want to talk about it any further.

As the silence between them became uncomfortable, she said, "Would you like directions to my place?"

He cleared his throat, adjusted his review mirror, glanced at her, smiled, and said, "Yes, I suppose that's important. I seem to remember you live in Barceloneta by the beach. Are you still there?"

"Yes, I'm still there. I had planned on moving, but . . . " She wasn't sure why she hadn't moved after Peter died. A fresh start was what she'd needed, but the timing had never seemed right and she loved its location next to the beach, so she'd stayed. She gave Roan directions then looking to fill the silence she asked, "Where is your cruise ship headed this time?"

"Parts of Italy, Malta, and Greece. I'll probably stay on the ship most of the cruise this time. I've done this cruise many times and, although, it's one of my favorites, I have a lot of work to catch up on."

"What type of work?" She assumed all his time would be taken up by treating patients.

"In addition to seeing patients, I'm doing a series of articles for a journal on travel medicine, ailments, diseases, and psychological impacts, etc." He gave her a wry smile. "Not the most exciting research for anyone not in the medical profession, but for me it's fascinating."

She was unsure how to respond because it certainly sounded boring, Sammy never liked science or anything to do with medicine, and after Peter died, she avoided it. But not to be rude, she searched for commonality, a way to connect while they rode to her house. "I'm kind of a research nut myself, but mainly travel sites and activities around Spain. This past summer I talked two of my friends into walking the *Camino de Santiago* through Spain into Portugal. It took us a month. We stayed in the villages along the way. Except for the crowds of people, the traffic, and commercialism it was one of the best adventures."

"Really?" He sounded dubious.

She had to laugh because she realized her description of the trip didn't sound like much fun. "Well," she paused trying to figure out why she had loved it so much, then said, "I spent priceless time with my friends, every small village was steeped in history so we learned a lot, and the food, like all of Spain, was to die for." She turned and studied him. "This is a very special country. But then you must know that you've lived here for a while."

He glanced at her, sighed, and admitted, "I haven't explored much. I'm on the ship a lot of the time during the cruise season which can be from March through December. So, is this trek you took something I should do?"

"I'd say do part of it. If you like mountains, spectacular scenery, and wildlife do the part through the Pyrenees. It starts just over the border in France and on the route you can stop in the midst of Spain's Basque country. You can go through Pamplona which is a feast for the eyes and," she paused, then added, "the stomach."

"How so? When I think of Pamplona I only think of Hemingway, bulls racing and fighting, and I admit that doesn't interest me at all."

"Oh, Pamplona is much more than that; it's the perfect wandering around the city. Hemingway wrote about it and loved it. Taking in the sites, stopping and nibbling *pinchos* in each bar is the best."

He glanced at her, raising his eyebrows. "Pinchos?"

She noticed his eyes for the first time—brown, a deep brown, deep-set with long eyelashes that most women would kill to have. Interesting—without his glasses, she could see them and decided he wasn't a bad looking man. Not that she was looking.

"Pinchos are similar to tapas. They're small slices of bread or toast topped with a variety of goodies and are usually secured with toothpicks so they're easy to pick up."

"Sounds like they'd be good with some Spanish wine. Now, that's something I've discovered about Spain. Their reds are first rate."

"True that. But you should try a gin and tonic sometime. It's become the national drink of sorts. And nothing like the ones you get in the states."

"I'll have to do that."

They made small talk until minutes later when he slowed the car.

"Well, here we are." He turned onto the street where Sammy lived. There was nowhere to park so he stopped in the roadway parallel to a line of parked cars. She reached down, picked up her purse, and opened her door anxious to get inside her building hoping to avoid an awkward goodbye.

"Thank you so much, Dr. Adair. I mean Roan. It was so kind of you to give me a lift."

She got out, opened the back door to get her bag, but he'd already taken it out. He walked around the car toward her as another car pulled up behind them, he waved at it to go by and she realized he was going to try to carry on their conversation. A conversation she very much wanted to leave in the car and forgotten. Anxiety about how to say goodbye to this doctor and their collectively sad past began to prickle so she quickly said, "Goodbye and thanks." She grabbed her bag from him and turned to go inside the building, but he caught her before she could get inside.

"My pleasure, Sammy. If you ever need a doctor, give me a call," he said reaching into his pocket, then he must have realized how that struck her because he stuttered, "I mean, well, here's my card. I don't know many people in Barcelona. The first year I was here I went home to the states every chance I had to placate my wife but since the divorce, I've been a bit of a recluse doing research. So, if you are ever so inclined, give me a call."

No, she wouldn't be doing that, but she took it anyway. "I'll keep it handy. Have a good cruise and good luck with your research."

And she rushed inside.

CHAPTER THREE

"Seeing him was a shock for sure," Sammy said and took a sip of her gin and tonic.

Danele did the same then said, "That bites. What'd you say?"

Ciara, made a disapproving sound and said as she grabbed a cracker and chunk of *manchego*, "What'd you expect her to say? Gee, doc, it's so nice to see you so you can remind me of the night my husband died."

Sammy's cringed and Ciara touched her arm. "Sorry, Sam, that was crass. But you must've been gutted." Then she looked pointedly at Danele and said, "I think she probably ignored him and she kept her eyes closed and he moved on. Right, Sammy?"

Sammy shifted and leaned back against the bottom of the couch. She and three friends were sitting on the floor in her apartment eating, drinking, and talking about Sammy's return trip from France two days ago instead of discussing the book they were supposed to have read. The coffee table was filled with drinks and food, the books forgotten and pushed to the side. "Actually, no. I didn't recognize him at first. Then when I did, images of Peter lying on the floor that night messed me up and I couldn't get my act together. Somehow I wound up inviting him to sit next to me."

"No! Why?" Ciara asked.

"Oh, I don't' know. He caught me off guard and he was nervous so I felt bad. Then we talked for a bit—at least I think we did. Once he left and went back into his train car," she closed her eyes, shook her head, "you're right, I was gutted. I'm not even sure why I let him take me home later except Javier was bearing down on us." This wasn't what she wanted to do this Tuesday night. For a change, she wanted to talk about the book and forget the weekend, but she made the mistake of mentioning her encounter with the doctor and that was all it took.

Sylvia joined them from a bathroom break. "What did I miss? Catch me—"

"Nothing. Look, I ran into him, we talked, he drove me home, he left. End of story. Now can we change the subject?"

Sammy stood, picked up empty plates, and carried them into the kitchen to clear her mind, quiet the memories, and find some peace, but in the kitchen, she was greeted by chaos. The counters were covered with a combination of last night's dishes and the aftermath of her last-minute shopping trip to get ready for tonight. Empty bags were intermixed with a plethora of open containers of olives, cheeses, and other typical Spanish tapas. As she moved things around to set down the plates, she came across her train ticket from Collioure, various receipts from her night out with Jim, and the doctor's card. She piled the receipts and train ticket together and threw them in the trash. She held the doctor's card trying to decide what to do with it.

In the other room, she heard Ciara say to Sylvia, "Don't ask her any more questions. When I picked her up at the hospital that night, I remember meeting the doctor. He was pretty torn up that he couldn't save Peter."

Sammy stared at the card and whispered, "But you should have." She started to toss the card in the trash, out of sight, out of mind, but hesitated and instead stuck it in a corner of one of the cabinets—somehow in some bizarre way it felt like tossing his card would be another goodbye and one of her last links to Peter. Saying goodbye in bits and pieces like she had done over the last three years: his clothes, his mail, his hugs, his Sammy dear, his voice, his face, his love. So much of her life given away in vanished moments and memories, and yet life had swirled around her taking her with it, an unwilling participant. Much of it defined by the 'before Peter' and 'after Peter,' so much so that it had become hard to remember when one started and the other ended.

Yet it *had* ended.

Leaning on the counter, she looked out the window over the sink and peered down onto the narrow street below where the headlight from a moped cast a beam across the sidewalk where a group of partying Spaniards laughed, pushing each other nearly coming into the path of the moped. That was her; her and Peter. Always with friends, out in the night dancing, meeting his work friends, being a couple. She raised her eyes and stared across the way where other lights flickered in apartments, and to the left between the buildings where more lights blinked out at sea and she felt her mood shift. She felt the tears rise. No, she wouldn't let that happen tonight so she rested her hands on the counter and shook her head until it hurt. Time to stop this. Onward. She wiped tears from her eyes, opened more containers, and focused on refilling the empty plates with a new supply of tapas: winter cherries, figs, some olives, and nuts that she had picked up at the local *fruteria*; the *Mahón* and *Arzúa- Ulloa* cheeses and some additional Spanish Ham, *jarmón Serrano* from the butcher. Jarmón was one of her favorites especially wrapped around a piece of cheese—so to redirect her senses she did that right now and put it in her mouth then she refilled her drink. She turned around and leaned her back against the counter, sipping her drink slowly, taking her time before heading back out there.

"Samantha! Get back out here. You can't hide in there. We know what you're doing," Danele shouted.

"Good lord, cool your jets. I'm on my way." Sammy grabbed a tray from the cabinet, put the plates on it, and went back to join her friends and be firm with them: no more talk of Peter or the doctor.

Luckily Ciara took that dilemma out of her hands. "Okay, girls, no more doctor conversation," Ciara said and turned to Sammy. "What did you do the rest of the weekend? How was the wedding and that hot cousin of yours?" Ciara twisted her long auburn hair into a knot at the nape of her neck, patted the spot on the floor next to her and said, "Sit, Sammy. Now tell."

Sammy set the tray on the coffee table and flopped down next to Ciara. "Well, girls, as you might guess Ian is still hot." She laughed, then admitted, "I'd always wished he wasn't my cousin. If you know what I mean—I crushed on him big time when we were teens and he'd visit our vacation home. But I'm happy for Ian and Cassie's a doll, perfect for him.

"The wedding was at this beautiful inn where Cassie lives. There were tons of sports celebrities, but I didn't really know anyone. Except for one very egomaniacal friend of Ian's and he took me —"

Danele cut her off. "What I want to know is what Javier was doing at the train station."

"I don't know, and I don't care."

"Yeah," Sylvia said, "I thought you were done with him."

"I am." Talking about Javier was almost as frustrating as talking about the doctor. Exasperated she said, "Damn it, could we please talk about the book for once?"

Sylvia filled her plate with more food, poured another gin and tonic and said, "Macy isn't here. We need to wait for her. We can talk about the book next time."

"Macy's not coming back you guys. She's locked up in that house with her *marido*." Danele puckered her red lips, ran a hand through her short-cropped black hair and made kissing noises. "Her everything. What bullshit that is."

Ciara popped an olive in her mouth and said, "Give her a break. She's a newlywed."

"For Pete's sake, Ciara, you always defend her."

Ciara glared at Danele. "And you're a hater. You're always slamming everyone."

Sammy's patience was gone. "All right, that's enough girlies. If we argue then the rule is no alcohol at these meetings. Remember our agreement?" She reached behind her, picked up two pillows off the couch and threw them at Ciara and Dalene.

Sammy loved these women. They'd been so much a part of

her life that she often wondered what she would have done if she'd chosen to teach at a different international school when she first moved to Barcelona. Sammy was closest to Ciara: red-haired, green-eyed, freckled, the skin of a porcelain doll, and genuine soul who moved here from Ireland after college to open the international school. Their personalities jelled immediately and it was Ciara who introduced her to Sylvia a stunning blond with the figure of a model and the quietest of the group. Originally from California, Sylvia left for a new start in Spain after a nasty divorce; she also taught at the school. Macy, absent today, was from Minnesota, also blond and beautiful in a classy, yet unassuming way, was a manager at Zara, a local department store and had come to Spain to find a husband, which she recently had. Fiery Danele, the only true Spaniard, owned a tour business. In fact, it was Danele who told her Max, owner of the flamenco venue, was looking for a dancer. 'I can't dance flamenco,' Sammy had told her.

Yet Danele was not dissuaded. 'You will learn quickly; Max is an excellent teacher.'

Max was and Sammy did.

These women had been through everything with her. They'd helped her find her first apartment and roommates, then this apartment when she decided she needed and could afford a place of her own. They listened when she complained about her dad, talked her out of a brief interlude with a much older man who used phrases like 'far out' and 'dude,' encouraged her when she stumbled at her first flamenco performance and brought her food when she sprained her ankle the next time because she miscalculated the edge of the platform; they'd insisted she remain in Barcelona when her gypsy mentality made her want to move to Turkey to dance, they chastised her for choosing the wrong men, celebrated with her when she found Peter, and cried with her when he died. They were her foundation, her rock.

"Okay, girls. Book talk. No more talk about my weekend, though one of these days I'll tell you about my quick trip to Paris on a private jet." Sammy took the books off the floor and handed them to each of the girls and said, "So, what did you think?"

"Oh, no you don't," Ciara said. "You can't leave us hanging." She tossed her book back on the floor and said, "Paris. Start talking."

Sammy told them about the night with Jim including the part where he had tried to seduce her and that he had a fiancée.

"Is he hot?" Ciara asked.

"He's definitely easy one the eyes," Sammy admitted.

"Photo?"

"No, Ciara, and he's a player. Forget him, girls."

"But *chica*," Danele said."I like a challenge."

"He's engaged and, besides that, he's back in the States. Moving on. Books?"

Danele stood. "Can't, sorry Sammy. I have a group scheduled for a tour of *La Sagrada* at nine." She downed her drink, picked up her plate and took it into the kitchen.

"Are you kidding me? It's only eleven. Sit down. Please stay."

"I have to go, too." Sylvia rose and went to find her coat.

Ciara finished her drink and stood.

"Ciara, stay. You own the dang place; you don't have to be there." Sammy said, "Please, please stay. I'm not tired. Are you?"

Ciara thought for a moment, shrugged, and said, "Sure, why not."

* * *

CIARA STAYED and before the other two left they all promised next month they would talk about this month's book. They decided to have it at Danele's who lived on the beach.

"No cop-outs now. Books, booze, beach, and food next month," Sammy insisted.

Once said their goodbyes, Sammy grabbed another drink, handed one to Ciara and sat on the couch. Ciara looked at her over the rim of her glass as she took a drink and said, "What's up? You aren't yourself and I'm guessing it's clearly not only about the doctor."

"It's dancing . . . and Javier. I've been thinking about it for a long time. I think I'm a little bored dancing the flamenco every night and the complications with Javier makes it nearly impossible. I want to do something else; I don't know what, or even how I'd survive without the job."

"But you're loaded. You can do anything."

Sammy stared at her and said nothing.

"Okay, I know it's your family's money, but you told me you have a trust fund from your grandfather you can tap into whenever you want. You're hardly destitute."

"Not something I'm going to do so my dad can say told you so. No, will not do that."

"Then what will you do? You can come back and teach at the school if you want."

Sammy thought about it and finally said, "Never mind. I'm going to stick it out. If Javier leaves me alone, I'll be fine. I love dancing no matter which dance. It's what I've wanted to do my whole life until I started listening to the old guy in my life. 'Get a degree, go to law school, be like me.' You'd think everyone was cut out to be a lawyer. He has three sons who joined his practice. He doesn't need me. No, I'll stick with what I know I'm good at."

CHAPTER FOUR

*C*iara burst into Sammy's room, pulling on her jeans, at the same time trying to button her shirt. "Good god, what time is it?"

"Go back to bed." Sammy moaned, pulling the covers over her head. She and Ciara had talked until two this morning. Ciara had fallen asleep on the couch until Sammy woke her up at around four and guided her into the guest room.

"No, really, what time is it? I can't find my phone."

"For Pete's sake, it's still dark out."

"No, it's not. I looked out the window. It's getting light."

Sammy groped around for her phone on the nightstand. "It's only seven-thirty."

"Oops, thought it was later." Ciara finished putting on her jeans, buttoned her shirt, and flopped on the bed next to Sammy.

"Go away. I need my beauty sleep." Sammy snuggled further down into the bed.

Ciara said, "Aren't you working today?"

"For God's sake, yes—at ten. Go make us coffee."

"Naw, I should go. I need to shower and change before I head to the school."

"Well, then, I guess it's a run for me." Sammy attempted to nudge Ciara off the bed with her toes. "Up girl."

Ciara stood. "I need my phone."

Sammy sat up and said, "It's on the table in front of the couch."

Ciara hurried out of the room and Sammy flopped down pulling the covers back over her. She heard Ciara moving things around and swearing, finally Sammy said, "Did you find it?"

"Got it," Ciara yelled from the other room. Then she poked her head into the bedroom. "Gotta go. See you this weekend?"

"Absolutely."

Ciara waved then Sammy heard the door close. The bed was so warm Sammy was tempted to stay there for the rest of the day. Through the open window above her head she heard the distant whish of the waves rolling in from the ocean. That sound often lulled her back to sleep, but today guilt tugged at her; she hadn't run in a week and already felt the difference in her body and energy. She threw off the covers, bounded out of bed, gave her teeth a quick brush, pulled on running shorts and grabbed a sweatshirt, tucked her hair under a baseball cap, put on sunglasses and headed out of her top-floor apartment taking the elevator to the bottom floor. The elevator softly bounced to a stop on the ground floor and Sammy struggled to open the metal accordion-style door chastising herself for not taking the stairs as she usually did. The door lagged as it screeched across the ancient track and when she finally got it open the scant scent of stale cigar smoke wafted inside. She stepped out into the apartment building's vestibule where the smoky-sweet aroma of tobacco was stronger. Emil Jessup, Peter's great uncle, was the only one who smoked a cigar and had been constantly warned by the manager—residents weren't allowed to smoke in the common areas. Emil was a sweet old man and lived most of his life in this building, but at ninety-two he could be grumpy and stubborn. Sammy had grown to love him like he was her uncle. If it hadn't been for Emil Jessup, Sammy would never have met Peter.

The morning she met Peter she'd just come back from her daily run and found a man pulling a suitcase, walking up and down the street looking down at his phone then up to the buildings and talking to himself. Sammy assumed he was searching for an address as it wasn't uncommon to see tourists absentmindedly wandering the street; finding addresses in this part of Barcelona was tricky—many of the buildings didn't have any. He walked by her mumbling to himself in rudimentary Spanish, dragging the suitcase that bumped noisily over the uneven concrete sidewalk, stopping occasionally to stare at the buildings' stone facades, peering around wood-cased windows and ancient doorways, many with rusted iron knockers, some rubbed shiny by residents, but none with any address identification.

Clearly exasperated he finally turned around and called out to her, "*Senor, help, por favor.*"

She hadn't known whether to be insulted or amused that he called her *senor*—she knew she didn't look like a man, but one could never be sure. He continued talking to her in stilted Spanish. She watched his face painfully contort while trying to get out the correct Spanish words interspersed with English.

"Sir, I can make it easier for you, I'm American, I speak English."

His face relaxed and he walked toward her, scratching his head. "I can't find numbers; these buildings don't have addresses." He shrugged, noticeably frustrated, but when he looked at her and smiled, she nearly lost her train of thought. He had spectacularly blue-green eyes that when he smiled brought forth such warmth that she felt like she had seen all the way into his soul. His high cheekbones along with the angular shape of his face, narrow jaw, and dark hair made him look like an Adonis. She hadn't meant to stare but found she couldn't look away. Something inside her stirred and she should have known at that moment she was a goner.

He handed her his phone and asked if she knew the address or someone named Emil Jessup. He explained that he was in Barcelona for business and was surprising his favorite great uncle with a visit. She told him she lived in the same building. They'd found Emil at home and before Peter closed the door to Emil's apartment, he'd asked Sammy if he could buy her dinner later to thank her. Her acceptance so quick, that Peter had laughed—obviously conscious of the effect he had had on her.

And that was that.

And that was then.

The air this morning was much like that morning: brisk and damp like a rain squall had passed through in the night. Still standing in front of her building she closed down her memory of Peter and Emil and focused on getting ready to run. She reached her arms high over her head, breathed in the morning air, grasped her hands together and stretched. A cold breeze whistled down from the end of the block where a peek-a-boo view of the sea met the horizon and a sliver of daylight eked through tiny spaces between buildings. The wind bellowed her sweatshirt; she pulled it tighter and zipped it up.

To her right, staff from the restaurant next door hurried in and out of the back entrance carrying in produce that an earlier delivery truck must have dropped off. Each time the door opened the sound and aromas of meat grilling and saffron sizzling spilled outside. Sammy said hello to several of the workers, turned left, and continued walking toward the beach sidestepping around parked cars, dodging bicycles, and occasional pots of flowers. As she walked, the personality of the neighborhood came alive around her, filling her senses with the cadence and rhythms of dawn. Further down the street voices drifted out of apartments and when Sammy glanced up she saw one woman hanging laundry on a clothes-line attached to her balcony. High above Sammy, the aroma of coffee wafted out another window followed by the hiss of milk steaming and a mother in a street-level apartment chided her child to come and eat his *pa amb tomàquet*—a piece of day-old rustic bread rubbed with garlic and fresh tomato and one of Sammy's go-to breakfasts. Right now, her stomach grumbled and she realized she never had dinner last night. Or, she wondered, was her stomach reacting to all the girl talk about the doctor and Javier. An aggressive run on the beach should take care of all of that; leaving girl talk, the doc, and Javier behind.

As Sammy neared the entrance to the beach, she increased her stride breaking into a jog to make sure her body would respond. She raced toward the edge of the sea, noticing as she ran, her body felt stiff; she stopped, bent over and touched her toes, and felt the slight pull of her calves and upper thighs, and a release in her back muscles. She straightened, grasped her hands behind her back, and tugged while staring out across the water to the horizon where the sun had started to rise creating brilliant striations of purple, pink, and aqua in the dawn sky, even the clouds that dotted the sky would have been worthy of a painter's palette with deep gray tinged with blue. It looked like a scene from a travel brochure and Sammy felt a surge of emotion that she often felt when experiencing the beauty of the *Catalan* region, whether at the shore or high above it at the monastery where the peaks of the *Monserrat* mountains rose up.

Further out she could see a cruise ship edging across the Mediterranean, apparently on its way to dock at the port. It looked like one of the smaller ones and she momentarily wondered if it might be the one the doctor would be on.

Fish vendors were beginning to set up along the board-walk behind her and lights from the distant hotel and other buildings further up the beach twinkled in the early morning sky. Energized by the beauty that surrounded her and the briskness and clarity of the morning, she took in a deep breath of the salty sea air and set out on her run.

IT WAS surprising how much a week's break from exercise, could wipe out years of consistent dedication to keeping fit. She opened the door to her building and noticed her calves felt tight and her breaths came in shallow bursts. Dancing would help and she had a performance tonight but chastised herself for being so lazy this past week. Determined to get back the time she lost, she took the stairs this time, two at a time.

The first thing she did when she got back into her apartment was down a glass of water, then filled the blender with fresh fruit, some yogurt, a splash of the juice from a fresh orange, a spoonful of wheat germ and lastly protein powder. There, that would take care of last night's drinking and her slothful behavior this past week. Buoyed by her run and the smoothie, she cleared the kitchen of all the dirty dishes and glasses from the book club gathering, straightened up the living room, and went into her bedroom to get ready for work when someone knocked on her door. Before she could answer it, she heard the apartment door open and Javier's voice, "Sammy, it's Javi. I'm coming in?"

She yelled from the bedroom, "*Do not* come in. Go home. You should not be here. How did you get in anyway?"

"You gave me a key."

She hurried out of her bedroom and found him standing inside the front door. He walked toward her; she put her hand up. "Stop, right there. Now turn yourself around and leave. Oh, and give me the damn key." She held out her hand.

"But, my love, I have told my wife about us. I told her I am leaving her so we can get married."

Exasperated, she said, "Now why would you do that? I told you from the beginning I never wanted to marry again."

He scratched his head. "Then why are you so angry?"

"Well, for starters you told me you weren't married, which means for the last six months you've lied about everything. Secondly, you told Max about us and now he keeps asking me if I can still concentrate on dancing since we're a couple. So now my job is in jeopardy."

45

"See, my love, it's all okay now. Everyone knows."

"No, it's not okay." She softened her tone. "Look, I don't love you, Javi. When I found out you lied to me, I realized I was relieved. I knew who you were, I knew you were a player. I was willing to overlook that because I was so skeptical about relationships anyway and," she admitted, "we were having so much fun. But never once did I think you were still married."

"But—"

"Now please go. I need to get ready for work."

He threw the key at her and began sputtering in Spanish, and though she was fluent, she only caught one word clearly, and that word was the worst thing a woman could be called. Then his eyes darkened and he said in English, "I'd never leave my wife for you anyway. Do you really think I told her? How stupid do you think I am?" Then he left.

Emotions ran rampant; the one that loomed the largest was fury. His arrogance and lack of remorse about lying to her and his infidelity to his wife reaffirmed the kind of man he was.

CHAPTER FIVE

Still reeling from her encounter with Javier, Sammy felt her fierce thirty-minute walk to work should have been enough to physically and mentally prepare her for seeing him again, but when she reached the employee entrance to the flamenco theatre Max met her.

"We need to have a talk," Max said,

Max led her into his office and before he said anything, she said, "We're done. I'm not seeing Javier. I'm fine with it and so is he. My focus is on my dancing and nothing will get in the way of that."

"I'm glad to hear you say that Sammy, but unfortunately it's gone beyond your relationship with Javier." He pointed to the chair in front of his desk and said, "Please sit. Business has taken a downturn since the other flamenco venue opened closer to *La Ramblas*. I have to let someone go and Javier has accused you of stalking him. He said you went to his wife and told her about the two of you. He said he has tried to break it off, but you refused."

She threw her head back and laughed. "You're kidding,

right? I had to throw him out of my apartment this morning. If anyone is stalking anyone, he's stalking me."

"It doesn't matter, Sammy. I have to let someone go and Javier has been with me since we opened."

"I'm your best damn dancer, Max. I've been with you for five years and never took a day off except when Peter died. I'm dependable and you know it."

"Look," he stood up and continued, "I had to make a choice and you are the junior member of this troupe and I can't have you and Javier fighting. Sorry, but I've already decided. I put Nia on tonight's performance in place of you. I'll give you a hundred days pay—twenty days for each year." He reached for her hand. "No hard feelings?"

She glared at him and said, "You're making a mistake." She ignored his outstretched hand and walked out of his office and went straight into the performance area to confront Javier. He wasn't there so she went into the men's dressing area and started yelling, "You POS. You lied about us and now you got me fired."

Javier came out from behind one of the curtained-off areas, smiling. "My darling, you got what you deserved."

She flipped him off and turned around to leave, nearly walking into several of the other female dancers who had been standing there listening. Nia was the first one to speak. "We are all sad you will be leaving. I fear we will all be out of a job soon. Max is not doing well. The new venue has taken many of the tourists, you should go there. They are looking for more good dancers." She came over to Sammy and kissed her cheeks then hugged her, as did the other dancers. Sammy turned to leave and noticed Javier watching her. She turned to the girls and said, "I love every one of you and so for your own good, stay far away from this one; he's still married." Then she walked out the front entrance.

The street clamored with busy shoppers, tourists, and traffic. Stunned at what had just occurred, Sammy walked to the curb and stood. In a daze, she watched as cars whizzed by in the frantic late morning commute. People going on with their lives: heading to jobs, parents taking kids to school, tourists flocking to cruise ships to whisk them away from the reality of their mundane lives and here she was, standing, jobless, wondering who she was now. She turned around and looked at the place where she'd spent the last five years, a place enmeshed with her identity—dancer, friend, employee, then lover to Javier—and now it was another piece of her identity she'd have to shed: first as daughter when her relationship with her father deteriorated then wife after Peter's death, now ex-girlfriend and dancer—unemployed dancer.

She moved back toward the entrance, trying to decide if she should go back in and fight for her job, but inside the window she saw Javier and Nia practicing for tonight's performance. Discouraged and exasperated, she threw her gym bag down, heavy with her clothes and shoes for today's rehearsal, and leaned against the front façade of the building. Her mind fogged with a jumble of the words spoken by Max including Javier's accusations and then fused with the penetrating reality that her job was no more. She needed to get away from here and think. She picked up her bag and purse to leave, looked inside the bag, stared at fragments of the last five years of her life, made a snap decision and tossed it all in the trash container at the curb. She might regret it later, but right now it felt like the right thing to do. Dancing for another

venue here in Barcelona was not an option she'd entertain
—not now.

Like someone else was controlling her legs she let them
pull her in the direction of home, not knowing what else to
do, yet the further she walked the more the idea of being
home today didn't feel like a haven from her anger, didn't feel
like the refuge she needed. What she needed was a place to
reflect on what happened today; to think about what the
future might hold for her and to see if there were mistakes she
made in the past that lead to this. Her heart raced, and she felt
panic rise—she tried to calm her breathing and knew she
needed solace and a quiet place to breathe the air and think.

The mountain. She needed the mountain.

It was strange how her sudden need for the mountain and
monastery instantly calmed her. It would be a long trek; first
taxi, then the train, then cable car—all in all, a full day. But,
she realized, it didn't matter—no job, no lover, not encum-
bered with anything—and suddenly she felt emboldened.
She'd faced worse dilemmas and Ciara was right, she was
financially secure and luckily didn't have to worry about
money and, she chided herself, it was last night in her conversations with Ciara that she had shared her own misgivings,
now the choice didn't have to be hers to make—Max and
Javier had made it for her.

She hailed a taxi and during the ride asked the driver to
stop so she could run into her favorite market to pick up
some food for the hour-long train ride.

"Ah, *Senorita* Sammy, how wonderful to see you. It has
been *too* long," the owner of the market teased.

She laughed and pretended to punch him. "Oh, Mateo,

don't try to make me feel guilty because I come here all the time. You are bad, *mi amigo*."

"You should cook for yourself. It is not hard, you know, and I do have the very best ingredients for the best paella in all of Barcelona. Fresh clams, homemade chorizo, and, the rice," he kissed his fingers, "is the best in all the world."

She rolled her eyes. "And the man keeps talking."

"I am a proud *Catalonian* and we are the best cooks, *miija*. Now what can I do for you today?"

"I'm taking the train to Monserrat so a ham and cheese sandwich, *por favor*."

Mateo shook his head. "No, no, no. I will make you the best *Bocadilla de Jamón Serrano Y Manchego* in the world."

"Mateo, dear Mateo, *jamón* and *manchego* are good enough. My taxi is waiting."

"And he will wait." Mateo stuck his head out the door and yelled at the taxi driver then came back inside. "Why didn't you tell me it was Lorenzo, he is my brother-in-law. He will wait until I tell him he can leave." He puffed his chest out and continued, "I take them food—the best food in all of Spain. He is grateful. Now, sit. I will make you a *café con leche* then the sandwich."

"*Gracias*, Mateo. Coffee sounds wonderful."

After a few minutes, he set the coffee in front of her and scoffed, "Ham and cheese. We do not do just ham and cheese in Catalonia—what is *jamón* and *manchego* without *piquillo* peppers and black olives? Tell me this *miija?*"

She raised her arms and said, "I give up. Do your magic."

He raised an eyebrow. "Finally . . . the woman, she surrenders."

* * *

Lorenzo dropped her at the train station an hour later. She'd finally left the market after forty-five minutes of Mateo's lectures on the beauty of the preparation of food, his insistence that she also take some empanadas, a leftover slice of a Spanish frittata, some deviled eggs, and while walking out the door he stuffed some churros in the picnic basket he also gave her. Then during the fifteen-minute ride to the train station, she listened to Lorenzo boast about Mateo's food, Lorenzo's own family, and his frustration with his in-laws. By the time she got to the train station her ears were ringing, she was exhausted and a little less committed to her journey. But the beauty of it was that during the time with Mateo and Lorenzo she hadn't thought about her job situation at all. Though right now sitting and waiting for the train to arrive memories and doubts swirled and she began to have second thoughts about heading to the mountain; the last time had brought unspeakable sadness. Other memories pushed away the bad and she remembered that in difficult moments the mountain had always provided her with clarity, a sense of peace and a feeling that she was not alone. Even in the beginning, it was the place that had given her a sense of belonging when she first came to Barcelona, her father's ultimatum still fresh.

"I'm not sure where your head is, young lady, but if you insist on dropping out of the law program and escaping to Spain, I'll have no choice but to cut off your monthly allowance," her father had ranted.

She'd fought the tears that threatened and lashed out. "I don't need your damn money. I'm sick of you holding it over my head."

Her mother had tried to intervene. "Samantha, your father is only looking out for your future. It's because of his dedication and hard work that we're able to afford the things we have."

Sammy was incredulous. "Please don't hit me with that bullshit. *Your* father was the reason we have," she swept her arms around the impeccably decorated living room in their seven-bedroom home, "all of this."

At that point, her father left the room.

Her mother put her arms around Sammy, hugged her, then stood back and said, "Look at me." Again sternly. "Samantha, look at me. Yes, I'm disappointed you won't be joining your father and brothers and yes, I'm worried you might be making a mistake, but you do what is necessary for your happiness and I'll support you. And, yes, my father did leave all of us very comfortable but remember your father has never touched any of that money. After we bought this house with it, he vowed to work hard for this family—and he always has." She touched Sammy's face and said, "I love you." Then she gave her a gentle push and said, "Now go on and live *your* life."

After living her entire life in the shadows of her brothers, it had been uplifting when Sammy's mother defended her, but sadly, it was the one of the few times her mother was supportive. It seemed to Sammy that since that moment every other conversation with her mother and her father had been laden with disappointment at Sammy's decision to move to Spain and to choose dancing as a profession.

And yet, Sammy rarely questioned any of those choices until now.

She boarded the train and as she searched for a seat, it struck her that she'd taken this same train with Peter the day of the wedding—Sammy dressed in an ankle-length champagne lace dress and Peter stunningly handsome in an impeccably tailored navy-blue suit. Her veil carefully stored in Peter's suitcase along with their clothes for the next few days. For their wedding night and the following day, they had planned to stay at *Hotel Abat Cisneros* which sat at the top of the mountain, a wonderfully isolated location and the only lodging at Montserrat. They'd decided it was perfect for a quiet mini-honeymoon and much needed after the frantic wedding preparations which were made with only a week's preparation. 'What are we waiting for Sammy, dear?' Peter had said, 'You love me, I love you.' She'd reminded him they'd only known each other for three months. 'Ah, but what a three months it has been,' he'd teased.

He was right, they loved each other so why not. Fortunately, when they'd tried to find a wedding venue on such short notice and couldn't, Father Thomas had stepped in assuring them, since Peter was Catholic, he could marry them at the basilica and it would be legal in Spain. Except for Sister Mercedes and Father Thomas, only a few friends knew about the wedding; she hadn't even told her parents. Sammy still held the joyful ceremony tenderly tucked away in her memory so now as the train finally pulled out of the station and picked up speed, a stillness settled. She relaxed, leaned her head back against the headrest, looked out the window and watched as the scrub along the edge of the tracks bent and twisted from the wind that had been predicted for today. The tension in her neck eased and her mind quieted as they shuttled through the city. Businesses, residences, and people's lives flew by with the ease of a hummingbird flitting from flower to flower, but there weren't many flowers on the back tracks of the industrial areas they passed.

Once they were on the outskirts, the scenery grew gentler. They swept by enclaves where houses were built into the hillsides, where tiny suburban villages were clustered and playgrounds were filled with boisterous energetic children. They traveled further and the topography changed gracefully to quiet, undulating golden hills. In the distance she caught a glimpse of the mountains of Monserrat, their peaks whispered by wispy, translucent low clouds then as they rounded a curve a blanket of fog ascended covering them. A moment later as if God's hand reached down wiped the fog away, the uniquely cylinder-shaped mountains completely reappeared as pillars reaching to the heavens. Cradled into the side of the steep mountainside still partially shrouded by the fog the tiny salmon-colored Chapel at *Santa Cova* built in the form of a Latin cross momentarily became visible. As the sun broke through, the Chapel was cast in almost celestial light as if giving a nod to its sacredness, an affirmation Sammy knew too well. With its remote location, it was the perfect sanctuary when she was having doubts about her move to Spain. And it was this chapel where Sister Mercedes found her during her first week in Spain.

She had not started her job at the international school yet and panic had set in. Sammy, still upset about her argument with her father, feared he might have been right that her move was foolhardy and her refusal to join him in his practice was pigheaded. She'd been feeling lonely when her roommates, whom she had just met, suggested a trip to visit Monserrat. She'd eagerly accepted. Once on the mountain as she walked around the spectacular, but somber retreat her earlier trepidation was replaced by a veil of sadness. Monserrat's beauty and religious attachments made her regret her estrangement from her father and she missed home, her family, and friends. As her sadness grew, she said goodbye to her roommates and headed back down the mountain for home. Ultimately, she took a wrong turn and instead of finding the cable car, she wandered aimlessly along a winding downhill path. Eventually she found herself at the entrance to the chapel at *Santa Cova* (the Holy Grotto) where the image of the Virgin Mary was once said to have appeared. Sammy entered and the chapel's beauty along with its serenity and grace overwhelmed her and as her chest filled with the spirituality of the place, she began to cry. That was when Sister Mercedes found her. With a hint of spunk and enduring compassion, Sister Mercedes helped her through that moment and many others during the years. Today, as the train took another turn and views of Monserrat vanished Sammy wondered if she'd see Sister Mercedes and if she could help her through this latest dilemma.

CHAPTER SIX

When the train ride ended there were several ways to get up to the monastery; the cable car was Sammy's favorite. It rose forty-five hundred feet in five minutes and hung, suspended above the valley, sweeping across the stunning scenery of the *Llobregat* River, the village of *Monistro,* and surrounding valley.

Today Sammy boarded the bright yellow gondola-type enclosure with a small group of tourists. In summer the cable car crammed as many thirty-five people inside and in those busy times, the ride up echoed with a cacophony of languages each with different cadence and volume. Today in the tiny space Sammy heard, peppered through the scraping and screeching of the gondola as it grated along the cable, several languages including a couple speaking English—obviously from the States so she asked them where they were from.

"The land of cheese, brats, and beer," the elderly man said and laughed.

"Ah, Wisconsin, I presume," Sammy said.

"Yup. We're takin' a cruise." He reached over and pulled his wife closer. "Me and the Mrs. are celebrating fifty-five years of wedded bliss. Isn't that right, Milly?" he said as he turned and kissed Milly's cheek.

Milly smiled up at him. "Bliss, honey? Let's see—seven states, thirteen houses and one rip-roaring life lesson living in Norway."

"Heck, it wasn't so bad," he said.

"True, we did survive."

Sammy was curious. "Oh, you didn't like it there?"

The husband answered, "We did, but dang nearly went broke. Never paid so much for a cup of coffee in my life."

"So where are you off to?" Sammy asked.

Milly answered, "Italy, Malta, Greece, and then back to Barcelona."

"We almost didn't make it, didn't we honey? Milly, here, got sick before we left with a bad bout of flu so we're a bit concerned about the health care aboard the ship, but the cruise line told us they have good doctors," the husband said to Sammy.

The wife then rolled her eyes and said, "He tried to leave me at home, the little stinker. You'd think he was trying to get rid of me."

The husband chuckled. "Well, you know, I could trade you in for two forty-year-olds." But then he hugged her and said, "Don't you worry Milly, I would never leave you behind."

Sammy laughed with them and said, "I happen to know a doctor on one of the cruise lines and from what he told me, they are extremely well-trained. You should be fine. It sounds like you might be on his cruise. He told me the route and I think it's the same one."

"Is he a good one? Can't be trusting any ole doc to my sweetie here?" the husband said.

She hesitated. He hadn't saved Peter. In her mind she knew no one could have saved him even though her heart sometimes told her something else. "I think he's quite good. You should be in good hands."

"What's his name?"

"Dr. Adair."

"Thank you. We're grateful for the information. Sure hope we don't need him." And the husband reached over and gave his wife another hug.

"I'm curious what made you come to Monserrat? It's quite a trip from the port of Barcelona," Sammy asked.

They told her that many of the ship's passengers were given destination packets and Monserrat was one of the 'must see' highlights.

"Before the ship leaves you must see *La Sagrada Familia*. It's Gaudi's famous unfinished Catholic church where construction has gone on for over a hundred years."

The husband nudged his wife. "Told you." He looked at Sammy and said, "After our last trip to the UK, Milly said she'd seen enough churches."

His wife turned to Sammy and asked, "What about the Picasso Museum?"

"Definitely! It's so worth it. This city is full of art; you must take it all in." Her love of art had blossomed since she'd been in Spain. She'd always been quietly passionate about art, especially paintings, but until she moved to Spain, she hadn't taken the time to explore. Ohio had many museums yet they hadn't interested her, and Peter had not been that into art. Even

Sammy's interest in architecture and sculptures had grown exponentially because of Gaudi's influence here.

The wife nudged her husband back and said, "Told you." Then said to Sammy, "He said *he'd* seen enough art museums after that trip."

"Okay, okay. I'll go with you, if you go with me," he said.

Watching them interact Sammy saw that they were clearly devoted to each other. She felt a twinge of sadness realizing this could have been her and Peter.

When the tram reached the top she wished the couple a good trip, quickly gathered her picnic basket, purse, and tentatively stepped out into the small station area where photos of the monastery and basilica hung on the walls. She tried not to dwell on the photos, too many memories pushed their way into her mind, but above the exit, a large photo of the famous *Montserrat l'Escolania* Boys' Choir hung. She remembered hearing them perform and it was a memory she cherished; an experience she'd never forget. So, she waited for the elderly couple and said to them when they exited the tram, "If you have a chance to hear the boys' choir perform it is an unforgettable experience. There is information over there on the rack."

While the couple picked up information on the choir, Sammy walked outside. She took a deep breath to quell the anxiety that immediately rushed through her body as she caught a glimpse of the spires of the church. She closed her eyes and willed herself to continue—she needed to do this.

The clouds had returned and a cool mist dampened her face and coated her hair as she started up the steep, paved walkway leading to the courtyard in front of the basilica. When she reached the top, she stood trying to get her bearings and bolster her confidence. It had been three years since she'd been here and as she stared at the basilica, the church where they were married and where they'd held Peter's funeral, memories of those two days clogged her mind and the sadness weighed her down. She willed herself to keep going, but her heart fluttered, her airway tightened and it felt as if an invisible force was holding her back and wouldn't allow her to go any further.

She couldn't do this right now.

Instead, she made her way to the overlook, set Mateo's picnic basket on the stone ledge, took some deep breaths and stared at the valley below. She'd focus on the positive, on this moment, and the beauty that lay before her. Mist circled and swept in and around the villages that dotted the lowlands. Ribbons of what must be the Llobregat river wove through the countryside, periodically disappearing only to reappear further out, eventually emptying into the sea. A gust loosened a bit of scrub that had clung to a boulder, rocking it back and forth until the bush tumbled down the hill. Off to her right, plants, flowers, and low trees had pushed their way through the tight rock crevices and ravines. Further up the hillside, the massive mountain peaks—made up of reddish, jagged, barren pinnacles—rose, dwarfing her, the abbey, and all of the visitors. She looked up at the sky, closed her eyes, and tried to let the stillness and solemnity of the place imbue her with confidence and take her sadness away. She stood there for several minutes, long enough for the sun to push away the clouds and allow its rays to warm her face. She opened her eyes as a breeze shuttled up from the valley and the mist disappeared. The sun appearing, the mist abating were just the signs she needed. Resolute and determined, she grabbed the picnic basket, and headed up the steps leading to the church. Yet as she climbed, she felt the strength in her legs weaken and her resolve wane. She moved over to the side, out of the way of passing tourists, sat, and while silently chastising herself for being so weak she felt someone sit beside her.

"I thought that was you, Samantha."

She turned; it was Father Thomas.

Seeing his face calmed her, so much so that any misgivings about her journey diminished and she reached over and hugged him. "My dear man, you are a sight for sad eyes."

"Are you okay my dear?" He frowned and searched her face. "I know this is not a happy place for you." He patted her hand and continued, "And if I'm not mistaken you haven't been here since the funeral."

"No, I haven't. I couldn't make myself come here, but then today . . ." She turned her head away from him to stare out onto the valley.

"And . . ." He waited for her to finish.

"I lost my job and the only place I could think of where I might get some perspective was here." She turned back toward him, smiled, and said, "I'd hoped I'd see you and Sister Mercedes. Is she here?"

"No, she's in the States visiting her sister in Seattle. She will be sad she missed you. But she'll be back next week. You must see her."

"I will. I've missed you both."

"Then we will see you at church soon?"

"Father, you know I'm not Catholic."

"God doesn't care."

"Oh, Father Thomas," she leaned her head on his shoulder and whispered, "how I've missed you."

From deep inside the church a dulcet melody floated above them. The sound of ambient organ music was soon joined with the fluid and harmonious voices of the boys' choir. Sammy let herself be taken away with the textured strains of a hymn that pulled at her soul with resilient clarity and she knew she must go into the basilica and face her fears, her loss, her heartache, and she knew she must conquer them today. Her reason for coming here became clear and she knew it wasn't because of the loss of her job, she knew it was the right time to put her past where it belonged—in the past. She would always love Peter and yearn for what could have been, but she needed to move on with her life and now that her job was no more, she could explore new ideas and face the days with a sense of expectation and not dread.

She lifted her head off his shoulder and looked at him, hopeful. "Father Thomas, will you escort me into the church? I think it's time I face it. I've been so fearful that I would fall apart if I came up here, yet seeing you I feel a sense of peace. The peace I used to feel and . . . I'm optimistic."

Father Thomas took both her hands in his and said, "My dear, I would be more than happy to walk with you . . . you know God is walking with you all the time. You must trust in his presence."

She'd never had a strong faith—she was spiritual, not religious—but Father Thomas's words strengthened her.

As they rose together to go into the church, the melody from inside the church surged with vibrant tenors singing hallelujah over and over again. Father Thomas raised an eyebrow and said, "See, my dear. He is everywhere." And he led her into the church.

When they opened the doors and the music flooded out,

she caught a glimpse of the altar, the place they had been married and she panicked. She turned to walk out, but Father Thomas held onto her arm and smiled at her. "Peter would want you to do this."

* * *

FATHER THOMAS HAD BEEN RIGHT of course. Peter would want her to live her life and be happy. In the end, confronting the past hadn't been so bad. She'd shed a few tears, lit a candle for Peter, told him she would always love him then she made her way down the mountain again. The return trip had seemed quicker. She contributed that to the lightness of her heart and eagerness to get on with her new life. With a sense of determination and purpose, she climbed up the stairs from Barceloneta metro station exit onto the street and was walking toward her apartment when her phone rang.

"Geez, Sam, I've been calling you all day. You leave me a frantic message about losing your job then you don't answer your dang phone."

"Oh, god, sorry, Ciara, I forgot I called you. I went up to Monserrat and I don't have good reception up there."

"Are you still there?"

"Nope, on my way home."

"Stay there. I'm coming over."

Ciara hung up before Sammy had a chance to tell her she was okay; that the afternoon had given her the clarity she needed. New life; new perspective.

It would take Ciara at least thirty minutes to get to Sammy's in the afternoon commute traffic, so Sammy stopped by a market adjacent to the marina, picked up a bottle of wine, and headed home. She'd just gotten into the apartment when the downstairs bell rang. Sammy buzzed her in. A few minutes later there was a knock on the door.

Sammy yelled, "Come in, it's open. I'm opening some wine." She finished opening the wine and walked out of the kitchen, "Boy that was fast. What did you do, fly? I can't . . . "

It wasn't Ciara, it was the doctor standing in the doorway. Hadn't she said goodbye to him and any future meetings? His being here threw her, but not as much as she expected.

"Hi, sorry to barge in on you. I tried to tell you it was me, but the voice mechanism didn't seem to work."

Weird that seeing him didn't send her into a panic or make her want to run. "It's broken. But that's okay. What brings you to Barceloneta?"

"A few days ago, I found these keys in my car," he said and held his hand out with a set of keys Sammy didn't recognize, "and no one has claimed them so I thought they might be yours."

She took them from him, shook her head, then looked more closely. "They're not for this apartment, but they look like ones from my old apartment. They must have slipped out of my purse. I need to throw them away, but for some reason, I don't."

"Memories?"

"No, they weren't . . ." But as she held them and looked closer she realized they were Peter's keys; not from her old apartment, from this one. She'd given them to him on a keychain with the FC Barcelona soccer team logo. A ringing in her ears drowned out the doctor's voice; he was talking but she wasn't hearing him. She allowed the emptiness to fill her and when she looked back at the doctor, she realized she was okay. "They were Peter's. Thank you for returning them. I don't think I knew I still had them. Strange how grief can make you forget things except the reason you're sad. It has fogged everything for me for a very long time."

"I'm sorry. I've seen that happen. The grief never goes away, it diminishes and life has a way of making us slog through it whether we want to or not." He shifted, seemed to struggle with what to say next, but continued, "By the way, I tried to call out to you up on the mountain, but you didn't hear me. Then you went into the church with the priest and I didn't want to disturb you."

"You were there? "

"I went up with a group early this morning and stayed around after they went back. I came around a corner and saw you."

"I didn't hear you, sorry."

"Was this the first time you've been back?"

"Yes, but I think I'm okay. It was what I needed." She realized she was still holding the open bottle of wine, so she held it up and said, "Would you like some? It's a Rioja and I remember you said you liked it."

"Sure, if I'm not imposing."

Now she was flustered and didn't know why. "Go ahead and push those books off the couch and have a seat while I get us some glasses."

"May I help?"

"No, no, please sit."

She went back into the kitchen and stood for a moment before getting the glasses down from the cabinet. Her heart was pounding and she felt flushed. Strange. True, his presence was unexpected, but she knew her reaction was different this time. Yes, he'd been the doctor who was there when Peter died, but the days following Peter's death his presence had been a blur; they'd had to interact and have conversations with hospital doctors and staff, the morgue, and the funeral home. He'd had to give his report to all of them, but she didn't remember him as a person, certainly not as a man. But seeing him today standing in her apartment in jeans and a white open-collar shirt with a bit of his chest showing, she realized what an attractive man he was and she felt a bit undone. In her mind she heard Peter's laughter and his voice chiding, "Sammy dear, you are alive. Get on with it."

She grabbed wine glasses and went out into the room where she found Roan sitting awkwardly between stacks of books, perusing one of them. She set the wine and glasses on the coffee table in front of the couch, picked up the stack of books from the couch and put them on the floor. "Now isn't that better? You have more room. Sit back. Relax."

He laughed, put down the book he was reading and, still looking a bit ill-at-ease, settled against the back of the couch.

She handed him a glass and filled it, filled hers then sat at the other end of the couch and watched as he quietly, covertly, took in the aroma, and then a sip. Much different from other men she'd known who felt as if it was an obligation to push their faces deep into the glass, make a production of breathing it in, swirling it around their mouth before responding with an exaggerated 'ahh.' Except for Peter. Peter was a beer drinker and grumbled about his distaste for 'the stuff.'

Roan let it rest in his mouth before swallowing and said, "That is quite good. Thank you." He looked at her over the rim of the glass, a smile twitching at the corners of his mouth, eyebrows raised, one eye slightly closed—was he winking at her—and asked, "I'm curious though; do you always greet guests with an open bottle of wine?"

"Only for handsome men." The words were barely out of her mouth when she wished she could take them back yet she felt like a schoolgirl flirting with the popular boy in class. And that was okay.

Roan tipped his glass. "Well, to handsome men then, I hope one will show up soon."

And that time he did wink at her.

There was scuffling at the apartment door, a yelp, then it burst open and Ciara walked in. "There's a goldarn hand truck at the top of the stairs, I nearly killed myself trying to go . . . " She stopped and stared at them. "Well, that's not nice. You started without me." She strode over, flopped down between Roan and Sammy, turned to the doctor and put out her hand and said, "Ciara O'Rourke."

"Hi, Ciara, Roan Adair, I remember you. I heartedly wish it had been a happier time." He turned to glance at Sammy presumably to see her reaction.

And while the memory held sadness, surprisingly she was enjoying this day and didn't want anything to ruin it. Sammy looked at both of them, the doctor frowning and now trying not to look at her, and Ciara, the memory obvious in her eyes, her smile tentative, as if she could vanish at any moment. Sammy sighed and said, "It wasn't a happier time, but that is life, isn't it? We celebrate the good times and grieve the bad. I'm okay, so please let's not avoid talking about Peter and what happened. He would hate it. It is, what it is."

Then she turned to Ciara and held up her glass. "Wine?"

CHAPTER SEVEN

*S*ammy was in her bedroom cleaning out her closet, throwing away all of her performance gowns and shoes. She wouldn't go back to dancing the flamenco; she didn't know what she was going to do, but she knew that beyond any doubt. When Ciara and the doctor were there, she'd told them about losing her job and though they helped her brainstorm some ideas of what to do next, all she wanted to do was cleanse herself of the last five years at Max's. Along with those gowns, any items that made her think of Javier she also tossed.

Although her apartment was compact, her closet was walk-in size—an oddity in most European spaces. She'd placed a large garbage bag right outside the closet door and pitched dress after dress in its direction. The last five years of her professional life cast away in a brilliant rainbow of candy apple red, dark sienna from the dress she wore the first time Javier kissed her, the cerise pink the first time she'd met Peter and he'd seen her dance, the daffodil yellow from one of her first performances, the Indian green, the celadon, cobalt blue, all cascaded in an amalgamation of colors with a false promise of a pot of gold at its end. Not that she regretted her time at Max's nor coming to Barcelona, it gave her a career and a love with Peter she could never replace, but those experiences and memories were extinct, ancient, in the past, a lifetime ago.

Once she finished with her performance clothes she stood back and took stock of what *was* left—mostly clothes and shoes that she still wore, but she realized they represented her life when she was in her twenties: stilettos, fake fur jackets, designer ripped and distressed tight jeans, tiny fringed shorts, midriff flaunting tops, a plethora of tank tops, colorful leggings, and a lot of boots. The boots she kept and some of the tank tops yet she had a sudden urge to purge, to upgrade not only her life but also her wardrobe, to modify to tasteful yet creative clothing and shoes—adapt to a sophisticated yet hip Barcelona style. Take some of the flamboyance, over-the-top playfulness out of her life and settle into her thirties with an internal stillness and comfort with the future, whatever it held.

In the past, she hadn't spent much time shopping for clothes in Spain. With so much of her time spent in performance clothes, her wardrobe had become outdated, and an upgrade had been unnecessary. But now it was time to spend some of that inheritance on fashion-first designers and exquisitely made clothes and shoes. Decision made, Sammy continued to selectively add to her giveaway pile and as she did an easy maturity settled, and eked its way into her consciousness. As the clothes and shoes in her closet dwindled, taking their place in the throwaway pile she'd grown excited about the opportunity to fill it again. All over Barcelona some young designers had their own shops full of ready-to-wear clothes and accessories. Also, there were chic shops hidden away on the less traveled passageways where she could uncover some real gems—shops that cater to women in their thirties—stylish, yet trendy, and extremely well-made. Spain was a fashion maker, but Barcelona was much more than that.

Although her closet was now sparse, seeing what she had accomplished gratified her. Old life—gone. New life—in the making. Giddy, she did a little tap dance then felt lightheaded and realized she hadn't eaten since those bites of Mateo's lunch so she reheated the frittata and empanadas he had given her, fixed a cup of tea, turned on her iTunes, flopped on the couch with a stack of Spanish fashion magazines and her iPad to scrutinize fashion sites and the latest fashion trends. Shopping would be on the docket for tomorrow.

SHE'D SLEPT WELL, unburdened, the lightness she'd felt after visiting the mountain and cleaning out her closet followed her into the evening and she woke this morning, rested, and ready to take on whatever life threw at her. Before heading to the shops, which didn't open until nine, Sammy decided to get an early start on the day. She left her apartment at eight and stopped at her favorite espresso café around the corner from her apartment and across the street from Port Vell, the waterfront harbor and marina. She ordered a *Café Cortado*—an espresso with a splash of milk— and treated herself to a *Xuxo* — a croissant stuffed with cream, deep-fried and sprinkled with sugar. Sitting on a high stool looking out the window of the espresso bar, she drank her coffee and savored every bite of her pastry until the night sky began to lighten. On the sidewalk outside the window, vendors set up souvenir kiosks and food trucks cranked out their awnings and huge chalkboard menus. Across the street in front of the marina joggers stretched and dog owners emerged, sleep-eyed with canines eager for their morning walk.

Drawn outside by the activity and anticipation of the beginning of her new adventure, Sammy asked the barista to put her drink into a to-go cup and she crossed the street. Out in the distance, she caught a glimmer of the sun's first rays brushing the surface of the sea. The sky, a hazy golden at the horizon with pink striations, fused into the deep rich indigo of the waning night sky. Sammy took a seat on a bench overlooking the Port Vell marina and breathed in the sea air. As she sipped her coffee, aromas of sizzling sugar and cinnamon from churros cooking up at the corner *creperie* food truck tickled her taste buds so much so that she was tempted to get another Xuxo, but decided against it.

Today was about clothes shopping.

The marina, its berths filled to capacity with fishing boats as well as luxury yachts, was her backdrop this morning for people watching and finishing her coffee. As the sun rose higher, she watched as fishermen and pleasure boaters boarded their vessels and loaded them up for a day at sea either for profit or for a day of relaxation on the Mediterranean. Sailboats, powerboats, and a scattering of yachts swayed, occasionally grazing each other with the sound of a soft thwap as the open sea rolled in. The benches around her filled with locals and the din of conversation rose with elderly men reminiscing about the good old days. Spurred on by the sudden activity around her and the itch to get her day moving, Sammy finished her coffee, walked to the end of the street tossed her cup into the waste receptacle and turned left down the expansive palm tree-laden promenade. The walkway meandered along the waterfront and paralleled the B10, a busy motorway on her right before ultimately connecting her neighborhood of Barceloneta to the bottom of *La Ramblas*—the pedestrian avenue that ran through the center of Barcelona and formed a boundary between the quarters of *Barri Gòtic*, to the East, and *El Raval*, to the West. The Barri Gòtic was Sammy's favorite for shopping and where she was headed today.

Sammy reached the top of the street, where the Columbus Monument stood, she crossed and made her way up La Ramblas. La Ramblas, she knew, had been an old riverbed until the end of the eighteenth century when it became Barcelona's only wide street—the rest of Barcelona encased in an intricate grid of narrow, dark, pathways. This morning the street lacked the crush of crowds that would come later in the day and yet there was plenty to watch. Along the sidewalk of La Ramblas, a plethora of oddities created a somewhat carnival-like, parade atmosphere. The menagerie consisted of vendors selling everything from books to souvenirs to food. Street performers danced, sang, and played instruments, and mimes attempted to attract the attention of those who passed. This group of performers tried to get her attention and distract her, but she was on a mission. Although shops and restaurants were plentiful along Rambla, Sammy's goal was to head to Barri Gòtic, and if she didn't find what she wanted there she would explore the *Eixample*—her other favorite shopping area. After a ten-minute walk, Sammy turned right into a narrow roadway, visibly not wide enough for a car, but she knew many traveled down it.

Initially, this particular passageway took Sammy past offices and other businesses then it opened onto a square where several avenues and pathways converged, anchored in the center by a fountain with bench seats encircling it. Today, the square was nearly empty with the exception of a couple wearing name tags, obviously from one of the cruise lines, dipping what looked like *melindros* (little ladyfinger type pastries) into cups of chocolate—a very Barcelona habit. They raised their hands in greeting, Sammy nodded to them and stood for a moment trying to decide which path to take; each direction would put her in the midst of fashionable shops and boutiques. She headed down one of her favorites.

Though stores wouldn't open for another fifteen minutes, she still got a thrill walking these narrow medieval stone streets; there was always something new to be discovered, something she'd never seen before. Century-old buildings were tucked up against the walkways and on the street level a plethora of stores, restaurants and trendy bars beckoned to patrons; apartments above the commercial buildings were filled with local families. This was where Barcelona came alive; this was its heart.

Sammy meandered, looking at window displays and, when she could, peeked inside closed storefronts making a mental list of the shops she would return to once they opened. Mixed in amongst the shops, museums, and cultural centers, modern-day artisans and merchants continued the traditions of generations past. She passed by the hat shop and saw the hat-maker through the window stitching a seam by hand. The leather shop that sold handmade purses, wallets, and briefcases had turned on its lights and she saw the owner working on a display. One of the shops, *Novedades Dorins*—a women's fashion boutique selling chic designs locally crafted from materials sourced in Spain, was closed, but Sammy would return to it. The lights were also on at *Efecto Limóna* a trendy zipper dress shop—though not her style anymore she'd purchased several zipper skirts from this designer in the past.

She walked further and before she knew it, she'd wandered outside Barri Gòtic area and found herself in front of Zara as it opened. Zara, where Macy worked, catered to a younger demographic. When Sammy entered the store, she found her decision to let go of old habits and styles was easy in theory, but harder to do when faced with all of the youthful trendy fashions. She ruffled through racks of clothes, naturally gravitating to the edgy ones and found herself indiscriminately grabbing things not unlike clothes she'd recently thrown away. When she got into the dressing room and rummaged through the items, she realized what she'd done and put all the selections back without trying them on. As she left, she mentally patted herself on the back for resisting old habits.

One of Barcelona's better-known young designers that also offered off-the-rack trendy, yet classy styles that were more closely tuned in to her age demographic had caught her eye during her wandering this morning so she went back. After trying on a few pieces the manager picked out for her, she got into a rhythm and before she knew it Sammy walked out of the store juggling five bags of clothes and two of shoes. She hadn't bought a coat that she really needed so she headed back to her apartment to unload her bags and come back after lunch. As she was passing under the *Pont del Bisbe*—

Barcelona's own Bridge of Sighs—a group of people surged out of one of the restaurants, chatting and not paying attention. They nearly knocked her over. While trying to get away from them she backed up and bumped into a man who was staring up at the bridge. She lost her grip on her purchases and the bags of shoes and two bags of clothes slipped to the ground; one box of shoes in the bags fell open and the shoes flew out. Frustrated, she turned to yell at the group, but they'd already moved on. When she turned her frustration to the man who was still looking up, he said, "Looks like you've been busy." He turned around and continued, "I see losing the job hasn't dampened your spirits." Then he smiled.

It was the doctor.

She felt her face flush as she grappled to gather her composure and her things.

"Here let me help you." He bent down and together they picked up her purchases.

She stood up, tried to handle them, but one of the bags kept slipping out of her grip; the doctor picked it up and started to hand it to her, but stopped and said, "How about I help you with these? Where are you headed?"

Where was she going? She'd lost track. "Back to my apartment to put these away before I head out again." Was she was stammering? Why was he suddenly having this effect on her? True, he towered over her, he was probably six feet or taller, but she'd dated tall men before, and yes, he obviously took care of his body because his shoulders filled out his leather coat quite nicely. The tan he must have gotten in Marseilles still lingered and his light brown hair still had those surfer-like subtle blond streaks making him look very hip and more like a California surfer than a doctor. And those brown eyes behind his glasses were now staring at her with such intensity she flushed.

"Here let me take a few more."

She handed him the bags of shoes and said, "Thank you."

As they walked, he commented on the Bridge of Sighs. "I was taken in by that bridge—architecturally magnificent—but that skull with the dagger out of its mouth was rather macabre."

Bridge? Somehow, she'd lost a sense of time and place. "Oh yes—our Bridge of Sighs. There are many legends about what the architect meant when he added that. I like the one that if you make a wish while walking backward under the bridge and look directly at the skull your wish will come true."

They continued their walk making small talk. Sammy tongue-tied or babbling about her purchases, Roan confident and so dang handsome that Sammy couldn't focus and several times she stumbled so that he had to hold her up and kept asking, "Are you okay?" Part of her wanted to tell him to go back to the ship and let her carry her own damn packages; the other half, well, didn't say a word. After they dropped her packages off at the apartment Roan asked, "Have you had lunch yet?"

"No, I was laser-focused on shopping. I think I'm obsessed."

"Well, if you're game, how about I treat you to lunch and then you can continue your recent obsession on a full stomach?"

"Sure, there's a restaurant on this block. It's family-owned and has fantastic local seafood. Does that sound okay?"

"Sounds great."

Sammy led him down the block a few steps from her

apartment where they went into the back kitchen entrance of the restaurant. The briny smell of the sea mingling with the unmistakable aroma of garlic simmering in butter and the sweet lingering whiff of saffron greeted them as they maneuvered around a stainless-steel maze of prep stations, cooktops, and the busy *brigade de cuisine*—the kitchen staff. Pots clanged, food bubbled on the stove, meat sizzled on the grill, and employees yelled over each other while waiters walked in and out loaded with trays of food. To anyone else it would seem like chaos, but to Sammy this restaurant and the people were as much home as Mateo at the deli, as Max and Javier had been at the studio, and as Father Thomas and Sister Mercedes had been at Monserrat.

"Hola, Sammy," several of the waiters and cooks called out as she and Roan walked through. The owner, Isabella, a short stocky woman with a penchant for bluster only surpassed by her warmth and passion for her restaurant and the food she served, pushed through the swinging door from the dining room, shouting orders to the waiters in Spanish. When she saw Sammy and Roan, she put her hands on her hips and shook her finger at Sammy. "So finally, you bring someone with you. And a handsome man, too." Then she winked at Sammy and said, "*Y una sexy.*"

Sammy felt her face flush, but took a deep breath and said, "Roan this is Isabella. She owns the restaurant. Isabella, Roan Adair. He's a doctor on the cruise ships. I wanted to show him what good authentic family-style Spanish food tastes like."

Isabella folded her arms across her ample chest and scrutinized Roan before she walked over and said, "Welcome, welcome." She kissed him on both cheeks then stood back nodding. "Yes, yes, you will do. Sammy here brings no one with her anymore. Always alone, she eats. And so fast! Always running, here, there," Isabella said while flaying her arms around. "Food needs to digest; wine needs to be savored. Tell her to slow down. Life is quick." She snapped her fingers, sighed, and said, "But it's good to see she has *amigos* after all."

Sammy smiled and shook her head. "I have lots of friends my dear Isa, but I keep your special place to myself. What would happen if everyone wanted to come here? Then I would have to wait for a table." Before Isabella could say anymore, Sammy grabbed Roan's arm trying to get him out of the kitchen.

"No, no, you cannot take him yet." Isabella took Roan's other arm and pulled him over to one of the cooking stations, picked up a croquette that had just out of the fryer and popped it into Roan's mouth.

His face turned red and he huffed while trying to chew, saying, "Hot, hot." When he finally swallowed, he said, *"Muy bien. Excelente."*

"You speak Spanish, Mr. Doctor?" Isabella said and nudged him to the next station.

"Yes, it's necessary for my job."

"Bueno, bueno," Isabella said, picked up a spoon, dipped it into a pot and handed it to Roan. "Taste." When he hesitated, she said, waving her arms at him. "Go on, go on. Taste." She shook her head. "Not hot."

Isabella leaned in toward him, watching him, her eyes glued to his face to see his reaction. Again, Roan huffed, but this time his eyes opened wider and he said, "That is fantastic."

Isabella straightened, suddenly appearing taller as if a puppeteer holding strings attached to her body had pulled her upward. She grinned broadly, turned to her staff, and said, "Whatever this man orders, it must be *perfecta*."

Sammy felt a rush of warmth and camaraderie being amongst her friends. Her confidence, now that she was on her home turf, and the awkwardness she'd felt with Roan earlier was replaced by a compelling desire to show him how unaffected she was by his presence. Because after all . . . she was.

They walked out of the kitchen and made their way through the crowded restaurant until Sammy caught the eye of Isabella's daughter, who pointed to several open tables and mouthed, "Anywhere."

She picked an open table by the window then instead asked Roan, "Do you mind if we sit outside? It's such a lovely day."

"Sure. You lead, I'll follow."

They went out the front door to the crowded patio area, but there weren't any empty tables. Roan walked up, stood beside her, and said, "It doesn't look like there are any tables. I guess we'll have to go inside." And he turned to head back toward the door.

"Wait, Roan. They always set up a table for me even when it looks full." Suddenly several waiters grabbed a table from inside and placed it on the other side of the front entrance and away from the other outside eating area.

"Well, I'm impressed," Roan said. "It seems we have our own special spot."

"Yes, they like me here." Then she laughed. "But I confess, they open this area up in the evening for dinner, they're just doing it early."

Roan pulled out her chair and stood beside her while she sat then took his seat. "So. What's good here?"

"Wine."

He laughed.

"No, I'm serious," she said. "They have the best wine list around. And they know what's good even if it's on the less expensive side."

"Well, then. Let's start there." He hesitated. "Unless you are in a hurry to get back to your shopping."

"I am, but a lot of stores close during the lunch hours. Do you think I would've forgone a chance to shop just to fill my stomach?" she teased, picked up a menu, and handed one to Roan who was looking at her curiously. "What?" She smiled at him. "I like to shop."

"That was clear by the number of packages I helped you carry," he chided.

They were flirting, this banter she realized, was fun. Then for a moment, she felt the familiar disquiet that whispered she was being disloyal to Peter; her heart beat faster and guilt infiltrated the joy she'd been feeling. She grabbed the glass of water the waiter placed in front of her, took a long gulp then a deep breath and let it fade.

"You, okay?" Roan asked, frowning.

"Oh, I had a moment. Peter and I came here all the time. It passed. I'm fine."

"I'm sorry. Being around me can't make it any easier."

"Nothing makes it easier, but time. I'm fine," she said. "Let's order." But the feeling of uncertainty remained. Should she make an excuse and leave? Before she could make a decision, the waiter brought them a bottle of *Albariño*—Sammy's favorite Spanish white wine—and poured two glasses.

Roan lifted his glass to hers and said, "To more shopping adventures."

"Yes, yes. Thank you." Sammy raised her glass, too, and searched for a neutral subject, one that didn't remind her of their shared moments at Monserrat and Peter's death. "Do you like paella?" Then without letting him answer, she plunged ahead. "Isabella makes *Arroz Caldoso* which is paella made with seafood—no meat—and it's a bit more like a soup than regular paella. You see there are many kinds of paella." She went into a breathy, lengthy explanation of the kinds of paella, where they came from, and way too much information most of which was unnecessary. It wasn't working, she was still feeling uncertain so she tried to relax into the moment and chastised herself—her anxiety was not Roan's fault.

"Seafood paella sounds perfect. When in Spain . . . as they say." He kept staring at her and finally said, "Are you sure you're okay?"

"My focus is on my lack of a job right now," she lied. "So, I'm compensating by shopping and talking too much."

"Ah, it's what we do, isn't it? Not shopping, but displacing our real emotions with something more tangible that has nothing to do at all with what we're feeling."

"Oh, my, is that what I'm doing?" She slowed her breathing and relaxed into her chair. "You sound like my old therapist"

"Sorry, the doctor took over for a minute. I planned on psychiatry when I entered med school, but changed."

"Why?" They were on safer ground now; small talk was easy.

He fiddled with his silverware and swirled his wine, then admitted, "I didn't excel. Psychiatry bored me and so my grades fell. I liked the challenge of emergency medicine; it's fast-paced and I liked the idea of being part of a team—so I switched to ER medicine with plans to work for Doctors

Without Borders when I finished. How about you, did you always want to dance?"

"Yes, but I was groomed to be a lawyer. My dad has a practice and my three brothers all went to law school then right into his practice. I headed that direction, too, until I realized how much I hate the law so I quit and moved here. It really upset my dad—he'd planned on my joining his practice. In fact, we didn't talk for a long time. Everything is good now."

The waiter showed up and after they ordered they continued to talk, Sammy telling him about Javier and the real reason she lost her job. "It's also the reason for my shopping trip," Sammy said.

"How so?"

"I threw away all my performance clothes and that led to purging a lot of my clothes that were ten years old." She shrugged. "I never shopped much for new stuff and didn't realize how outdated my clothes were. And," she continued, staring out at the marina and the sea across the street, "it's about new beginnings: job, closet, life. Out with the dance, in with everything new—whatever that will be. That's something I've yet to figure out."

Roan leaned back in his chair and said, "You know, I don't know if you're open to it, but I had a thought about your job."

Sammy felt at ease now, she knew that her initial panic was due to her mixed feelings about being around Roan and trying to separate the doctor who couldn't save Peter, from the attractive, intelligent man she was beginning to like.

"Yes, please share."

"Didn't you tell me you occasionally teach dance?"

"Yes, I teach a class here and there for friends, and friends of friends who want to learn the flamenco. But nothing very organized or on any regular schedule. Why?"

"Ciara mentioned you have a substantial inheritance. Well, have you ever thought about opening your own studio?"

Her own dance studio? Of course! She felt a surge of glee, her heart beat fast, her stomach flip-flopped, she felt a buoyancy she hadn't felt in a long time, a very long time. It was the answer—the perfect answer. This was the answer. And kids, she'd do it with kids. She jumped up, rushed at Roan, and kissed him on the cheek.

"Oh, my god, how could I have not thought of that?" She nearly jumped up and down. "It's perfect, Roan. Thank you so much." She giggled, did a quick twirl and flopped back in her chair, grabbed her glass of wine, leaned back, closed her eyes, and took a long sip. Then she opened her eyes and grinned at Roan.

But he was flushed, looking quite embarrassed . . . and shocked—there was that.

He cleared his throat, cocked his head, and said, "Happy to be of service."

"No, really, you don't understand. It is PERFECT."

And a voice somewhere deep in her psyche whispered, and so is he.

CHAPTER EIGHT

*T*hey said goodbye at the restaurant. Roan had to get back to the ship to prepare for its departure in a few days and Sammy's enthusiasm for her new project completely dismantled her plan to shop.

"When you return, I'm taking you to dinner to thank you for making my day and possibly my future."

"No need, but, yes, let's get together when I return. I'll be eager to hear what you've come up with." He leaned in to give her a quick hug, but she surprised him again with a quick kiss on his cheek.

"Truly, Roan, your idea and willingness to share it with me means a lot. I know our past is complicated and I'm sure it will be confounding at times, but I like you. So, let's stay connected."

He reached out and touched her arm then took hold of her hand, and said, "Okay, then since I've gotten your approval, I'll be calling." And he surprised her by leaning over and lightly touching her lips with his, winked at her, and walked away.

She stood there taking in this feeling, this new feeling, a

feeling that she had thought left her a long time ago. It surprised her that she had begun to care about him so quickly, so soon, and if she was honest, he stirred in her a longing, a desire to be loved again.

But she couldn't let that feeling linger.

Right now, she had work to do.

When she got back to her apartment, she went through her packages, hung up her new clothes and put away her shoes. Then immediately formulated a plan to see if Roan's suggestion was even feasible. Should she rent a studio or buy? That would depend on Spain's rules on owning a business as an American. First call was to parents about the trust. She explained to them what had happened and what she wanted to do with some of her trust fund. Surprisingly, they were both supportive.

Her father initially had tried to play tough guy by grumbling, "Just come home? There're plenty of spots here to open a studio."

"Dad, we've had this conversation. I love it here; I'm staying."

They bantered back and forth and traded gibes for another few minutes before her father capitulated. "Well, at least your knowledge of the law and negotiating skills will come in handy."

"Okay, Dad, I'll give you that, but you do know the laws are different here."

She heard him chuckle, then a bit of mischief and a whiff of sarcasm filled his voice and he said, "It's quite possible you won't be able buy property in Spain. You'll have to research the laws. I might see you back here soon." Then she heard him whispering to her mother, loudly enough for her to hear, "Get her room ready. She'll be back by Thanksgiving." She heard a slap and her mother say, "Stop it, Stuart."

He came back on the line and said, "It's your trust fund, honey. I wish you every success. I'll send the paperwork out."

And that was that.

Obstacle one: overcome.

Obstacle two that her father pointed out concerned her; she grabbed her iPad and did some online research which showed that since she already had an EU permanent residency permit, she would be able to buy property and open a business.

Obstacle two: overcome. Another hoop she didn't have to jump through.

And yet the search also showed that opening a business could be arduous and somewhat complicated. She punched in Ciara's number. Ciara had had to go through a lengthy process to start her international school and Sammy wanted to pick her brain about finding a studio space and what the advantages were to rent versus buy.

"What's up?" Ciara answered sounding breathless.

"You busy?"

"A little. Ran to grab the office phone. Why don't you call my mobile?" she grumbled. "You keep calling my office line. I'm never in the office, my cell is always with me."

"Wow, geez, grumpy. Should I hang up and call your mobile or just hang up?" Sammy's joyful mood slipped away.

Ciara sighed. "Sorry. Work stuff. Kids, if you want to know."

Kids. Maybe she should rethink her idea about teaching kids to dance. Deflated she said, "I had some news I wanted to share, but, well, never mind. Call me when you are in a better mood."

"That's probably for the best. It's been one of those days; if it's not the parents bitching, it's the kids acting out. Actually, it's the parents. Talk soon." Sammy knew Ciara often had issues with parents of the kids in her school and at times had thought about selling the school.

Ciara's testy response put her off, but Ciara was Sammy's rock and had always been there for her. They'd been best friends since their first meeting. Ciara's story, like Sammy's, followed the common thread of many ex-pats who came to Spain; they came to escape, to begin a new adventure, or a desire to search for their roots. Ciara came to Spain from Ireland where she grew up and where her parents and eight siblings still lived. She'd confided that those tight family ties became oppressive and their demands on her time and their insistence she help in the pub they owned became more than she could handle, so she left not long after college to move here. It was Ciara who was there when Peter collapsed, took Sammy home from the hospital the night he died, who called the others to tell them about Peter and stayed with her in the weeks following, making sure she ate, and helped her arrange the funeral. So, she'd let Ciara have her grumpy time.

Sammy grabbed the iPad again and decided to do her own research until she could talk to Ciara. She learned that a cash purchase of a space would pose less of a problem than trying to find financing, but now she needed to decide whether to do that or lease. Next, she sent emails and texts to friends and acquaintances who had children to see if they would be willing to sign them up for a class. As she was finishing the last text her phone rang; a number she didn't recognize.

"Sammy, it's Roan. Not disturbing you, am I?"

"No, not at all. I'm doing some research on your idea."

"Great, I was worried I'd overstepped."

"Actually, I'm very grateful." As he was saying something her phone clicked like she had another call. She briefly pulled the phone from her ear and saw it was Ciara. "Say, Roan, would you hold for a minute, Ciara is calling me."

"Go ahead and take it, I'm prepping for the cruise anyway. Your number was still in my phone from . . . ," he hesitated, "before, but I wanted you to have mine. You've got it on Caller ID now so give me a call periodically and let me know how all the research is going. I have coverage at sea. Good luck, bye now."

"Say wait . . ."

After he hung up, she clicked over to Ciara feeling a bit out-of-sorts thinking about that kiss Roan had given her when they said goodbye at the restaurant. She was distracted, but it didn't matter because Ciara, in a rush of apologies, rambled on about why she was so messed up when Sammy called earlier.

"Sammy, are you listening?" When Sammy didn't answer she continued, "Look, I said I'm sorry. Get over it."

Sammy laughed then. "Leave it to you to give an apology in one breath then take it away with another. It's fine, silly. I had an unexpected call from Roan. I was talking to him when you called."

"Do tell. What did the hunky doctor want?"

"Well . . ." She started to try to explain to Ciara, but changed her mind. "Say, what are you doing right now? If I came to the school, could we talk a bit?"

"Hold one, let me check this afternoon's schedule." The

phone went quiet for a minute then Ciara was back. "Clear. My afternoon's clear. Come on over."

* * *

SAMMY WALKED into the international school and immediately ran into some of the teachers she knew including her friend Sylvia who, as usual, looked like she'd just stepped off the runway.

"Hey, what are you doing here? Ciara told me about your job; I'm sorry. I know how you love to dance. Are you coming back to teach?" She locked arms with Sammy and they walked through the halls, past classrooms, until they got to Ciara's office.

"No, I have a few things to talk to Ciara about. I'll tell you about it when I see you at book club."

"Oh, yeah, I forgot about it. Where is it?" Sylvia asked.

"Danele's."

Sylvia glanced at her watch at the same time the class bell rang. "Gotta run before the kids have a free-for-all."

Sylvia left and Ciara got up from her desk and gave Sammy a quick hug. "I'm sorry I was so bitchy this morning. It's been one of those days." Ciara pointed to one of the two chairs in front of her desk and said, "Sit and tell me what's going on with the doc." Then she closed the office door and sat down next to Sammy in the other chair.

"It's not about the doc. He had an idea and I wanted to talk to you about it and pick your brain."

She told Ciara about Roan's idea. "I'm so excited, but there's so much I don't know. I've never started my own business."

"With all the bullshit I went through today I'd tell you to forget it and go work for someone else. But most days I'm happy."

They talked about Sammy's options and when Sammy got to the part about buying a studio or renting a space, Ciara jumped up. "Oh my god, I can't believe I didn't think about this earlier. We have space."

"What do you mean?"

"There's an empty, warehouse-type room upstairs that we've never used. It would be perfect for your dance studio. You game?"

"I don't know. I'd have to see it."

Ciara grabbed her key ring and said, "Let's do this."

* * *

THE ROOM WAS PERFECT. As soon as Ciara unlocked the door and they'd walked inside, Sammy knew. She could already see it filled with students: girls and boys at a practice barre along a wall of mirrors, a piano in the corner for dance classes and recitals, turn boards for training. She saw it all, and she loved it. The last time she was this excited about her future was when Peter proposed.

The room was vast with a high wood-beamed ceiling and rustic wood floor; tall wood-cased windows on the eastside framed a view of the distant Mediterranean and the ones on the westside looked out over the rooftops of Barcelona. The room was empty except for several iron rope rings that hung from the ceiling, an old scale, a rope ladder, and two vaulting horses. Ciara told her it was once a gymnasium for the school but after they added a new gym in the eighties the old one had remained unused. There would be a lot of work that needed to be done, but Sammy loved it. The floor needed to be refinished to make sure it was smooth so barefoot dancers didn't get splinters in their feet or trip if they were wearing shoes and yet the floor couldn't be too smooth so the students would lose their balance and fall. She would install a ballet barre, mirrors along two walls, and paint the grey walls a bright white. She couldn't contain her excitement so when she and Ciara went back to her office and Ciara gave her a rental rate, Sammy quickly agreed.

"Are you sure? I want to be fair, but the school could use the extra income."

"It's perfect. I want to get started as soon as possible. The floor will need to be refinished and I will have to have other work done. Would that disrupt the school?"

Ciara frowned. "I didn't think of that. Having equipment and contractors coming and going wouldn't be good." She paused a minute then reached behind her, opened drawers on a large bookcase and pulled out some paperwork. She rummaged through a few stacks. "Viola," she said, "as I thought. There's an old outside exit and back staircase up to the room. Let's check it out."

They headed outside, to the side of the school where they found the door. It took several pulls to open it. Sammy made a mental note to have the door fixed. They entered a dark entry, flipped the light switch, but nothing happened—another addition to her list. Using their cell phones as flashlights, they walked up the narrow unlit stairway feeling with their hands along the dark paneling. The stairs seemed stable beneath their feet, but the left-side handrail needed to be secured in places. They reached the landing at the top and searched for a door into Sammy's new studio space. In the darkness, they ran their hands along the walls hoping to find a handle and after a few times walking back and forth Ciara yelled, "Found it." She yanked the door and light flooded in from the studio. "This is perfect for contractors and even for the students who will take your classes, Sammy."

Sammy was elated, rushed into the room, pulling Ciara inside with her and said, "Come on dance with me."

And they waltzed to imaginary music.

CHAPTER NINE

*S*ammy filled the following days with planning and initiating several aspects of those plans. She reached out to Macy's new husband, Tomas. He was a general contractor and had done work on his and Macy's house; he also had a crew of sub-contractors that did specialized work around the city. She hired them to fix the electricity at the back entrance, add a new exit door with a secure lock, add new lighting so the back entrance wouldn't be so dark, repair the handrail, clear the room of the leftover equipment and take down the rope rings and ladder. Once they finished there, she would have them start on everything else.

She also laid out a marketing plan that she would launch a month before her opening. Timing for her marketing blitz depended upon the efficiency of the workers and the absence of major structural issues. After a brief inspection, Tomas told her the space below the studio was a storage room for the school so if any problems arose with the joists or beams or bad planks when refinishing the floors, the subs could get at them. With a targeted opening of January, two and a half months away, she'd begin marketing right before the holidays with early sign-up discounts in hopes that parents might add dance classes to their children's Christmas gift list. Sammy already had confirmed five registrants, children from women she had taught in the past, but she knew in order to make a go of this endeavor before she ran through her budgeted funds, she'd need many more students.

By the end of that week, both exhausted and hopeful, she crossed off several of her to-do items and was sitting in her apartment at her desk adding new ones—it seemed that for every task she crossed out she added two more. She was excited about her new venture, but also exasperated as the list grew. She sighed, leaned forward putting her elbows on top of her desk, resting her chin on her hands and stared out the window at the dark clouds that had begun to form. The weather report was for an unseasonal storm that would bring excessive rain and choppy seas. A metaphor for what she was feeling right now: turbulent excitement, brooding waves of emotion, and oppressive clouds of trepidation. She looked out over the rooftops as an influx of grey formed on the tops of the structures and beyond white chop formed on the Mediterranean in the distance. Across the street, laundry on clotheslines stretched across balconies billowed and flapped in the wind. As the storm approached from the east, Sammy heard wind wheezing and felt it seeping through the gaps in the single pane window in front of her. Windows. Darn. She added those to her list. The ones in the studio were old and would need to be replaced or at least weatherized and caulked. She was adding to her list when her phone rang and she answered without looking at the caller ID.

"Sammy?"

"Yes."

"Sammy, it's Roan. How's that project of yours going?"

Hearing his voice unnerved her. She'd thought about him many times since they'd talked briefly before he left and more than once her thoughts lingered on the memory of the kiss he gave her as they parted at lunch. Her mixed feelings about it, guilt and desire, beat an opposing drum in her heart. But hearing his voice made her smile.

"Well, I found a studio space and I'm making a list as we speak about all the things I need to do." She shivered as the wind outside picked up sending a wisp of cold air into the room and rain began to pound on the window. She pushed back from her desk and stood.

"Well-done, Sammy. Where?"

"Ciara had an empty room at the school—and it's perfect. It has the most beautiful floor, and big windows so there is a lot of light. It's old, but has so much character."

"Definitely sounds perfect. You're leasing it then. Not buying a place?"

"I couldn't decide, but once I saw the room at the school I knew."

"How will that work within the school's hours?"

"Perfectly actually, it has its own exit; the dance students can come and go without disturbing classes." Now she couldn't contain her excitement and realized how much she wanted to share it with him, and she began pacing while talking. "I can't wait to show it to you. I've already started a long list of what needs to be done, but . . . the darn thing keeps growing."

"I get it. That happens with my research. One new fact or

discovery leads to another. It can be daunting at times. But you've got this."

"Yeah, I know, but dang it, you are right—it's so darn unnerving." Just then her list fluttered to the floor. "Say, it's really cold in here. Hold on I have to make sure my window is closed."

"Of course."

She laid the phone down, closed the window, picked up the scattered pages of her list off the floor and flopped on the couch wrapping herself in a blanket. "By the way, thanks for the confidence in me. I've been second-guessing myself."

"You shouldn't. From the little time I've known you, you seem like a pretty determined woman." He hesitated then said, "And I like that." He cleared his voice and rushed on. "Say, we had a pretty good storm that ran through here about an hour ago. Did it come your way?"

"It's hitting us now. Do the ships get a lot of turbulence?"

"This one was rough, but these ships are steady. They have stabilizers so typically we rarely feel rough seas. This one we felt." It sounded like he covered the phone and spoke to someone then to her, "Say, I gotta run. Patients are lining up."

She was disappointed. "Okay. Well, give me a call when you get back."

"Call? I thought you promised me dinner? You're not bailing on me, are you?"

"I promised to *take* you to dinner—believe me you don't want me to cook."

"Okay it's a date then—no backing out now. I return in a week. I'll give you a call. Or . . . " she heard a smile in his voice, "maybe I'll just show up. Take care."

"You too, Roan." She hung up. For some reason she felt all

warm and fuzzy. Roan: She liked the sound of his name on her tongue and liked hearing her voice when she said it. She snuggled deeper into the blanket and an image popped in her head of Roan sitting next to her on this couch. And the kissing . . . there was that.

* * *

SEVERAL DAYS LATER SAMMY, back from her run, had just finished making a protein drink when the intercom rang.

"Yes?"

"I see they fixed the intercom."

"I'm sorry, who's this?"

"It's Roan. I told you I might show up."

"What? Wait, aren't you supposed to be out at sea?"

"I had a little accident and . . . Hold on, is this a bad time? I can come back."

"No, no, come on up." She pressed the button to let him in then realized she was a mess from her jog. She ran to the bathroom and looked in the mirror, took her hat off, fluffed her hair then grabbed some product and tried to repair the damage her hat had done. She washed her face and put on a bit of mascara, pinched her cheeks, rolled on some deodorant walked into the living room to wait. Still flustered, she paced, glanced around the room, quickly gathered together discarded clothes, threw them on her bed, swept her arm across side tables to wipe off the dust then brushed the accumulated dust off her sweatshirt sleeve as Roan knocked on the door.

She opened the door and was shocked to see him standing

there with his left arm in a sling. "Oh my god, what happened?"

He shrugged. "Apparently I'm a bit of a klutz."

She waved him inside. "Come in."

"Thanks."

She moved back to let him get by, but when he slid past her in the tiny doorway his hand brushed hers and the scent of his cologne, a clean, fresh woodsy aroma, sent an unexpected thrill through her body. He walked into the room then paused and turned towards her while she closed the door. She'd noticed he wasn't wearing his glasses so this morning those deep-set eyes seemed to hold the slightest bit of mystery —or was it seduction? He was clean-shaven, something she hadn't noticed before, unlike most men now who sported either a designer stubble or full beard. His high cheekbones were still a bit rosy from the cold day. She didn't understand why he was having this effect on her and she tried to avert her eyes but found herself staring at him instead.

Today, his unexpected presence in her apartment unnerved her.

She wanted him.

He stared back at her, eyes questioning. Then he looked embarrassed and said, "Am I keeping you from anything? I was out driving to the store to pick up some food and realized I was by the marina and decided to say hi. But like I said I can come back."

She shook her head and tried to find her voice. "Just got back from my morning run. That's all I've planned for the day except some paperwork for the studio. Please take off your coat and sit." She walked over and stood next to him. He slipped his coat off his left shoulder and as he struggled to get his right arm out, she reached over to help him they bumped heads.

"See I told you I was a klutz," he said and rubbed his forehead. "Are you okay? We hit pretty hard."

Her head hurt too, but what she really wanted to do was grab his face and kiss him. She suppressed the urge and laughed instead. "Yes, I'm fine."

They moved into the room and sat across from each other: Sammy on the couch, Roan on a chair. "So, what happened?"

He scratched his head and said, "I'm still trying to figure that out. I'm usually very steady on the ship. I'm very fit you see." He flexed his other arm and grinned at her. "When the storm hit, it hit fast and there were several people outside that needed to get inside. I went out to help an elderly woman at the same time we hit a roller and down we both went. I dislocated my shoulder."

"Ouch. How's the woman?"

"She's fine. In fact, later that day she thanked me and when she asked my name, she said she knew about me because a woman had told her when she was up on Montserrat. She said your name was funny like a man's. When I suggested Sammy, she said I was right, so thank you for putting in a good word."

Had she? She couldn't remember and didn't think she'd do that. Then she remembered the couple from the trip to the mountain. Of course, she had.

"Anyway," Roan continued, "they won't let me work until it's fully healed so I'm on medical leave for a few weeks."

"You didn't say anything when I talked to you a few days ago."

"I was in denial. Ha, I figured I was tougher than that. I

convinced myself it was a muscle pull until the other doc pointed out my shoulder looked deformed."

"Is it painful?"

"Only when I do this." He started to lift his arm out of the sling.

"Stop!"

He stopped, a playful smile twitching at his lips—kissable lips, the bottom lip plump, ripe for tugging on with hers. She blinked, trying to regain control.

"I'm messing with you; I'm a tease—or so my wife used to say. But to answer your question, it's more like a dull ache now. I take anti-inflammatory meds if it gets too bad. Luckily, it's on my left side; I'm right-handed."

"One of my brothers broke his shoulder once. He said it was pretty painful." They sat there looking at each other for a few minutes before Sammy continued, "How bad is it? I mean how long before it's healed?"

"Sixteen weeks, but I told them as soon as I can lift my arm without it killing me, I'm going back. They're short on doctors. We airlifted my replacement, but she is due to go out on maternity leave in a few weeks. I'll be needed."

He leaned back into the chair, crossing his leg, settling in. Sammy, with a start, realized he looked like he belonged here. But he couldn't. That was Peter's chair, the soft leather still molded to Peter's body. The man who couldn't save him shouldn't look so relaxed in Peter's space. But he did and his being there fit somehow.

She cleared her throat and started to say something, but Roan interrupted her. "Enough about me, tell me all about your project. You said you found a space at Ciara's. How's renovation coming along?"

Her excitement over the new business took over; she relaxed into the moment. When she finished telling him about what had been done so far, she told him about her progress with the marketing plan and timeline for the rest of the work. "The floors will be done by the end of the month but will need to cure through November isn't the best month to open up windows. When they are ready then we do the next round of painting and installing the mirrors. I hope to have all of that done by Thanksgiving, Christmas at the latest, and open just after the first of the year."

"That's pretty ambitious, but it sounds like you've got this under control. I admire you. I can't imagine starting my own business alone. Even my practice was opened with another doctor." He leaned forward and started to get up. "Well, time for me to hit the road and get that food back to my place." He rose and grabbed his coat. He slipped his right arm in and when she rose to help him with his left one, he said, "I got this. I think I've proven how inept I am at trying to help someone or letting them help me." He laughed and said, "I think you should keep a safe distance."

She moved closer to him anyway and reached around him to help him pull up his coat over his injured shoulder. Their faces inches apart and when she looked up at him, his eyes were on hers, his mouth so near. In that moment, she realized she didn't want him to go. Her sudden desire for him overwhelmed her; her confusion over her feelings for him and how quickly those feelings had materialized confounded her but she said, "But what if I don't want to?"

"Want to what?"

"What if I don't want to keep a safe distance? What if I don't want to keep any distance at all?"

She took his other hand, lifted it to her lips and kissed it; she stared at him while she did it and this time, she clearly saw seduction in those eyes.

"Then it's a good thing this arm is healthy." And he wrapped it around her waist, pulled her tightly into his body, bent his head and kissed her. Not a light touch this time, this time slow and soft at first then teeming in passion, and with an unspoken promise for more. Her body relaxed into his and she allowed the sensations of his body pressing into hers and her mouth exploring his to make everything around her disappear. She wanted him and she wanted him now. She began unbuttoning his shirt, but he pulled back, gently brushed a wisp of hair out of her face and, his voice gruff, said, "This is unexpected."

She didn't want him to go, that kiss, her desire for him had risen to such a level that reality and common sense fused to the back of her mind. But he had pulled away and she was confused, so she stepped back. "I'm sorry, I guess I thought you were . . . "

"I am, Sammy. I'm drawn to you in so many ways. But . . . " he hesitated, looked at the ceiling, closed his eyes and said, "Are you sure this is what you want? Our history is complicated."

She wasn't going to take the time to think about any of that right now and to prove it to him, and to herself, she took his hand and led him into the bedroom.

* * *

THEY'D FALLEN asleep hours ago and Roan was still asleep when Sammy slipped out of bed and walked toward the bathroom, hoping not to disturb him. She was confused, filled with guilt and remorse. The sex had been glorious and Sammy had given herself to him in ways she hadn't since Peter, but her conscience nipped at her that she'd slept with the man that couldn't save Peter. Her mind told her he couldn't have, but her heart beat with the resolve that he should have. She felt disloyal to Peter and angry at herself— not just because of the sex, but because there were feelings involved that she couldn't quite explain. She'd always steered away from anything too deep, love meant loss, even with Javier, yet with Roan, this felt different.

"Are you okay?"

She jumped. Roan was standing behind her with his hands on her shoulders.

"I'm fine," she lied, walked into the bathroom and closed the door. She stared at her reflection in the mirror above the sink and in her own eyes she saw the truth: she was beginning to care about Roan and she was being disloyal to Peter. She knew it made no sense—it wasn't like she hadn't slept with a man since Peter died, but this was different. This time remorse rose through her body in every place the doctor had touched. She willed the tears away but when it got to be too much, she slipped to the floor quietly sobbing.

After a few minutes, Roan tapped on the door. "Sammy?"

"I'll be right out." She made herself stand, blew her nose, turned on the water and rinsed her face.

He tapped on the door again.

She opened the door, walked around him, grabbed her clothes off the floor and dressed. Then she sat down on the bed and forced herself to look at him. He had also dressed while she was in the bathroom but now stood with his back to her peering into the bathroom where the floor was laden with used tissues, where water still dripped from the faucet, where the white towel she'd used to wipe her face was spoiled with the black from her eyes and red from her lips—colored evidence of her betrayal. He turned to face her but avoided her eyes. His eyes downcast, his body shifting from one foot to the other, he took a deep breath, finally raising his eyes to meet hers and said, "You were crying." He shook his head. "I was afraid of this." He took a step toward her, but she held up her hand. Resigned, he raised his arms then let them drop to his side. "What can I do, Sammy? How can I fix this?"

Sunlight poured into the room from the window above the bed sending sharp shafts of light onto crumpled sheets, pillows, and comforter they'd tossed on the floor in their frantic desire for each other. Streams of sunlight also spilled through the window landing on Roan's troubled face, his brow furrowed, the corners of his mouth drawn down. As she looked at him, she wished she could disappear into this bed and hide under the covers until he left—into this bed where years ago she'd made love to Peter and where today she'd had sex with this man; this man who was kind, who awakened in her feelings she thought were gone forever, romantic feelings that, if she was honest, she didn't want to have anymore—for anyone. Yet, while her soul spun guilt, her desire for him still simmered.

Roan walked over, sat beside her on the bed, stared at his hands then took one of her hands in his. "Did we make a mistake?" He paused, looked at the ceiling then continued, "I don't know. I have my own doubts, too." He looked over at her and she saw the truth along with distress in his eyes. He looked weary, but she couldn't find any words or the desire to comfort him, so he continued, "But we took a moment that we both felt and acted on it. We can't take that back, but we can move on. We can take the time to think about it and decide what we do now. Right?"

She wasn't sure. Since Peter's death, she'd come this far without romance, without deep feelings or someone to care about; with caring, came loss she'd learned that when Peter died. Yes, she'd begun to open up and felt safe again, but was there safety in caring about Roan, about having a relationship? She wasn't sure. She slipped her hand out of his, stood, her back to him and closed the curtains on the window above her head, smothering the light, the truth, the reality. The room darkened, and she paced. Images of Peter flashed in her memory and angst filled her. She tried to talk, to express to Roan what she felt but the words stuck in her throat and all she could do was nod.

"You're thinking of Peter, aren't you?

Again she nodded.

"You know I couldn't have saved him, don't you?"

Like he could read her thoughts. The fact that he saw through to her innermost thoughts terrified her. Sex was one thing; this was different it seemed. She turned away from him, hiding her face so he couldn't see the truth outside of what she said which was, "I know you couldn't, Roan." Then realizing he deserved the truth, she turned back to him and said, "In my mind I know that." She shook her head as if to clear it. "But my heart," she touched her chest, "well it hasn't fully connected with my brain yet. And it's not just that, Roan, it's something else, too. I'm beginning to care about you and it scares me." She tried to smile, but her lips quivered. Head down she walked over to him. When he stood up she wrapped her arms around him and rested her head against his chest. "I want to get there; I thought I had, but I need a bit more time."

"I think we both do," he said, his voice full of emotion. Then he stepped back, drawing the back of his finger down her cheek, he smiled and said, "We jumped into this rather quickly; perhaps a friendship is what this," he spread his arms to include the two of them, "needs. We could take a step back. Would you be open to that?"

Her voice barely above a whisper, she said, "I think so."

He put his hands on her shoulders, looked down at her, and gave her a timid smile. "I don't know how it will work or if it will work, but I want to keep getting to know you."

She raised her eyes to him. "I want to get to know you, too, but outside the role as my husband's doctor. I'm not sure when I can get there." She sighed. "Or if I can," she took a step back, frowned, and continued, "I'd like to try, though. Let's meet for coffee in a few weeks and see how we both feel."

"Or dinner," he said and winked, "—you do still owe me dinner. So when you are ready *and* if you decide you want to keep our friendship, I would welcome that. I like what we started and I'm always up for a free meal—friends or lovers either way." And he turned to walk out of the bedroom.

She followed him. He grabbed his coat and as he headed for the apartment door, she moved in front of him. Sharing her misgivings and hearing his own concerns as well as his attempt at humor, lightened her, so she touched his hand and shared, "Be patient with me, please, and I'll be patient with you. If we both want it, we will find that place, that place which works for both of us."

He tilted his head and he said, "I really like you and hoped we could find each other devoid of our history, but maybe that's being too optimistic."

She desperately wanted to hold him to keep him from going but knew he was right. She regained her composure and confidence, outstretched her hand and said, "Deal. Now let's shake on it." When he took her hand she pulled him toward her, looked into his eyes and said, "I don't want to blame you for anything, Roan, I like you."

THE SILENCE in her apartment after Roan left wrapped her in a fog of confusion. And yet his voice echoed in her head spliced with hopefulness and a degree of pessimism. 'I really like you and hoped we could find each other devoid of our history, but maybe that's too optimistic,' he'd said. Part of her wanted to fight his cynicism, ignore her own misgivings about getting involved with him in the first place and charge with abandon into the future.

She walked back into the bedroom and faced again with the evidence of the last few hours; she began ripping the sheets off the bed. Determined to start the day fresh, she shoved those sheets in the washer, put new sheets on the bed, threw the tissues away and cleaned up the bathroom then got into the shower.

She'd keep her emotions about Roan tucked away for today and worry about them tomorrow.

CHAPTER TEN

That tomorrow morphed into days. Sammy purposely wouldn't let herself go to that place again—to examine what feelings towards him were real and which were because of their past. So, with the studio renovation still underway she stopped thinking about Roan, deciding to examine her feelings once things settled down with the studio. And as each day went by, it became easier. Though she'd had one call with no caller ID and no message, as far as she knew he hadn't tried to connect with her either. If she became tempted, she pushed through it, and soon bigger issues with the studio occupied her time and her thoughts.

Those issues began the afternoon after Roan left her apartment. She'd gone to the studio and found the crew pulling up the wood floor. Frustrated and still in a fragile state after being with Roan, she yelled at them demanding to know what they were doing. When they told her their instructions had been to pull up the floor before adding a new one, she was furious.

"You are not to touch that floor except to refinish it." She tried to breathe through the jumble and confusion of her rising emotions and demanded to know who had told them to take it all out. The foreman explained that some floorboards had seemed to have rotted in places and the only way they felt they could make for a smooth transition between the old floor and the new one was to pull it all up and lay a new floor. If they didn't, he explained, the grain of the new wood would not be the same as the grain and texture of the old one.

Exasperated she immediately called Macy's husband, set him straight then handed the phone back to the foreman who listened intently, nodding periodically. When he finished, he handed the phone back to Sammy, apologized, and told her they'd only replace the bad ones and then refinish the entire floor.

To ensure there weren't more mistakes she went to the studio early every morning before the workers arrived. Gratefully any thoughts of Roan were overtaken by her need to make sure the studio was finished correctly. Once she felt comfortable that the new boards would be added without taking out more, she moved on to the next task on her ever-growing list—to make the private back entrance safe and welcoming to students even during night classes. She conferred with the electrician on the selection and installation of light fixtures to the outside of the entrance and up the staircase; she also had them add an electronic keyless entry locking system. Under her supervision, another worker fixed the handrail and painted the stairwell and upper landing. Upstairs in the studio, she directed them to set aside space that would be walled off as a place for dancers to store coats, purses, and backpacks. As she imagined dancers coming into the studio getting ready for classes, she realized they might need a bathroom too, but she couldn't see any place where it would fit. Then she remembered seeing a couple of closed and locked doors at the top of the international school's internal staircase that led back down to classrooms. She asked Ciara about them and found out one of the doors was indeed a bathroom that they didn't use anymore. The bathroom had been locked up so the students wouldn't go up there to use it or hang out unsupervised. She added a small bathroom remodel of things that needed to be done.

Finally, it was time for the crew to begin work on sanding and staining the entire floor. Sammy felt the remodel was in good hands, so she took a breath and admitted to herself that she still hadn't sorted out her emotions about Roan. What to do about her attraction to him, her hesitation to get involved with anyone again, and the lingering guilt she felt from the last time they were together? So, she did what she had been doing the previous week, she let it fall to the back of her mind. And again, justified it by reminding herself he hadn't called her either. The further her emotions about Roan drifted and the more she avoided them the less important they felt and she wondered if that meant that her feelings about him didn't matter either.

To keep busy, she focused on marketing by creating an announcement postcard with her contact info, tentative opening date, projected class times and options, and included an invitation to an open house for the week before classes would begin. She sent it out and began reaching out via social media, and in doing so caught a post about an offer for a cruise out of Barcelona. It just so happened it was on a morning when she found herself with nothing pressing that needed to be done, and seeing the post about a cruise made her realize it was time to connect with Roan. But when she called him, it went straight to voice mail. She fumbled through an explanation and said she hoped they could continue to be friends while deciding what other, if any, direction they should take and then she invited him to dinner. Somehow, she'd expected a quick return call and received none so after a few days she tried again and got the same result. Confused and irritated she assumed he'd decided that she wasn't the one for him so she stopped calling, and maybe that was okay. No involvement, no disappointment, no love, no loss, no having to say goodbye.

* * *

IT WAS time for book club again, and they were gathered in the sunroom of Danele's house on the beach making another attempt at discussing the same book they were supposed to discuss last month. And yet no one had been able to stay focused on the book nor seemed to remember much about it. Catching up, gossiping, eating and drinking had taken over. Sammy wondered if this was how all book clubs went—an excuse for people to socialize, eat, and drink.

Sammy was deep in her own thoughts, the book not even a glimmer in her memory. This allowed her to sit quietly in the corner of the room half-listening as the girls jumped from one subject to another, talking over each other, each one raising their voice louder than the other to be heard. For that reason, they didn't seem to notice her lack of participation. Most of the time she absentmindedly nodded and smiled at her friends so they wouldn't notice her preoccupation. In moments of the animated chatter, Sammy easily found herself either gazing out the floor to ceiling windows at the sea or staring at the floor; her mind wrapped around thoughts of Roan, her pent-up emotions, her anger that she seemed to care and that he hadn't called her back, all of that mixed up with her guilt about Peter. Her thoughts tumbled, swept in and out like the seagulls being tossed around in the thermals above the surf just outside the windows. Yet, foremost in her mind was a missed phone call she'd received this morning; no called ID again and no message. She wondered if it might have been Roan yet the fact that she cared annoyed her.

Suddenly the conversation in the room stopped and Sammy turned around from her seat to see the others staring at her.

"What is going on with you?" Danele pressed her. "You've been out of it since you got here."

"Yeah, Sammy, even lately when you're at the studio working, you're not yourself. Are you having regrets about the business, because I hear from all the mothers and even the kids, they can't wait until you open in January?" Ciara said.

"And the studio looks amazing," Sylvia added. "I peeked in and saw that the floors are done and drying. Aren't you happy with how it's turning out?"

"Yes, I am, the floors are spectacular." They were perfect in fact they gleamed with a rich honey color. Everything in truth had turned out better than she thought it would. The custom mirrors would be ready and installed before Christmas, and the partitioned alcove was ready to be started with the addition of a vinyl floor, hooks for coats, and cubbies for storage; next she would have them start on a remodel of the bathroom.

"Then, what's up?" Sylvia asked.

She wasn't sure she wanted to talk about it; she hadn't figured out what she was feeling. Her emotions spiked with the highs and lows of her non-relationship with Roan, its uncertainty with no identity, no moniker, and his recent silence. It had been a few weeks and she hadn't heard one word from him. At times she felt strangled, strapped by her past, and skeptical on any future relationship.

And that unanswered call loomed.

Right now, she resorted to the only platitude that made any sense. "It's complicated." She looked up, and saw they were all confused, except for Ciara.

"It's about the doctor, isn't it?" Ciara asked.

Sammy nodded. Again, the book discussion tabled. Sammy told them about Roan's visit and where it took them and her regrets about it, and how he'd not returned any of her calls, but she left out the part of today's missed call. "I think I should forget about him and go back to finding someone to provide sex when I need it and that's it. He's obviously forgotten about me."

"What if something happened to him," Macy said. "You'd feel terrible if you wrote him off then found out he was hurt."

"I say use him for sex, if it was good," Danele paused, staring at Sammy and asked, "Was it?"

Her body tingled remembering that morning. She still hadn't gotten over how good he'd made her feel. "It was good," she whispered. "It was too good."

It was then that she broke down.

They all gathered around trying to comfort her, which made her cry even harder. Between wiping her eyes, trying to breathe and between breaks in her sobs, she gulped, "I don't know what's happening to me."

Ciara moved so she knelt in front of Sammy; she took Sammy's hands in her own and said, "Of course you do." Sammy objected, but Ciara put her hand up. "Think about it a minute. In the last," she paused, thought about it and continued, "about month and half, you went to your cousin's wedding which brought back memories of your own, you ran into the doctor that was there when Peter collapsed, you lost your job, you went to the mountain where he died, you said goodbye to him, you started a business, and a new relationship." Ciara stared at her and wouldn't let her look away. Ciara's eyes dared her to deny it.

Sammy searched for a tissue and when Sylvia handed her one, Sammy pushed back. "But, damn it, I'm stronger than that." She hiccuped and demanded, "Why am I being so damn needy? Tell me that?"

Macy reached over and took her hand. "I think you like the man more than you want to admit."

"But," she protested, "I don't even know him, really. And do I want to? What if I have to say goodbye to him, too, like I had to with Peter?"

"Sammy," Ciara said quietly, "you can't go through the rest of your life pushing potential love away. And for that matter you knew everything you needed to know about Roan the night Peter died. He showed you that night and in the days that followed the kind of man he is."

Sammy shook her head. "I don't understand."

Ciara stood up, pulled a chair closer to Sammy, sat in front of her and said, "Well, for one thing you already know he's a good man, right?"

Reluctantly, she nodded.

"Geez Sammy, don't be so enthusiastic," Danele chided.

"Even I know he's a good man and I only saw him for five minutes at the hospital."

Ciara continued, "Remember when you wanted to go with Peter in the ambulance and they wouldn't let you? Well, the doctor tried to convince them and when that didn't work, he climbed in and said he was going. Later the paramedics told me that on the way, Roan was in constant contact with the hospital. He told them to prepare for an emergency procedure. He thought it was an aneurysm."

"Yes, but it didn't matter, did it?" Sammy said. "Peter died anyway."

"Look, Sammy, you can't keep blaming Roan. That's what you are doing right?" Ciara didn't wait for an answer. "And look what's happening to you? You're not moving on. You have a good man who seems to be interested in you and you in him."

Sylvia walked over and touched Sammy's arm, quietly interjecting, "Sammy, you can't; he's a caring doctor. He was devastated when he learned Peter died. When Macy and I got to the hospital, we saw him wandering around outside. Then after Ciara told us Peter had died, I went out and found him slouched over on a bench, head in his hands covering his face. He saw me, jumped up, and immediately asked how you were doing and if they were able to save Peter. When I told him no, he walked away from me and went into the hospital to find you."

"I never saw him."

"No Sammy, you didn't. He found me," Ciara said. "And I told him to leave you alone. I remember he nodded, shoved his hands in his pockets then went on to say when he was in med school, he'd lost his first patient to an aneurysm and had never gotten over it. Then he turned to leave the hospital. I tried to stop him to thank him. When he turned back to me, I could see his eyes were damp. I remember I reached out to comfort him, but he shrugged and said 'I've never gotten used to the dying' then he walked out."

"That's a good man, there, Sammy," Macy said. "I've found one and I think you have, too. You need to let him in."

Sammy, dried her eyes, stood and said, "It's all bullshit anyway. He's not returning my calls. Who needs someone like that?"

They all yelled at the same time, "Sammy!"

It was then her phone rang.

She stared at it.

This time the caller-ID clearly said Roan Adair.

"It's him," Sammy said to the group.

"Answer it," they chorused.

She shook her head. "I'm not ready. Not after all this. I need to think. I need to go."

CHAPTER ELEVEN

The sun had begun its descent at the edge of the sea when Sammy tore out of Danele's house with her friends begging her to come back inside. Instead, she fled and drove toward home with her hands tight on the wheel and at a pace that matched her innermost thoughts: fast and furious. Fast through the streets of the community where Danele lived and faster as she reached the outer limits of town where the setting sun flashed by as it reflected off the darkened windows of empty restaurants and tapa bars, places that in a few hours would be packed with families and young Spaniards looking for a Sunday night of food and drinks. Empty like her heart felt after rushing out on her friends. She hadn't stayed for Danele's lovely buffet, hadn't given them a proper goodbye, but there was nothing to do about it now. She'd left—getting home was her goal.

She wove in and out of traffic to get home to her safe place, her neutral spot to process her thoughts without the girls making her feel guilty for not letting Roan fully into her life. Furious, because she was angry with herself for allowing the unanswered phone call to occupy her thoughts so much that it complicated the vow she made days ago that she was done with Roan. She was angry too at the girls for not understanding and angry at Roan for his disappearing act.

Her frustration rising, she realized any normal attempt to calm her emotions was futile so at the next stoplight she turned off the residential road to finish her trip home along the beach. The sea, like the mountains, always seemed to quiet her anxieties; bringing lightness back into this day became paramount—the water would give her that. Within five minutes the Mediterranean came into view and she instantly felt her tensions ease. She rolled down her windows and breathed in the saltiness of the cold November air, watching as the wind swirled the sand on the deserted beach. Except for a few joggers no one had ventured out but she felt the pull of the ocean and decided she needed to get out and walk—walk and think. She drove a bit further before she turned into a spot off the side of the road and stepped out onto the sand, pulling her coat tightly around her. She buttoned it bracing herself against the bite of the wind and curled and tucked her hands further up into the sleeves to keep them warm. At the shoreline waves slapped at the sand and in the distance, Sammy could see the white chop of the sea. As she walked, the sun began to set and kissed the horizon with an arched rainbow of gold, coral, then orange and lastly crimson.

Then her phone rang.

Roan.

She hesitated, watched caller-ID flash on and off, listened to the shrill tones permeate the quiet evening, staring and willing something to tell her if she should answer it. And yet the thought of connecting with him made her realize how much she'd missed talking to him these last few weeks. How could she explain to the girls that it wasn't only about the sex, he'd become important to her life? And that terrified her. But they knew didn't they—it was Sammy that didn't fully understand until this moment.

It rang a few more times before she quickly made a decision and with her heart pounding, she said, "Hello."

"Did you think I'd skipped town?" He chuckled.

Confused, her warm feelings tempered at hearing him laugh and it annoyed her. She felt her indignation rise and couldn't stop herself from lashing out. "Well, if you were trying to play hard-to-get, I should tell you, I don't play those games. It doesn't work on me and I can see right through them."

For what seemed like minutes there was silence on the other end, then his voice was cool as he said, "I don't play games." And he was silent again.

His tone threw her and she couldn't decide if that made her angrier or if she was afraid she'd pushed him away. She started to say something, but before the words came out of her mouth he said, "Got you." And she could hear the smile in his voice. Then he continued, "But Sammy, you need to know I don't play games; I'm an open book. Words and deeds matter to me."

A gust twirled the sand at her feet, tugged at her jacket, and fluttered her hair; she turned around so the wind was at her back and with her head down, she began walking back toward her car. "They matter to me, too, Roan, but you disappeared. Didn't even return my calls." She realized she was more hurt than angry.

"I did I . . ." Loud noises in the background then a loudspeaker and high-pitched ring downed out the rest of what he said.

"I can't hear you, Roan."

"Sammy, I gotta run. They're calling my flight. I'm in New York for my connection to Barcelona. Long story. My ex-father-in-law died suddenly. I've been trying to call you since I left; cell reception was horrible. I'll call you when I'm back."

"Wait, wait," she blurted then wished she hadn't because she couldn't gather her thoughts enough to know what she wanted to say.

"Yes?"

She said the first thing that came to her mind, "Come by when you get back. I'll take you to dinner."

"It's about time." He laughed. "I deserve it, you know."

"Hey don't mess with me or I'll take you to McDonalds."

"Oh, no, you don't. The cost of my brilliance is going to include expensive wine and the full array of Spanish delicacies."

They were flirting again and it felt good. Then she heard the loudspeaker again.

"Really, Sammy I gotta run. How about next Saturday? This coming week is busy, too much going on."

What was she doing next Saturday? It didn't matter she needed to see him. That works."

Then he was gone.

For the first time since Roan left her house that day when they made love, she felt buoyant, reassured that having him in her life was a good thing. Joy replaced misgivings. Not that the creation of her new dream of the studio hadn't given her those feelings of joy; they'd given her a sense of purpose, and movement to the next phases of her life. But the joy she now felt after talking to Roan opened up other feelings. The future felt promising again, there was a lightness that she could see. Open to all kinds of possibilities, she felt herself starting to soften toward him again, releasing those unnerving emotions that played the yin and yang with her head. She hoped it would be the last of those contradicting feelings because what she felt right now, with the cold beating at her body and face, was the warmth of an unlikely friendship with a man she realized she truly cared for. And she needed to keep telling herself that his existence shouldn't be connected to the loss of Peter. After all he was just a man, an ordinary man that she liked and one that made her feel excited about embracing what was now new in her life—just a man, a good man, independent of her past, independent of Peter.

And it wasn't as if he was like Peter anyway.

They were different.

Peter had been outgoing, confident, excitable, enthusiastic, and owner of a small export trading company based in the United States—a business he loved. Every time he had a new idea his voice quickened and he would talk endlessly about it. Peter was a charmer, everyone who met him felt instantly drawn to him and yet he always seemed unaware of his charm and good looks. And despite all the opportunities that came his way with women flocking around him, he was a one-woman-man—loyal to her in every way.

And yet, like Roan, he was kind, self-deprecating, and humble.

Unlike Peter, Roan was quiet and her attraction to him came from this quiet confidence—an innate sexiness to his strength of character and intuitive nature—especially when it came to his sensing of her feelings and doubts. His genuineness and thoughtful conversations excited her. When she thought of him now and tried to bring his face to the forefront of her memory, she realized there was no one physical feature that made Roan so handsome, though his eyes came close—from them came an intensity, an honesty, and a gentleness. He epitomized the strong, silent type with the complete absence that he was hiding something. She could trust him.

But she wanted to find out more about him beyond their past connection. That would take time. That empty space in their friendship would have to be rectified the next time she saw him.

Next Saturday.

She'd see him in six days.

Her body flushed with anticipation and as she cradled that feeling she watched the sun make its last appearance on the day as it fell into the sea and twilight was captured by the night sky. Within moments the stars flooded the darkness, twirling and dancing with the bright full moon acting as the parent overseeing the spectacle. Behind her along the waterfront, restaurant lights flickered then lit up, out at sea the lights of ships and pleasure boats illuminated the water's surface glistening and shimmering in the sleekness of what had turned into a calm night, and as she walked back to her car, lights from passing cars on the road behind her scanned the beach and people began parking and going into restaurants, voices crowded her thoughts, but that was okay.

It was life.

There was life in the sky as the stars played in the night, there was life behind her and life out there at sea, and there was Roan on Saturday night.

* * *

SAMMY RETURNED HOME STILL cold from the walk along the beach. She rummaged through her cabinets looking for the containers of loose tea she bought at a tucked-away tea shop in London years ago. Owned by an elderly woman who convinced her that tea was the ultimate beverage for many reasons—one of those reasons she chose to share with Sammy. In her very English accent, she looked at Sammy's face closely and said, 'My you're a lovely little thing. But, dear, drinking tea is like sitting in the thermal baths in Bath so sit down and have a cuppa and those bloody spidery things by your eyes will fade away like the smoky *smirr o* rain does in May.' Sammy had been so stunned at the woman's directness that she did as she was told. It wasn't long before she was charmed by the woman and not the least bit offended by her observation about the tiny lines that had started to form around Sammy's eyes since Peter's death. When Ciara arrived in England later that week to travel with Sammy, Sammy asked her what 'smoky *smirr o* rain' meant. Ciara laughed and told her that in England it meant drizzle like a 'soft day' does in Ireland.

Sammy pulled out Earl Grey—the ultimate English tea the woman had told her—plugged in the tea kettle, packed loose leaves in the tea infuser, and waited. She'd call Danele as soon as the tea was done.

Sammy was curled up in Peter's chair sipping tea, legs tucked under her, calling Danele. "I'm sorry."

Danele laughed. "When my phone rang, I told the girls that's Sammy calling to apologize."

Sammy took a sip of tea then tried to explain. "But, I'm really sorry. I—"

Danele interrupted her. "*Tia*, we love you. Tell her girls."

Sammy heard them all yell, "We love you."

"See, I told you," Danele said.

The tea was warming her body, and the sound of her friends reaching out with love warmed her soul. "Did everyone stay? I should have. You made—"

"*Si*, you should have. I made *croquetas*, *albondigas*, and *churros*. I worked hard for you, silly girl." Then Danele laughed. "No, no *chica* it's *bueno*. Ciara left, too, but *she* did not leave before eating."

"Ciara knows better than to leave when there's food involved. Like me, she doesn't cook, but at least I can make a few things. Which I'm going to do right now. I'm starving and this cup of tea isn't doing the trick. Love you, *chica*. See you soon?"

"*Si*." Then to the girls, she yelled, "Tell Sammy goodbye." And a chorus of voices surged through the phone.

Sammy hung up, set her tea down, and leaned her head back against the back of Peter's chair then ran her hands along the cool, plush leather, the price of the chair far beyond what Sammy had felt was reasonable—'we could buy a houseful of furniture for what that cost' she chided him. But Peter had insisted—it was their first purchase together and since they were to be married soon, he said he needed to have something in the apartment that was only his.

She stood, and as she always did, kissed her fingertips, warm from holding the teacup, then lightly touched them to the place where Peter always rested his hand, a place close to the TV remote, always handy for his obsession with catching every televised FC Barcelona match. The memory of him sitting there either shrunken with frustration or chest out praising the team for its shrewdness in executing a play that resulted in a goal made her smile and she felt no lingering sadness. In fact, the anxiety and rumblings in her stomach now were from hunger, but as she went into the kitchen to find something to eat the intercom rang.

"Let me in. I come bearing sustenance." It was Ciara.

Sammy opened the door to her apartment, stood in the doorway, and waited; moments later Ciara burst out of the elevator, carrying a bag and arm full of stacked containers. "I have food!"

"You are a godsend," Sammy said. "I'm starving."

"Here, take these before I drop them." She handed Sammy some of the containers.

They gave each other a quick air kiss and went into the kitchen where Ciara plopped a bag on the table and said, "My god, the things I do for you."

"I'm famished! How did you know?"

"Duh. You walked out without touching a bit of food. That is not like you especially when Danele makes her croquetas."

"I just talked to her and she never said a word about you bringing food."

"As I was leaving, I told her when you call to apologize—like we knew you would—not to tell you."

"I am sorry; truly sorry. I'm sick of being weak, uncertain, so I've decided to go with it and see what happens."

"Go with what?" Ciara opened the bag and pulled out manchego and bread and said, "Where are your plates?"

Sammy took out some plates and a knife. "Roan, Ciara. I'm going to embrace the feeling, . . . and maybe him!"

"Well, it's about time." Ciara piled their plates with everything Danele had made and they moved into the living room to eat.

"Drinks?" Sammy asked.

"Water. Had enough alcohol at Danele's."

Sammy grabbed two bottles of mineral water and gave one to Ciara. "Were the girls mad when I left?"

"Not even a little. We're concerned about you, silly."

"He called."

"We know. You left."

"No, on my way home."

"You talked to him?"

"I did. Like you said, he's a good man. I like him. In fact, I like him a lot." She let that feeling settle and went on. "We both know it might not work, but I'm willing to try and I think he is, too. I'm taking him to dinner on Saturday."

Ciara took a bite of albondigas, frowned and said, "Why hadn't he called, though? That did concern me. You don't treat people like that."

"He said he tried. His father-in-law died . . . well, his ex-father-in-law—and he had to go to the states. That's all I know for now, but I trust this man."

"Then I trust him."

They continued eating Danele's food and Sammy told her how she'd made tea before Ciara got there and how that had made her think of their visit to Ireland and Ciara's family.

"Remember how shocked your dad was when I refused to drink Guinness or any other beer?"

Ciara's eyes narrowed and she glowered at Sammy. "How could you? Nobody dislikes beer in Ireland. I think you might have insulted the whole country."

"It's gross. And Guinness is worse. So bitter." She grimaced and went on, "And since we are talking about Ireland, how is Mr. Sean O'Sullivan?"

"Married."

"Yes, but the last I heard you said they were thinking of divorcing."

Ciara glowered again, then frowned. "They have a child. Sean wants to stay married."

"But wasn't she unfaithful?"

Ciara put up her hand. "Don't want to talk about it."

Sammy had met Sean when she and Ciara took a trip to the UK and Ireland after Peter died. Sammy always felt Ciara had regretted leaving Ireland and Sean. Sammy could tell this weighed on her. "I'm sorry."

"My own fault. I left to come here. We're friends. That's fine with me. I have a business and a life here." She paused. "Now can we change the subject?"

"Sure."

"So where are you taking that hunky doctor for dinner?"

"Maybe I'll cook."

Ciara laughed. "You can't cook."

Ciara was right.

But maybe she'd try.

CHAPTER TWELVE

*T*he sweet aroma of saffron filled Sammy's small apartment. In the kitchen, several chicken thighs and piles of mussels, clams, and prawns lay atop wax paper wrappings for the paella she decided to make tonight for her evening with Roan.

After trying to figure out where to take him, she decided it was time she took Mateo's advice and leapt into the unknown and frightening world of cooking. She was leaping into the unknown and frightening relationship with Roan so why not go all in.

She stopped stirring the *sofrito*—the flavor base for the paella made of tomatoes, onion, garlic, some dried sweet pepper called *fiora*, and sweet Spanish paprika—to rewrap the seafood and meat she bought at Mateo's shop and put them in the refrigerator. She'd bought everything she needed from him this morning and right now as she eyed the rice also cooking on the stove, his words of advice rang in her ears. 'The secret to paella, *mi querida* Sammy—*el arroz debe ser perfecto*. If rice not good, paella not good.' He proceeded to lecture her on the merits of cooking and he congratulated her on finally coming around to his way of thinking. Then he sold her the most expensive paella pan he had along with other utensils, but when he tried to sell her a gas burner stand to cook it on, she drew the line.

"That won't fit in my apartment let alone on my tiny balcony."

When she went to purchase the rice from him and picked up a standard long-grain, he shook his finger at her and chastised, "No, only from Valencia's rice fields. Here take this. You are a beginner, this is best."

She looked at the label, then the cost. "Twenty Euros for rice?"

Mateo shook his head and grumbled, "Do you want mush? We are making a masterpiece, not food for cattle."

To seek more advice, on her way home from Mateo's she'd stopped at the restaurant to ask Isabella if she had any secrets about making paella. Isabella gave her the same answer about the rice, but added, "You are brave to try to make this. Even the best cooks," she stopped and stood taller, "like me, have had years to master it—the *socarrat* must be perfect or it is ruined."

Exasperated Sammy said, "I thought it was the rice, Isa. I'm so confused. I'll never get this right." After Mateo drummed into her the importance of the rice now Isabella was telling her it was something called *socarrat*. "Please. What is *socarrat?*"

"Ahh, *socarrat muy importante.*"

Frustrated, Sammy repeated, "What *is* it?"

Isabella's face relaxed, her eyes took on a dreamy look, her mouth puckered and she raised her hand to her lips and kissed them. "*Si*, the rice— but the rice must crunch on your first bite of paella. It takes time. With love and patience, you can make the perfect *socarrat* and your man will make passionate love to you."

"Isa, please. What is it and how do I make it?"

"Love? How do you make love?" Isabella teased.

Finally, she told Sammy that *socarrat* was the crispy bottom that was created when the rice caramelized and toasted, and the key to make the rice perfect and therefore the paella perfect. Then Isabella said, "Wait. I have something for you." She rummaged through the restaurant's kitchen then disappeared for twenty minutes before returning with a book she shoved in Sammy's hands. "Take this. Best paella recipe." Then she shook her finger at Sammy and warned, "You must not burn the rice."

Right now in her tiny kitchen, Sammy, hot and frustrated, continued to stir the sauce that wasn't thickening like the cookbook said it should: 'This mixture should be thick enough to hold its shape on a spoon.' While the kitchen smelled heavenly, she was starting to panic and grumbled to no one, "What the hell was I thinking." On the other burner, in the flat paella pan a small test portion of rice simmered in fish stock infused with saffron, it was reducing and had started to crisp. She was experimenting with the rice so that later today when she cooked the dinner 'el arroz sera perfecto.' As she turned from stirring the sofrito to take the pan of rice off the burner before it burned, she knocked over an open can of tomatoes which tipped over the bottle of fifty euro saffron and the Spanish paprika, all coalescing together in a puddle on the counter. Her stomach fluttered and her heart pounded, and she felt the panic rise, but she was determined to make this work. Taking deep breaths, she calmly cleaned up the mess trying to save as much of the saffron as possible then she took a dishcloth and slid the rest of it into the garage telling herself mistakes were all part of the learning process: failure and success were only separated by attitude. And if it didn't turn out at least she'd bought an expensive Rijoa, a loaf of *pa de pagès català* from her favorite bakery, asked Mateo to make pinchos and purchased desert from Isabella—Isa's famous *Crema Catalana.*

The sofrito finally thickened and the rice crisped enough to satisfy Sammy that she could do it again tonight. Roan would be here at eight and though it was only noon, the anticipation she felt was dampened by the fact she still had so much to do. She cleaned up the kitchen then looked around the rest of the apartment and decided it was time for a change. She hadn't made any changes since Peter died, and she was ready.

First, she tackled the bedroom. If there was to be any romance tonight it needed to look different from the last time, the time she'd panicked. She also knew the bedroom needed to be the bedroom of a single woman, not someone still married and not a widow. She wanted to approach tonight's visit with Roan that way—new outlook, new bedroom, new woman. In many ways, she realized, she'd been living as if Peter was still alive, making time until he would reappear like she was living in the shadows of her life waiting for him to re-emerge. Not living *her* life, she was living a life of what could have been and in some warped reality, what still might be. Like he was still alive and refusing to come out of the darkness.

Her bedroom needed a total makeover. Everything wouldn't get finished today, but at least she'd begin. She kicked the small area rug in front of her bed out of the way and moved both the chair and nightstand out. Next the bed. Her mattress rested on a frame with wheels so she used her arms and pushed, then bumped it with her hips across the old wood floor until it was on the opposite wall across from the window. That window, which was narrow and high up on the wall, always caught the first light of morning. By situating the bed across from it, when dawn emerged, she would see it.

Next, she tore off the old sheets, blankets, the duvet cover and pulled out a new bed ensemble that she'd never used. She'd bought it on an impulse when Danele talked her into it. Sammy loved bright colors, but these were different, not the oranges, reds, and yellows she'd become accustomed to since moving to Spain, the backgrounds on this comforter were bright yellow with splashes of cyan and mint green flowers.

She made the bed with the new linens, slid the antique armoire to the other wall under the window where the bed had been, relocated the side table and chair into the corner, kitty-corner from the bed. Then as she walked into the living room she paused in the doorway, looked back into the bedroom and decided to paint the opposite wall, either yellow or aquamarine. She nodded; this was more like it. This was her.

The living room was another story and while she stood mentally rearranging furniture, she decided it was time to put Peter's chair into the guest room and take the yellow lounge chair out of there and bring it into the living room. Peter's chair had always been too big for this room anyway. She moved the lounge chair into the living room then she tilted Peter's leather chair on its side and maneuvered it through the guest room doorway and pushed it next to the bed. The

yellow chaise lounge next to her white couch worked especially well when she threw two white pillows on the lounge
then remembered a soft chenille throw blanket she never used
that had both specks of yellow and teal in it. She rummaged in
the guest room closet, found it, brought it out, threw the
blanket on the couch and stood back. Perfect.

By the time she was done with the living room, it was five
o'clock. She needed to shower, dress, and figure out where
they would eat since the tiny table in the kitchen would not
do. She remembered a small round drop-leaf table she kept in
her storage unit in the basement—it might work. She rushed
downstairs and opened the storage unit, pulled out her hand
truck and maneuvered the table into the apartment, pulled the
chairs from the kitchen table then centered the table and
chairs up against the wall slightly outside the kitchen with
enough room for her to go in and out. She'd set it later, but
first she needed that shower.

After her shower, it took thirty minutes to decide what to
wear, spending most of the time overthinking it: Sexy?
Uptight schoolmarm? Sophisticated professional? Flirty
flamenco dancer? Casual—to show him this is no big deal?
She had all those bases covered with her new clothes, but in
the end, she decided she needed tonight to be an unspoken
friendship theme—so casual but with a flirty spin. After trying
on many things, she decided on several of her new pieces:
black palazzo pants, a casual coral cropped top, new chain-
embellished black pumps with a chunky heel and added flirty
drop earrings. She loved how she looked and felt, she loved
how the pants flowed when she walked and how they brushed
against her legs with fluttering softness, like butterfly kisses.
But time was quickly getting away from her and she began to

panic and question whether an hour was enough time to get everything else ready.

* * *

AND SHE WAS RIGHT—AN hour wasn't enough time. He'd be there in ten minutes and nothing was ready. And damn it, the rice wasn't crisping and even if it did, she couldn't figure out how to keep it that way and warm while they had drinks. Thank goodness at least the sauce was abundant, spectacular, and simmering on the stove. She'd cook the seafood at the last minute so it wouldn't be overdone—a tip she learned when she'd tried to cook shrimp once and they turned out like rubber.

But the table wasn't set, appetizers were still in boxes from Mateo's, and she was still obsessing: when he arrives should she offer him gin and tonic or Sangria or should she take it slow and offer a traditional Spanish aperitif of sweet vermouth? Which dishes should she use on the table; should she add flowers—she'd bought them and was now having second thoughts? Is that too romantic? How about candles? Her anxiety rose to the point that she was doubting everything: the meal, her decision to cook, the way the apartment looked, her clothes, and even her reason for seeing him again. She'd decided to call him and cancel when the intercom rang. In complete resignation that tonight would be a disaster, she pushed the button to let him up. By the time he got to her door she was doing all she could to stay calm. He walked in, looking all handsome and expectant, with a big smile on his face and flowers in his hand then he took one look at her face, set the flowers down and wrapped her in his arms.

"You're upset. Should I go?"

She nuzzled her face into his shoulder, the nubby parts of his wool jacket scratchy on her face, he smelled of the sea and a deep masculine musky, earthy aroma that made her want to remain right where she was. He tightened his grip on her and stroked her hair, whispering in her ear, "Please don't be sad. I can go. We don't have to do this," which released the tears she was holding back. Nothing was the same anymore. Everything was different: her apartment, her bedroom, her clothes, Peter's chair, and damn it she was cooking. She *never* cooked, not even for Peter. What was she thinking? She snuggled closer to Roan, felt his heart beating, felt the pressure of his hand on the back of her head while he continued to stroke her hair, she suddenly realized she felt at home there which confused her even more. She leaned back and looked into his eyes while he wiped the tears from her cheek. No glasses tonight, his deep brown, full lashed, concerned, and kind eyes stared down at her and she suddenly knew tonight would be okay. She stepped back from him slowly releasing her arms from around his waist, sniffing and whimpered, "It's the damn rice." Then realizing how ridiculous that sounded she began laughing which made him look even more concerned because she couldn't stop.

He tilted his head, squinted at her and said, "Are you sure you're okay?"

She took in a long breath, nodded, and repeated, "It's just the damn rice." And she giggled again.

"I don't understand. But really, I can go."

"No, you are *not* to leave." She backed up, took in a few more deep breaths and continued, "I'm fine." She resolved then to relax and enjoy the night, and said, "I had a moment."

He looked uncertain but smiled. "If you're sure."

"You're damn right, I'm sure, Dr. Adair. Now come in and sit while I get us drinks and something to eat."

"Wait, I thought you were taking me to dinner. You're not copping out, are you?"

"Perhaps." She grinned at him, feeling mischievous and flirty. "But don't worry, you won't starve." Then to herself, "I hope."

"Hmm, you're being a bit cagy, but I do smell something fantastic."

"Shit! The rice. I didn't turn it off." She hurried into the kitchen but over her shoulder, she said, "Sit. I'll be right back."

She grabbed the pan of rice, took it off the burner and set it aside. She didn't have the nerve to see if it was burnt, instead she made two gin and tonics, sorted the appetizers and took them out to him.

He was sitting awkwardly on the lounge chair and when she came in, he said, "You've changed the room. I like it, but where's that nice leather chair that was so comfortable."

"It was Peter's, Roan, and I thought it was time I moved on. It's in the guest room."

"I'm sorry I asked. Is that what's bothering you?"

It wasn't. Seeing him sitting there looking out-of-sorts and so damn handsome made her want to drag him into her newly decorated bedroom and forget about the damn sofrito, paella, socarrat and satisfy her need for him right now. But she didn't. She handed him a drink, sat on the couch, waved him over to join her and set the plates of tapas on the table in front of them.

"No Roan, nothing is bothering me. Now let's talk. I was

sorry to hear about your father-in-law. How are your ex-wife and the rest of the family doing?"

"It was expected, but sooner than they thought, so they're still having a hard time." He reached over and picked up one of Mateo's special pinchos—crostini spread with fig jam, manchego and topped with Spanish chorizo all held together with a toothpick.

She noticed it then. "Your arm! It's not in the sling anymore."

He popped the pincho into his mouth and grinned, "Yup earlier than expected, but all good." Then he rotated his shoulder, grimaced and said, "Well not entirely all good. Ha, but much better. They still won't let me work quite yet, but at least I can move it."

"Well, if I remember correctly, you didn't have any problem moving either arm the last time you were here." She was taking a chance bringing up the memory that was difficult for both of them, but she knew if she didn't address it, it would hang over the mood the rest of the night. "So maybe you never hurt it at all and just wanted me to feel sorry for you so you could get me into bed." She winked, and with that she headed to the kitchen to start the seafood and try to crisp up the rice if it wasn't burnt. On her way she turned back to see how her statement had affected him.

He took the lead, feigned shock and disbelief and said, "Ah, but if I do remember correctly, it was you that insisted on having your way with me. But you are right, no, it didn't encumber anything we did. Would you like a replay, because my arm is better than ever and my hands, well, you remember, don't you?"

He had her there. And over her shoulder she said, "Well you're a bit full of yourself, aren't you?"

She ducked into the kitchen for refuge and from any further banter that might result in something neither of them was sure was a good idea. Of course, the kitchen didn't look like any refuge, it looked like it had been hit by, well, Sammy trying to cook. She shuffled stuff around on the counters, pulled the seafood out of the refrigerator and it promptly fell out of her hands, plopping on the floor.

"Shit."

From the bellows of the other room he called, "Need some help in there? Ready, willing and certainly able."

"You stay right there. I've got it handled." She picked up some of the shrimp that had fallen out of its paper, stood in front of the sink and rinsed them off.

"Say that G&T was really good, I can see what you mean. How about another? Never mind, I'll make myself one. Because," his voice grew closer, "I'm quite capable."

"Now, darn it, don't come in here. It's a mess.

"Baby, nobody puts Roan in the corner."

"Oh groan; I see what you did there. Dirty Dancing, really?" She turned around, her hands full of packages of seafood, and he was leaning against the doorframe empty glass in hand, grinning at her. If only . . .

"If only what?" he asked.

Had she said that out loud? "Ah, if only, if only, ah, if only I'd started this earlier." No, not really, but it was the best she could do because the real 'if only' was if only he wasn't so darn good-looking and sexy standing there—there was that.

He winked at her and grinned. "I know we said we'd take this slow, but I have no problem skipping dinner."

She was speechless.

"Oh shit, I'm kidding. See. Look at my face." And he pointed to his face.

She couldn't; wouldn't look at his face. She was too afraid she'd take him up on the skipping dinner part and head right into the bedroom. But she wouldn't, she shouldn't.

"Now, here's the gin," she said and shoved the bottle at him along with the tonic and a lime, "go make your own darn drink and let me destroy this dinner in peace."

CHAPTER THIRTEEN

*H*e did.

And she did.

Dinner wasn't the success she'd hoped for, but they made light of the clumpy rice that Isabella had told her must fall gently one by one, 'It should be dry, not sticky.' And, of course, in parts Sammy had burnt the bottom of the rice—no sofrito there. While the chicken was perfect, the seafood was so rubbery that Roan offered to take it to his place to feed the hungry pigeons that congregated outside his apartment. But they had both finished another G&T and polished off nearly two bottles of Rioja so Sammy knew the night wasn't a total failure. And the best part, besides Roan being there, was the sauce and the bread. She wound up dumping the extra sauce in a bowl and they made a meal of sopping up the sauce with chunks of the hearty bread.

Roan leaned back in his chair, patted his stomach, grinned and said, "That's the best meal I've had in a long time!"

She picked up a piece of bread and threw it at him.

"How dare you waste that good bread," he said and

proceeded to pick it up off the table and swiped the rest of the sauce with it.

"Hey, you didn't leave me any?"

Before he put it in his mouth he got up, walked over to her, tore off part, then leaned down and gave her the rest, then lightly kissed her. "See, now you have some, so quit complaining," he said.

She couldn't stand it any longer. She stood and pulled him towards her, losing herself in everything about him.

"We shouldn't you know," he whispered.

"I know, but . . ." Reluctantly she took a step back. His eyes told her the truth; the desire was there, but so was the hesitation.

He sighed and tapped her nose. "We agreed." He took his glass of wine and moved to the couch, sat and said, his eyes locked on hers, "Not that I'm happy about it, but, Sammy it's the right thing to do." He hesitated and continued, "For you, it's the right thing for you."

She saw it again, the kind man, the gentleman, not one of weakness or trite politeness, but one of great spirit. What he was, what was beautiful about him, came from deep within— and deep within her she was grateful.

"Okay, so we take it slow." She agreed and flopped down next to him, a safe distance so she wouldn't be tempted. "But I want to know everything about you, Roan. Tell me."

He told her he was thirty-eight, and grew up in Indiana, the youngest of four kids, and had three sisters. "My parents had me when they were older and have since passed away. Growing up, my sisters were merciless, they were either teasing and tormenting me or smothering me with kisses. They loved to pretend I was their baby or their patient.

Pretending they were doctors and nurses was their favorite pastime. I think that might be where my desire to become a doctor came from because it's the only thing I remember ever wanting to do.

"I married young, right out of college after graduating from University of Indiana and then enrolled in med school. I was lucky, my wife had a job that paid well, and I had a grant both of which allowed me to finish, take my boards, and head out into the world of medicine."

It was the first time he'd mentioned his wife since he'd taken Sammy home from the train. "You said you were divorced and it was complicated. What happened?"

He frowned, rearranged the pillows, crossed one leg over the other and said, "I guess it's not so complicated, disappointing though. I'm not crazy about failure in my life." Then he shook his head, as if to clear his head, and continued, "Once I got my license I hoped to work with Doctors Without Borders, but I guess I never shared that information with her —just assumed she'd be okay with it. I was young and had a different mindset about marriage. Rather archaic actually: me boss; you follow. You can imagine how that might put a strain on any marriage. I could be a little hard-headed." He looked at Sammy over the rim of his glass as he took a sip. "Not that person anymore."

"I can see that," Sammy said.

"We had quite a row one night until she reminded me, I'd promised her she could quit working once I was out of med school. She was right. I was wrong. In the end, I didn't join Doctors Without Borders." He took a breath and went on, "Since I still had some debt from school, and to fulfill my commitment to her, I entered into private practice with a friend of hers. It was rewarding at first and our practice grew quickly, but sadly profitability became the focus for both my partner and my wife. Eventually, I realized I wanted to do more with my life, at the very least quell some of the intensity of private practice, and the focus on wealth and status. For my partner, it had become less about care and how many patients we could fit in a day."

She waited for him to go on, but instead, he stood, walked over to the table, picked up the bottle of wine and said, "Would you like more?"

"Sure."

He came back over to the couch, poured the rest of the wine in her glass and then his, and sat again. She was about to ask him to go on, when he said, "When on one particularly packed patient day, my partner misdiagnosed one of my patients, I told him I was done. After selling my share of the practice to him, I finally persuaded my wife to come with me on this journey as a cruise line doctor. I told her we'd see the world. I did; she didn't. She spent most of her time flying back and forth to the states and eventually after a year of doing that, we parted ways. She and my old partner are together now."

"I'm sorry. I've come to realize that losing a spouse whether by death or divorce is still painful and difficult to get over. Have you?" Sammy asked.

"Gotten over it? It's been two years now and I've had a lot of time to think. I'm not sure we were ever right for each other, but . . . ," he finished his glass of wine and continued, ". . . I'm pretty darn happy with my life, right now." He looked at her then, as if waiting for her to say something. When she didn't, he stood and said, "I'm sorry, I've rambled on. I should get going."

"No, please stay. When you said you were happy with your life, it struck me rather unexpectedly that I'm happy with mine, too."

"Well, then, I won't go yet. And if you are okay with it." He seemed to scrutinize her face before asking, "I'd love for you to tell me about Peter."

She couldn't help but smile when she thought about Peter. "Oh, he was one-of-a-kind. I think I'm okay talking about him to you, but if I need to stop, I'll tell you." She tucked her legs under her, settled into the corner of the couch, and said, "He filled a room, and people gravitated toward him. He was dynamic, good-looking, and kind. My past relationships were disastrous and my relationship with my family wasn't the greatest so when I saw myself leaning into him emotionally, I was skeptical and wary. I kept asking myself, was he another player and could I trust him? Was he so full of himself that nobody else mattered?"

Roan leaned toward her and touched her hand. "I bet that he wasn't, Sammy, or else you wouldn't have married him. I think you're the kind of person who wouldn't tolerate that in anyone. Am I right?"

"You're right, I saw how he handled people, especially women, when they fell all over themselves to get to him. Bottom line, he was a good man, a good person." And probably the best man she'd ever known, although she had a sense that Roan was close. "Don't get me wrong we had issues. He was hardworking and if there was anything that didn't always work between us that was it. The success of his company was, at times, more important than time with me, but we worked on it and by the time we got married we were heading in the right direction."

They'd continued to talk through the evening getting to know each other better and before they knew it, it was one in the morning. She'd told him more about Peter, but she also talked about her trepidation in the success of her studio, her past frustrations with her parents and how she'd always felt like an outsider in her own family.

"Being the only girl, no one took me seriously. It was all about the boys' sports, my dad's job, and my mother's social calendar. It was part of the reason I needed to get out of Ohio and a lot the reason I never told them about Peter. The truth is, my parents have never supported me and when I'm around them they can drive me crazy."

Roan shared a bit more about his childhood, which seemed idyllic, then he talked about his own insecurities about leaving his practice and venturing out into the cruise line business, but how much he loved it. He told her one of the other reasons he and his wife didn't work out was because he'd always wanted children and she hadn't. He thought once they were married, he was out of med school, and their lives took on a routine with more financial security she would change. She didn't.

"I have eight nieces and nephews and the one thing I regret about moving to Spain is that I don't get to see them as much. How about you? Were you and Peter going to have kids?"

"I'm trying to remember if we ever had a specific conversation about it. I think it was always a given. We would say things like 'when we have our kids' or 'I'd never let our kids do that.' You know that kind of talk."

He nodded.

"But," she teased, "if what you are really asking, Roan is if I want kids, yes Roan, I want kids."

"Ha, looks like my attempt at taking the circuitous route didn't work—you saw right through that one. I'll have to watch myself in the future—no one is going to pull the wool over your eyes," he joked.

She frowned, tilted her head, crossed her arms across her chest, tried to sound annoyed and bristled, "Why would you want to?"

"Want to what?"

"Pull the wool over anyone's eyes."

"I'm teasing you. I didn't broach the subject of kids so that I could get an answer from you. If I wanted to know I would ask you."

"Right, sure you would have." Her attempt to look and sound mad was waning.

"Sammy, look at me, I mean it."

She couldn't hold it in any longer and began laughing. "I'm messing with you."

"Messing with me, were you? Well, I teach you." And he moved toward her and began tickling her, growling like a wild animal.

All she could feel besides the luxury of the tickling sensation was his breath on her neck, the smell of his aftershave, and the intensity of how much she desired him at that moment. But then she was laughing so hard that she couldn't catch her breath. In an attempt to slither away, she fell on the floor. Finally able to breathe, she looked up at him and said, "You better watch out, buddy, payback is a bitch and I'll get you when you least expect it."

He threw his head back and laughed. "I'll be waiting. Here

let me help you up." He leaned over, reached his hand down to her but instead of pulling herself up, she pulled him down to the floor. He toppled over and fell hard on his side and hit his head on the side table.

"Oh, god, I'm so sorry." She crawled over to him. "Are you okay?" She tried to get a look at his face, but one of his hands covered it and the other rubbed his head. "Please let me see. I'm so sorry, I was—"

In an instant his hands were free and his arms were around her as he pulled her on top of him. Desire rose in her and any rational thoughts floated away as soon as his lips found hers. She wrapped herself in the moment and let all doubts and trepidation disappear. His lips urgently pulled at hers and he slipped his tongue in her mouth and she nearly lost consciousness. She tried to quiet her need for him and then he whispered, "Sammy," his voice shaky, coming in shallow breaths. And she slipped her arms out of her shirt and started to take it off. Suddenly he pulled her hands down and he gently rolled her off of him.

She flopped to her back, pulled her top back down, threw her arm over her face, and said, "I know."

He turned on his side and faced her. "I didn't say anything," he said, he voice tender, but thick with emotion.

"But you were going to. And I know you're right." She rolled to her side, faced him and touched his cheek. "But I hate this."

He touched her hair and pushed a strand off her face. His fingers soft against her cheek, she took his hand and touched his fingers to her lips, then kissed the back of his hand before sitting up. She turned and smiled at him. "Rain check?"

He stood up, reached down to her and helped her up. She

bounced up next to him, kissed his cheek and said, "Thanks for being the level-headed one."

"Yes, well, next time you better look out, because you'll have to be the one to stop this, because I won't be so gallant." He tilted her chin up so she was looking into his eyes. "Sammy dear, somehow, someway, you've captured me." And then he gently kissed her. "To be continued." He turned, walked toward the door and grabbed his coat. As she followed him, he said, "How about I take you to dinner this week? A less seductive location might be good."

He'd called her Sammy dear, something only Peter called her, but she didn't care. Somehow coming from Roan, it seemed perfectly normal. She wanted him, oh how she wanted him right now. It was crazy how much she trusted and desired him. "I have a better idea. Macy and her new husband are having Thanksgiving at her house this year with a large group, would you come with me?"

"Thanksgiving already? It can't be soon. When is it?"

"A week from Thursday."

He reached for her hand, covered it with both of his, and said, "Do you really think I'm going to wait that long to see you again?"

She had to smile at that one. "Do you think I would let you?"

They stood looking at each other, neither one wanting to say goodbye. She couldn't take her eyes off of him; he looked like she imagined he would have as a young boy. His hair had taken a hit when they tussled and tufts of it stood on end, his face was ruddy, and he looked like he might not have shaved this morning as his face had taken on a somewhat scruffy look making him look incredibly masculine. He lifted his eyes to meet hers, shook his head as if to clear his mind, and said, "I gotta get out of here. You are a minx."

Reluctantly she dropped his hand and sighed. "So, if we're not going to wait, where are you taking me and when?"

He tilted his head to the side and thought. "Good question. Let's see, now. Hmm. Well, have you been to Dali's Museum in Figueres? I've been wanting to go since I moved here."

"No, but I love art. I've been to most galleries in Barcelona, but isn't Dali's far?"

"Two hours tops. We could make a day of it. What do you say? Game?"

She thought about spending the entire day with this man; she knew the studio would be okay without her, Ciara had been checking on it when Sammy wasn't there. She looked up at him, smiled, and said, "I'd love that. In fact, if it wasn't Sunday morning already, I'd say let's go today. But Tuesday, let's go Tuesday. That will give me time to sleep today and time on Monday to clear up some stuff for the studio."

"All right then. How about we get an early start and have breakfast on the way up? Pick you up at eight."

"I like that plan."

"Well, I better get going so you can get some sleep. Thank you for dinner. It was . . . " he rubbed his stomach and said, "a gastronomic delight. I think you should be a chef instead of this silly dancing nonsense." He opened the door and ducked behind it as she lunged at him. Then he feigned seriousness and put out his hand. "Since we're taking this slowly, I think a handshake is in order."

No, a handshake was not in order, not at all. But it was the safest thing to do right now, so she extended her hand. Instead of shaking her hand, he raised it to his lips, kissed it and said, "Until Tuesday." He turned to leave then abruptly turned back and said, "Oh the hell with it." And he grabbed her, pulled her to him, wrapped her in his arms and kissed her in a way that made her want to keep him there forever. Then he turned and walked away.

She wanted more—more of him, more of this feeling, more of the life that now stood before her. She closed the door and turned back into the room. It felt empty and foreign. Over the past many hours, she had gotten used to his presence in this space. She liked the feeling it had given her—life in this room where, she realized, at times had felt lonely and without purpose. This room, this apartment was meant to be filled with love and passion again.

CHAPTER FOURTEEN

*S*ammy woke to the warmth of sunlight pouring through the bedroom window later that morning. Its rays rested on her face and warmed her body. Light shimmered through her closed eyelids until bit-by-bit she opened them. She rolled away from the light, tugged at the covers and covered herself into a cocoon of quiet reflection. Last night Roan called her 'Sammy dear' and that had been okay with her. He'd said, 'Sammy, dear, you've captured me.' The reality was, *he* had captured *her*; disarmed her, and made her begin to hope again for that love she once had. As she lay there in the twilight of the morning, she knew all of her past trepidation about Roan had been released in the night. This longing for him was different from any she'd had for other men; this longing, this desire cosseted with emotions she had yet to identify.

But today, she didn't want to think too long on what these emotions might be; instead, she threw off the covers, sat up, stood, and stretched her arms in front of her then lifted them over her head. She rotated her head, releasing the stiffness and kinks in her neck and shoulders. Then remembering the array of dirty plates and glasses on the table in the other room and the chaos in the kitchen with pots needing soaking and scrubbing from the burnt rice, she nearly slunk back into the bed. But she didn't. Not to be dissuaded nor discouraged, she pulled on comfy socks, picked up her sweatshirt off the floor and slipped it over her head.

As she turned to leave the room her eyes scanned it, this was good—the new arrangement, the new bedding, everything new except that part of her past which quietly rested on top of her dresser. She reached over and picked up the photo of Peter and touched his face. "I will always love you," she whispered, "but it's time for new beginnings and maybe it's time to love another." She kissed his face, put the photo back down and grabbed her phone to see the time. It was nine already and while her bed begged her to return, she needed coffee.

Feeling particularly joyful and lightened, she danced her way into the other room where aromas from last night's meal swirled more memories in her head. She took deep breaths letting the ambiance fill her senses: garlic, saffron, the wine, and then Roan's aftershave which immediately heightened her desire for him and the memory of his body pressed against hers as they wrestled on the floor almost made her pick up the phone and tell him to forget this foolishness of waiting and to get over here right now. But she didn't.

The kitchen was a disaster, but she managed to find the French press, boiled some water, made a cup of coffee and carried her cup back into the other room to plan her attack. On the dining table crumbs from the crusty loaf of bread were sprinkled across the red, green, orange and yellow paisley tablecloth and dried splotches of red sauce and red wine made it difficult to discern what was food and what was cloth. Red wine still remained in the glasses on the table in front of the sofa, her enthusiasm to clean waned, she flopped on the chair and sipped her coffee when her phone rang. It was Ciara.

"Top of the morning to ya. How was dinner?"

Sammy couldn't help but laugh. "Well, it wasn't a success, but then part of it turned out exceptionally well."

"Ah, you must be talking about the good doctor part. Did he stay? Is he there?"

"Nope, he left and we only shared a kiss—maybe a bit more." She couldn't help but smile just thinking about their romp on the floor. "But it's good, very good."

"Spill Sammy."

They talked for the next hour and Sammy told her all about rearranging her rooms, what she wore, the night, the meal, and what nearly happened with Roan.

"I'm determined to let all of our past baggage take a trip somewhere else."

"Finally. Now that's the Sammy I know. That Sammy has always taken charge of her life."

"Yup, and he's picking me up on Tuesday and we're taking a little day trip to see Dali's Museum."

"You'll love it. Dali's paintings and the museum are the perfect mix of weird, brilliant, and otherworldly. But you will spend the night?"

"No, Roan said it is easily done in a day trip."

"Sure, it is."

Sammy could hear the dubiousness in Ciara's voice and it

caused her to retort. "We will *not* be spending the night. We are waiting for all of that."

"Uh, why? That's kind of archaic thinking, isn't it? We live in the twenty-first century not the eighteen hundreds. Besides you already did the dirty deed. So, get on with it."

"Oh, Ciara, you are so . . . well, you are so . . ." Pushy, Sammy wanted to say and to chastise her for not taking her own advice in the past with Sean, but as Ciara was her good friend Sammy only repeated, "Like I said, we will wait."

"Sure, Sammy, whatever you say."

"Oh, for Pete's sake just take my word for it, we shall just wait a bit."

"Silly girl, get that man before someone else does."

But she wouldn't. Not yet.

After Ciara hung up, rather than clean up, Sammy grabbed her iPad and began making a list of the things she needed to do at the studio the next day. She wanted everything done by Tuesday so she wouldn't be distracted when she was with Roan. The studio was nearly ready except for finishing the coat and bag area, the bathroom and some painting. She'd spend tomorrow making sure those tasks were getting done and return calls to people who had inquired about classes. The first class of the year—and of her business—would be beginning ballet for girls and boys aged three to four. She'd also recently brushed up on her contemporary dance and thought of opening that up to older girls and women. There had been a time in her life when she hoped she was good enough to become part of a Broadway troupe of dancers that would travel the world, but her entree into dance had been too late in her adolescence and also too sporadic, so she'd never been good enough. Perhaps her calling all along was to teach young hopefuls and help them succeed.

The rest of the day she kept busy cleaning and doing dishes. When she was finally finished, she again stretched out on the chair and felt a pressing desire to call Roan.

"Miss me?" his voice hoarse, like she'd woken him.

"Oh no, did I wake you?"

"Are you kidding, this perfect specimen of male fortitude has been up since six. How are you, my beautiful chef extraordinaire?"

"Hey don't mess with me. That sauce was perfection. Next time I'll feed you bread, if I even *let* you back in this apartment."

He said, "Ah, next time. So, there will be a next time? Something to look forward to—bread, water. And yet Sammy dear, I don't care as I'm with you."

She felt the glow of his words, but just said, "Until Tuesday."

CHAPTER FIFTEEN

*H*er alarm had gone off at six, but she'd wondered why she set it at all. She'd hardly slept all night. A jumble of emotions and anticipation about spending her day with Roan kept her awake most of it. And then it seemed as soon as she fell asleep her alarm woke her— too early, way too early.

Her excitement propelled her through a hasty shower and after getting dressed she still had an hour to spare so she flipped on the news and paced, flipped off the news, watched a few minutes of a rerun of a local food race show with participants frantically flying across Europe in food trucks while trying to win a million dollars, flipped it off, flipped on the news, made coffee, changed what she was wearing, made her bed, looked at her announcement for the studio, endlessly changed and rearranged the layout of the announcement and now with less than five minutes until Roan was to arrive she panicked and contemplated changing her clothes again. Instead, she waited.

And waited.

When he rang the intercom she jumped, looked in the mirror, momentarily thought she should change again, got pissed at herself for being so indecisive and instead of pressing the intercom to let him in she went down to meet him. She pushed open the entry door to the outside and saw him leaning against his car which looked like it had been newly washed because remnants of soap suds and water spray still remained. He looked massively handsome, freshly scrubbed, shaved, and as she got closer that musky-smelling marvelous aftershave that he wore sent her reeling back to the memory of their tussle on the floor a few nights ago. Her face grew hot as she remembered and felt it flush as she raised her eyes to his. He was staring at her, his eyes perusing her body. He whistled and said, "Looking mighty fine there, Ms. Driscoll."

Though she was pleased, she pretended to shrug off the compliment, retorting, "Was there any doubt in your mind Dr. Adair?" Confident now in her new wide-leg jeans and pleased with herself that she hadn't given in to her last-minute panic to change again. He, she noticed, also wore jeans, a white henley, and what looked like a black cashmere jacket.

As she approached him, his eyes moved up to her face and he grinned. "Your carriage awaits." He bowed ceremoniously, reached for her hand and helped her into the car. The inside was as clean as the outside and smelled like pine. She glanced around, his glasses were on the dashboard, map on the seat, overcoat in the back, and along with what looked like a cooler. She loved that he was prepared for this day.

When he got into the car she asked, "So where are you taking me to breakfast?"

He started the car, turned and looked at her, and said, "It's a surprise."

"But . . . "

"Yes?" He challenged her.

"Where . . ."

He tilted his head, raised his eyebrows, and said, "Yes?"

"Couldn't you . . ."

He took his hands off the wheel, hung his head then turned to her, his jaw set but his eyes amused and he said, "It's a surprise. No more questions."

Damn it, she didn't like this loss of control. And yet, he was sexy as hell when he was forceful. "Okay you win."

"Good, because, Sammy dear, you are my captive. You're not going anywhere. Sit and relax and enjoy the ride whether I take you to McDonalds or drive you to Paris for dinner at the Eiffel Tower."

She tried, but fidgeted and didn't like the uncertainty that apparently was spread out before her. This loss of control unnerved her; she was the one who planned holidays, outings, book club gatherings, and even planned her wedding to Peter when they'd decided in only one week to take the leap. She didn't like to relinquish so much to the universe and for that matter another human being. So, after they were driving for a while when she expected him to jump on the motorway and he didn't, she said, "I think you missed the turn onto the motorway."

He put his finger to his lips and said, "Shush. I am your leader; you must follow. Relax. Enjoy."

Her mouth twitched with the words she wanted to say, but she quieted that response and said, "Okay if I must, but you need to know this is not easy for me."

He looked over at her his eyebrows raised, and said, "You think I don't know that, which, my dear Sammy, makes it so much more challenging." Then he winked at her and continued, "And exceedingly more interesting."

"You might be the master of my day now, but let me remind you, there might be a price to pay at another inopportune time . . . and when you least expect it."

He looked over at her, taking in the length of her body, his eyes locked onto hers. "I'm not sure you want to mess with me girl. But I'm up to the challenge."

Twenty minutes later he turned off the busy main road onto a road populated with commercial buildings, hotels, restaurants, and tourist venues. A minute later the road branched off to another she was unfamiliar with. Though this street seemed less crowded, rail tracks supporting the *Renfe*— the Spanish rail system—ran along the side marring the view to the ocean on their right. The scenery was muddied with cables and fences on the Mediterranean side and more buildings tight against each other on the west side of the road. None of these places looked like somewhere she'd like to eat. Eventually Roan turned off onto a narrow side road that crossed over the tracks then dipped downward towards the sea leaving the busier sectors of the city and the tracks above and behind them. After a few downhill sharp turns the road opened to the expanse of the Mediterranean Sammy thought, this is more like it. She immersed herself in the beauty, easily forgetting her need to direct the day. She opened her window breathed in the salty freshness of the sea, watched as the sand spun, and gulls swopped, picking up shells off the sand. A gulp of cormorants flittered along a floating log close to shore. And yet, except for the birds and a small structure in the distance, today the beach is vacuous compared to the summer months when beach umbrellas and bronzed bodies captured spots on the hot sand.

Moments later Roan turned into the sand-filled driveway of a flat-roofed white stucco dwelling. Pots filled with flowers lined the entrance and window boxes bursting with carnations and begonias hung from windows; a sign in front named the restaurant *Cafe En La Playa*.

Sammy quipped, "A café on the beach—well that's original."

"Oh, but wait my dear, you will see this isn't just any old café on the beach." He pulled into a space, stopped and said, "I hope you're hungry because they make the best brunch in all of the *Costa Brava*."

Teasing, she said, "Of *all* of the *Costa Brava*? Are you quite sure about that?"

He nodded, "I am." He cocked his head and said, "Now you're not going to give me any trouble, are you? Remember. You agreed to relinquish all control and put yourself in my very capable and masterful hands."

"I have no such memory. I think you're delusional." She opened her door and got out before he could correct her. Behind her in the driver's seat, she heard him mumbling so she poked her head back in and said, "I capitulate. This looks lovely and it's on the water. I'm willing to give in to anything when I see the ocean."

As he was getting out of the car, he winked at her and said, "Anything? Really? Are you sure you want to make such a bold statement because I might have to take you up on that later?"

And she might let him.

A puff of wind swirled the sand at her feet and she caught

a whiff of something delicious cooking just inside. They approached the large, imposing wood carved entry doors where on either side, soft, gauze-like white curtains billowed out two open windows. That perfect dichotomy beckoned to her and she had a feeling this was a special place.

Inside to the left of the waiting area stood a long wood bar, the shelves above it laden with an abundant stock of different types of liquor. Beyond the bar the room opened up, banked by a wall of floor to ceiling windows that took in the full breadth of the ocean. Inside, diners were dressed casually in light clothes because warmth came from tall heaters scattered randomly on the shiny concrete floor. Waiters scurried in and out of an open side door bringing food to the diners outside. Outside patrons occupied stainless-steel tables that were set up on a makeshift slate patio around the perimeter of the restaurant. One of the things Sammy loved about Spain was that even though it was November people were still able to enjoy places like this open-air restaurant.

A waiter waved them to sit anywhere they liked. There was an open table in the corner by the windows and Roan cupped her elbow and guided her towards it. As they sat a waiter brought them the menu and asked if they would like coffee. They both ordered a cappuccino.

"How is the studio coming along? Did you get everything done yesterday?"

Just thinking about the studio and the steps she was taking for her future flooded her with both trepidation and excitement—her enthusiasm won out. Positivity surged through and she gushed, "Roan, it's going to work. I just know it and right now in this fantastic place and this glorious day, how can I be anything but positive? So yes, to answer your question, I got everything done at the studio. Now I just need to get the registration info out. "

"When do I get to see the studio? It was my idea after all."

"Soon. I'm not quite ready for anyone to see it yet. I've only let Ciara in once because it's her school."

"When you're ready then." He paused, took a sip of his cappuccino and said, "So, how do you like the day so far?"

"Well, I don't know, you got a little bossy there for a while, " she teased.

"Hey, I'm a man, Sammy, it's what we do, isn't it?" Without waiting for any answer to his obvious rhetorical question, he reached for her hand and said, "Besides I like the idea of taking care of you," he said, "not that you need it. You're a strong, independent woman."

She fondled his hand, aware of how his touch just now had set her on edge and filled her with desire. "And that's just the way I like it."

"And it's one of the things I like about you, Sammy. That," he leaned forward, "and you are one of the most beautiful women I've ever known."

Beautiful is not a term anyone had ever said about her, not even Peter who had told her countless times how pretty she was and now with her shorter hair she wasn't even sure about that. But she let the warmth of Roan's words wash over her and she settled in the confidence that today was going to be a good day. "You wouldn't say that if you saw me at six this morning. But thank you."

"I'd love to see you at six in the morning, Sammy."

This doctor, this man's presence in her life filled her with, she suddenly realized, feelings that might be bordering on love. It unnerved her and to hide her eyes from him because he would surely see it, she looked down into her cappuccino and took a sip. To get a grip, she quickly said, "My that's one of the best cappuccinos I've ever had."

"Well, I'm happy you like it, but," his voice quickened with excitement, "wait until you taste the food."

But she was already taking in the best food for her soul and for her life.

* * *

"Would you mind a quick walk on the beach?" They'd finished eating and Roan had been right about the food, everything had been delicious. And now she needed to feel the ocean.

He looked at his phone and said, "Our time at the museum will be tight, but sure. Whatever you like. For the next few minutes or so, I will relinquish control."

"Oh, so now it's 'whatever you like,' she scoffed. "Before it was, grrr, I am caveman; woman must follow."

"Well, then . . . " He pulled some bills out of his wallet, left a tip, stood up, held out his hand and said, "Woman, we are taking a walk on the beach whether you like it or not. Come NOW."

She took his hand and they walked out the side door onto the sand. She took off her jacket, slipped out of her shoes, and let the sand tickle her toes while they walked. "C'mon now it's your turn. Get those shoes off. The sand is warm and glorious."

"Now who's being bossy?" he chided her, but he did it anyway.

A thought had just occurred to her, "You know I don't

have anything I need to get back for tonight, so if we really do get pressed for time, we could always stay." He looked quickly at her and before he could say anything she added, "Two rooms of course."

He picked up a rock and tossed it in the ocean, cocked his head, looked at her and said, "You're one surprise after another." Then he grinned and said, "But of course two rooms."

CHAPTER SIXTEEN

*T*hey'd already spent hours in Dali's Museum and as they walked into the last exhibit, they found themselves surrounded by massive photos of Salvador Dali—photos taken of him at various ages and stages in his life included a collection of the images of the different phases of his characteristic mustache. Roan stopped in the middle of the room, his arms crossed with one hand on his chin, face pensive as he pointed at one in particular and said, "Fascinating. It's perplexing how his different personalities show up not only in his work but in all of these self-portraits. In this tiny room alone, we see the deviant Salvador to more normal staid, romantic Dali."

Sammy loved this conversation and watched Roan's face animate as he described his love of this museum. With each contact whether the other day having lunch in Barceloneta, sitting in her apartment, walking on the beach, or even walking through this museum she was learning about so many of the facets of Roan and she was loving it, especially his apparent love of art. Peter never enjoyed it as she did, frequently groaning when she pleaded with him to see the Picasso exhibit or take in more of Gaudi around the city. Though he might have enjoyed this one because from the first exhibit to the last Dali had not disappointed, and nor had Roan's thoughtful and intellectual observations.

"I agree, he was an artist before his time. Much like Andy Warhol; Dali paved the way."

"Absolutely. I was mesmerized by the intensity and diversity of the artist: macabre at times, sometimes enlightening, always exhilarating with multitudes of curiosities whether in sculptures or paint medium and all were stunning works of art." Roan moved away from a crowd of people who had gathered in the middle of the room. He leaned against a column at the perimeter and motioned for Sammy to join him. When she did, he continued, "I mean his work was surrealistic and yet with a penchant for romance. He was skilled not only in his ink drawings and paintings but sculptures, jewelry, and other visual arts. To say nothing of being provocateur as well as just uniquely strange. Thank you so much for coming with me."

They moved toward the exit when they both stopped at one particular photo of Dali with his arms wrapped around Gala, his muse and the love of his life.

"I've read they had a very unorthodox relationship, but were devoted to each other," Sammy said.

"Yes, I heard that, too. She was quite unique in her own right." He turned to her. "Ready to go?"

"Yes."

Roan held her elbow and led her out of the entrance. "I still can't get over it. As soon as we entered the museum, I was awestruck. And the car that rains inside. Can you believe it? What a mind he had."

"I'm happy you suggested it. I'd heard about the museum, but would never have taken the time to come up here if you hadn't suggested it, so thank you."

As they walked, Roan grew quiet, then said, "You know it is kind of like us."

"What is? Certainly not his work." Sammy was confused.

"No, no. You said he and Gala had a very unorthodox relationship. As we do."

"Goodness. Not like that. She was—"

"I know, I'm kidding. Well, not really. Because, you know Sammy, I think we've done a pretty damn good job moving this relationship on, as unorthodox as it is." He took her hand and leaned down to look into her face. "We have, haven't we? Today was a good day."

She let her hand rest in his, embraced the joy of being with him and let it radiate inward. She smiled up at him and said, "Today was a fantastic day."

He squeezed her hand and when they got to the car he said, "One of these days I'll have to get you over to my place to show you some of my art."

"Like I haven't heard that line before," she teased.

"Ah, so you're a woman of the world, eh?"

She winked at him and said, "Dr. Adair, you have no idea." Then she laughed and got in the car.

Roan got into the driver's side and said, "Well then Ms Driscoll it looks like this journey we are on is going to be more fun than I thought."

"Again, Roan, you have no idea." She turned away so he couldn't see her smile. Or see the affection in her eyes. She knew it was there because she felt it surge through her body and felt it filling her eyes.

He started the car, looked at his watch and said, "It seems it's already near seven and we haven't had anything to eat since this morning. I did put some crackers, cheese, and wine in the cooler, but I think I'm ready for a full meal. Are you up for a little dinner before we head back?"

"That sounds lovely. I'm starved."

"Okay then, I know a place about forty-five minutes from here where we can have a 'lovely' dinner overlooking the water and it happens to be an inn if it gets too late."

"Two rooms, remember?" She wasn't sure that she would be able to stick to that stipulation, but she would try. Things were going well and she didn't want to ruin it. But darn, it would be hard.

"Of course, two rooms." He looked at her, his jaw set, eyes intense behind his glasses, his mouth firm and he continued, "I'm serious. I'm not messing this up again."

* * *

NEITHER ONE OF them needed to worry. It turned out even after dinner and wine at the spectacular Michelin-rated restaurant overlooking the Costa Brava, it wasn't very late after all. They could drive home and still be back by midnight. And yet in this romantic five-star inn with its setting high on a cliff looking out onto the vastness of the night sky, where outside spotlights shone down toward the ocean's edge, where soft lighting tucked into the salmon-colored walls around the perimeter of the dining room and candles in the middle of the table flickered, setting off a glow over Roan's face, Sammy was tempted to insist they stay.

"This *is* lovely, you know. I can't think of a better word to describe this room." She spread her arms out to encompass all of it. "The setting, the . . . well everything is perfect." The day, the night, this room, this inn, and the wine. Everything made her emotional and the wine certainly hadn't helped keep her heart in check.

"I was pretty sure you'd like it," Roan said.

"I have, I do, and," she gazed down into her glass of red wine getting lost in her thoughts for a moment, then she swirled it, took a sip, and said, "I haven't had one moment of guilt, or trepidation, or any negative feeling about this entire day nor any longings for Peter." She glanced over at him, staring, and said, "My only longings tonight, or maybe it's desire, Roan," she hesitated, "have been for you."

She watched as his face flushed, even in the candlelight she could see her words had affected him. He cleared his throat, took off his glasses, set them on the table, rubbed his eyes then looked at her with such intensity and purpose that she had to look away because what she felt for him at that moment seemed impossible.

"That makes me very happy."

"Well, then I think we should stay here," she said.

"That's not a good idea."

"It is and I don't mean two rooms." When he didn't answer she continued, "It's late and I'm really tired. You shouldn't drive, you've had wine. We should stay. We *need* to stay, it's safer." When Roan still didn't answer she said, "Well, then," she was getting irritated, "what do *you* think we should do?"

He thought for moment then replied, "What should we do?

We don't tempt fate, that's what we do." He tipped his wine glass at her and said, "Drink up, if we leave soon, we could be home in an hour."

The wine had definitely taken a toll on her inhibitions, she was a little bit drunk and a lot turned on, and she wanted him. "Let's stay. C'mon." And she tried to put on her sexiest face until she saw she wasn't succeeding when he burst out laughing.

"Nope. No deal. I'm taking you home. And if you noticed I only had one glass. You, my dear, on the other hand, had the rest of the bottle."

* * *

ON THE WAY HOME, she fought to keep her eyes open to stop from falling asleep she talked. "Tell me—" She stopped, her brain had taken a momentary pause, so she concentrated until she remembered. "When do you go back to work?"

"They called me yesterday and want me back the Sunday after Thanksgiving. A cruise is heading out then."

She yawned and felt herself nodding off, but asked him, "Do you ever have to work holidays?"

He took one hand off the wheel, reached over and stroked her hair and said, "Sammy, you are exhausted, you don't have to talk to me; I'm fine driving. Lay your head back and sleep. I'll wake you when we're in Barcelona."

The gentleness of his touch awakened more than her eyes and she regretted letting him talk her into driving back rather than staying at the inn. All she wanted right now was to fall into his arms. Instead, she stretched and she said, "If I sleep now, I won't tonight, so let me jabber. Okay?"

"Jabber on." He put his hand back on the wheel and continued, "Yes, sometimes we have to work during holidays but don't worry, I'll be here for Thanksgiving so I can meet all those friends you keep talking about."

"You already know most of them, but there will be a few you don't know. In fact, there might be a few I don't know." She pondered on that for a moment thinking about who that might be. Then she asked, "Will you work over Christmas?" Waiting for his answer, she fought again the heaviness of her eyelids.

"Probably not. I worked at Christmas last year. And honestly, I've actually been thinking of not going back to the cruise line someday."

That last part of the sentence floated somewhere in her semi-conscious state and she couldn't bring it forward. The only words that resonated were 'not going back'. "Home? You're thinking of not going back home? Where would you stay tonight?" Now she was awake. "With me? Well, sure I—"

But before she could finish, he started laughing. "Relax, Sammy. I was talking about not staying in the cruise industry. Changing where I doctor." His words became a serenade for her fatigued body and mind. They floated somewhere in the recesses of her mind and she fought to listen to him.

"Since I've been away from the cruises because of this shoulder issue . . ."

She'd given up and let her eyes close and his voice continued and blended into the hum of cars passing in the other lane. The only part she clearly heard was when he said, "What do you think?"

To which all she managed to say was, "Yes."

She heard him chuckle and was about to protest, but after

that, she didn't remember anything else until they had pulled to a stop and Roan had turned off the engine and said, "We're here sleepyhead. You're home safe and sound."

He helped her out of the car, asked her if she wanted him to make sure she got into her apartment okay and when she mumbled, "I'm good. You go."

He kissed her goodnight, and she held on to him a little longer, deciding whether to make him come inside so she could have her way with him, but she was exhausted from their day and, she rationalized, there's always tomorrow.

CHAPTER SEVENTEEN

*A*s she suspected even that little snooze in the car messed her up and at two AM Sammy was fully awake. Either the short nap in the car, too much wine and food, or her frustration that she went to bed sexually unsatisfied made it nearly impossible for her to quiet her mind and relax. She had lain there, wide awake staring at the ceiling, rolling from side to side, covering and uncovering herself, opening and closing the window, in fact she was so desperate at some point she'd gotten up, taken a shower, and put clean sheets on the bed hoping that would help—not tonight.

The one thought that gave her the most aggravation was the unfulfilled night in the romantic inn that she should have had with Roan, but all that did was make her desire for Roan bloom to almost the breaking point so much so that she nearly searched for her vibrator. Instead she got up, took a sleep aide finally falling asleep into a fog of images that made Dali's mustache take on comical contortions chasing her as she tried in vain to get away driving in a car that rained inside.

She woke late the next morning feeling like she had a hangover, which she knew she didn't because regardless of what Roan said she only had three glasses or four. Okay, well maybe she was a little hungover. Later, after her run she called Roan.

"Well, good morning sleepyhead," his voice groggy.

"Say, I'm heading over to the studio in a bit to check on some things, do you want to go with me? If you don't have any plans."

"Hmm, so what changed between yesterday and today?"

"What do you mean?"

"Yesterday when I asked you said you weren't ready to let me see it. Or is it because I was so witty and charming the rest of the day that you decided you can't be without me?"

"Aren't we full of ourselves? Actually, I need your opinion."

"I'd like to see it. The studio was my idea after all."

"Ha, okay, I see what kind of guy you are. One who throws an idea out there and then takes credit for it. Ah-ha, I see that now."

"How well you know me already."

"So, if you're game, why don't I meet you there in say an hour and half?"

"Address? Or should I pick you up?"

"I'm walking over. It's only a couple miles. It's close to *La Pedrera*."

"Got it. Text me the address and I'll be there. Coincidently La Pedrera is a few blocks from my place so I'll just walk over, too."

* * *

THEY ARRIVED at the school at the same time. She'd approached from the side of the school and he was in front so he couldn't see her, but she could see him. He was dressed in tan sweatpants, dark blue canvas slip on shoes with no socks, it looked like he'd rolled up the sleeves on his untucked, wrinkled, blue shirt, his hair tousled, his eyes sleepy, his face flushed like he might have jogged over. Actually, she thought, he looked like he should be taken back to bed and she was sure she was up for the challenge.

She held back a bit to watch him as he nodded to students and teachers entering and exiting the front entrance of the school. He seemed relaxed, a natural with other people. Like Peter, he seemed comfortable in his own skin. The only time he appeared unsure was when Sylvia approached him and began talking to him as if they were old friends. His face first questioning then a look of recognition crossed his eyes and Sammy heard him say, "Sylvia—right! Sorry I didn't recognize you at first."

Then she heard Sylvia say, "Yes, I think the last time was at the hospital when Peter—"

Sammy popped out from around the building and said, "There you are, Roan. I see you two have met. Sylvia, do you want to come up to the studio with Roan and I? I'm showing him how his great idea turned out. And you haven't seen it in a while, right?" Sylvia shook her head. "Perfect, let's get crackin'." And she took hold of Sylvia's arm and pulled her around toward the side entrance.

Roan looked at her, perplexed. "I thought it was at the school." He reached out, touched Sammy's forearm and pointed. "Don't we go in this way?"

She lightly patted his hand as you'd pat a child's and said, "You'd think so, wouldn't you? And yet," she grinned at both of them, "there's a separate entrance. C'mon." She waved at them to follow her.

Sammy was a taking leap of faith, but could hardly contain her excitement. Before she unlocked the side door, she made them stop and admire the newly poured sidewalk that led out toward the back parking area behind the school.

"Isn't this cool? Now when I have night and weekend classes people will have a place to park and won't have to walk around the school to get here." Her enthusiasm didn't seem to have spilled over to Roan or Sylvia; they just nodded. "Okay I can see you're not impressed, but watch this." She punched in the code to the key-code door lock and they all heard a click. "Pretty cool, huh? Now it's secure unless you have the code." At least this time she was rewarded with quiet mutterings of approval.

They entered the entry alcove and immediately their presence initiated the motion detector light, turning on to show off a newly painted brilliant white entry. "Impressive, right? The motion lighting! Another security measure," she smiled brightly at them, waiting for a response. Roan's raised eyebrows seemed to be poking fun at her overenthusiastic fervor. He gave her a wimpy thumbs up, obviously not sharing her excitement. But she got it; everyone had their own passions and this was hers. She started up the stairs and waved them on. The stairs had been refinished and gleamed in a deep mahogany color. Treads had been added in a vibrant colored mosaic so there would be no risk of students falling; the handrail had been secured and periodically up the steps a motion detector triggered cam lighting that had been added into the previous dark brown beadboard walls that were now white. The lights turned on as they climbed.

Sylvia said, "Wow, this is really impressive. I remember telling Ciara when I first started at the school that this should all be boarded up, but just adding white paint sure lightened it up."

Sammy tried to catch Roan's eyes to give him a 'see someone appreciates what I've done' look. Again, he gave her a raised eyebrow, bug-eyed, silly grin, thumbs up. She glared at him.

"I'm kidding you. It's really quite impressive," he capitulated.

"Of course, it is," she quipped.

"Nice work Sammy, it used to be so creepy. I hated coming out here when we had to get something from the storage room." Sylvia looked down at Roan coming up the stairs behind her and continued, "You should have seen it before, Roan. Sammy has done miracles with this."

Sammy was grateful to Sylvia—that's what friends are for. Sammy looked at Roan again to see if Sylvia's words had affected him and saw him nodding, finally obviously impressed.

"So Roan, what do you think so far? Do you think this is welcoming and safe enough for students to come if I offer night classes?"

"Yes, I'd say this will do the trick." He grinned up at her. "Very impressive Ms. Driscoll."

They'd reached the landing, the door to the studio in front of them. Sammy's stomach was doing flip-flops. She was nervous and realized getting Roan's opinion was more important to her than she thought. Before she opened the door she cautioned, "Now though the floors are cured and dry, but let's walk around the perimeter."

They nodded and Roan said, "Do you want us to take off our shoes?"

"Naw. All's good." She felt a tremendous amount of pride in what she'd accomplished these last several months and as soon as she opened the door and glanced around the room, she nearly wept—it was so perfect.

She glanced at both of them to see their reaction.

"My god, Sammy," Sylvia said, "you've done miracles with this old space." She turned to Roan and said, "You should have seen this before, Roan. It was a big empty room with no character, grey walls, beat-up floors, and look at it now. Sammy, I love it."

Roan nodded. "I don't know what it looked like before, Sammy, but Sylvia is right, this is, well, quite impressive, nicely done."

The wood floors gleamed, the mirrors along the wall to their right reflected the light coming from the windows on both sides filling the room with the perfect brightness for day classes. She flipped the light switch to make sure the lighting at night would also provide the same. The Cam lighting in the ceiling would work well at night. At the back half of the room tucked in the corner sat a piano; she closed her eyes and envisioned students and couples dancing to ballads or jazz being played on its keyboard by an accomplished pianist that she'd yet to hire. Her own piano skills might not be up to the task, but there were times when she longed to feel the smoothness of ivory under her fingers and hear the cords of music they elicited and listen to the melodies of life. Music had always done that for her. Her need to dance was as much invested in her love of music as it was in her love of feeling the movement of her body. Right now, she resisted the urge to play with the keys, but was overtaken by the desire to take advantage of the gleaming floor and expansive room. She took off her shoes and pirouetted from one end to the other, letting the skirt of her dress flare out and brush her thighs as she danced. Then she waltzed over to Roan and grabbed his hand. "Take off your shoes, we're going to dance."

He looked pained and averted his eyes. She reached up, took hold of his chin and tilted his face down so he couldn't avoid looking at her. She resorted to something she'd always chastised other women for doing and pouted and pleaded.

He shook his head and said, "That wasn't fair." He sighed and said, "But if I must, be warned though, you might regret it." He took off his shoes, straightened his body, his face serious, he held out his arms and said, "Shall we dance?"

She moved into him and gazed up at him and said, "But *can* you dance?"

"How could you possibly doubt it? I'm a man of many talents." He began to hum a waltz and with the grace of a gazelle he swept her effortlessly around the room. Every once in a while, Sammy caught a glimpse of Sylvia, her face alight with obvious pleasure as she watched them. They moved around the room and Sammy became very aware of Roan's arms wrapped around her and the closeness of his face to hers. It took everything she had not to stop and kiss him, but that brief interlude with her imagination interrupted her concentration and she missed a step and tripped, landing hard on the floor. Well, she thought, that had never happened before.

Roan bent down to pick her up, looking at her a bit perplexed. "Did I do that?"

She brushed his hands away and turned to Sylvia. She wasn't going to let that momentary mental distraction stop her from feeling those feelings of freedom and artistic release again, she wanted to keep dancing. "C'mon Sylvia, time to—as they used to say—cut a rug." She bounced up from the floor, grabbed Sylvia's arm and said, "Pretend, we're back in the twenties and Count Basie is playing a boogie."

Sylvia pulled back. "You've truly lost it, Sammy. Not only am I not going to dance I have no idea who Count Basie was, where he was a Count, and what the hell is a boogie?"

Sammy threw her hands up in the air, exasperated she turned to Roan. "Please tell me at least you know what I'm talking about?"

"Cut a rug? Of course, I do." He grabbed her and as they danced all she could think about besides making sure she didn't fall again was how much this man had been surprising her. He liked art and she'd be darned if he couldn't dance, and dance really well. She'd always had to beg Peter to dance; he'd told her he didn't like to make a spectacle of himself. And yet here was Roan showing *her* up.

When Roan finally stopped and she caught her breath, she stood back, put her hands on her hips and said, "What the hell. Where did you learn to dance like that?"

He looked at her, a mix of cocky and confident. "I told you, my dear Sammy, I'm a man of many talents. Some of which, I might add," he winked, "you haven't even discovered yet."

"Well, let me tell you, Dr. Adair, I'm impressed with your

dancing abilities. Sylvia, don't you think . . . ," Sammy turned to talk to Sylvia only to find she'd left.

Sammy turned back to Roan, shrugged and said, "I guess she found us boring. But really where did you learn to dance like that?"

"Cruises. I was one of the lucky ones who had to . . . well, actually I volunteered, to be an extra should any of the older women need someone to dance with. And boy, let me tell you, did they teach me a thing or two. More than half the crowd was over seventy and, boy, can they really dance, and those older women," he paused as if looking for the right word, "those women are very persuasive."

Sammy doubted it took much persuasion on their part, it was apparent to her that Roan was an easy target and one that was willing to be taken captive—and a handsome one at that. Right now, she couldn't think of anything better than letting herself be taken captive.

As if he'd read her mind, he held out his hand, and said, "Say since Sylvia's gone, do you want to stop by my place on the way home?" His face, mischievous, almost demonic. "I could show you my etchings?" He grabbed her, swung her around and continued, "Unless you'd like me to show you more of my moves?" Then he dipped her and planted a kiss on her lips. "I have many more, you know." And pretended to let her drop, caught her as she fell, wrapped her in his arms and kissed her hard.

A kiss that she definitely returned with all of the fervor that she could muster. Going to his place after this was probably not a smart idea, but she pulled away while trying to catch her breath and said, "And that Roan was unfair of *you*," and she tweaked his nose. "I'm not that easy, you know. As if a little showmanship and dancing skills would let you take advantage of me." She did a little tap dance moving a safe distance away from him. "I'd love to see your place. But," she was firm, "you should leave that charm and all those talents you say you possess right here, mister."

And his face took on an innocence she knew was false.

CHAPTER EIGHTEEN

*H*is apartment was what she'd expected in that it was impeccably, tastefully, and expensively decorated, masculine and minimalist, so much so that in a way it didn't look lived-in. There were very few photographs and though art did occupy some of the walls they were sparse and without, it seemed, a sense of continuity in their subjects or color palette. But the completely open floor plan, with dining, living, and kitchen all strategically laid out with easy flow from anywhere, allowed one to appreciate the vastness in the impressive yet unpretentious surroundings. The contemporary vibe throughout with its almost loft feel was contrary to most apartments in older buildings in Barcelona, but it was exquisite.

"This is lovely."

"We were lucky, it had been newly renovated and the seller was motivated. We got it for a lark and with the sale of my practice, we were able to pay cash. Then of course my wife immediately went about ordering furniture from all over Europe and had it delivered."

"And she left it all behind?"

"She didn't want anything except *out* she said, so," he spread his arms to encompass the room, "she's out and this is all mine. But, I'm rarely here to enjoy it."

"Well, it's gorgeous."

"I haven't had the time nor the inclination to arrange the art in this room. My wife didn't have the eye and she started hanging my art collection without any input from me. But she had great taste when it came to the furniture and decorating."

An overstuffed sectional with modern clean lines covered in a nubby taupe fabric sat in front of large floor-to-ceiling industrial-looking graphite casement windows. The windows looked out onto a substantial terrace—also rare for Barcelona—filled with foliage and some flowers that looked as if they needed a drink or two. In front of the sectional two small contemporary round tables with black tops, edged in light wood trim that complimented the light wood floors held an abundance of knick-knacks including books, a few plants, an empty coffee cup and a French press. Over the back of the sofa a contrasting darker taupe-colored throw and a variety of brightly colored pillows in orange and red, both solid and in various patterns, were randomly strewn about.

Sammy was impressed and it made her think about her own apartment and realized that her space could do with more sprucing up. Until recently, she'd never been interested much in decorating. Watching her parents obsess over the placement of each piece of furniture and insisting on the most expensive pieces had left her empty. That they cared so much about status and keeping themselves among the elite of their Cleveland suburb had always annoyed her. Roan's space was so understated but obviously done with high-end furnishings and exquisite taste.

Right now, Roan seemed flustered and began randomly straightening the pillows while he picked up the coffee cup and French press. "Looks like I didn't clean up after myself this morning."

His nervous energy started to make her feel tense so she said, "Stop, Roan. I love it. You must be very comfortable here. It's so darn beautiful."

His hands full on his way into the kitchen area, he stopped mid-stride, his face pensive as he perused the room. "It is, isn't it?" He nodded as if noticing for the first time, then turned to her, set the cup and French press down on the kitchen counter and clapped his hands. "So . . . what can I get you to drink?"

"How about that Rioja you mentioned?

"Now you're talking. It's after one. Drinking time—or so I've learned since moving to Spain. If you're hungry I have a refrigerator full of leftover tapas that if I don't eat will go bad. I went to my favorite market a few days ago and the owner wouldn't let me leave without two grocery bags full of food."

"Sure, I've got a few last-minute things to do at the studio but I'll do them tomorrow, and . . ." she grew very serious, "it would be a travesty to let the food go bad."

"Now, that's the spirit. How about we start with vermouth instead of wine. Never drank it except in a mixed cocktail until I came to Spain. And recently I bought a light, dry variety the guy at the local shop recommended. I've been dying to try. You game?"

"Start? How long do you think I'm going to hang around here anyway?"

He winked. "As long as I say."

"Oh, I see macho man is back. I suppose you think now that you have me here you are going to entertain me with your etchings, eh?"

"But of course, and coincidently most of the good ones are in the bedroom."

"Etchings—bedroom. How original."

"Worried I might try to seduce you?"

Trying to look indignant, she said, "Not even a little. You turned me down last night, so maybe it's time I called your bluff."

He came back from the kitchen carrying a tray of tapas and two glasses of vermouth, set the tray down on one of the tables, handed her a drink, picked up his and said, "Follow me."

"Lead the way Tarzan."

She followed him down a long hallway lined with a masterful mix of vibrant colored paintings and pencil sketches. When they reached the end of the hall, she caught sight of what looked like a Peter Max painting over a large king-size bed and the closer she got Max's unique signature was evident.

"Oh, my god, is that an original?"

Roan grinned at her, his pride of ownership, obvious. "You bet it is. Well, original in that he painted it, but there are variations of others like it. I bought it from a collector before it was rumored Max stopped painting. I heard by 2012 dementia had hit him pretty hard and some of his stuff was no longer painted by him; just signed by him."

"Well, it's stunning. I love his work. I have some of his

prints, but nothing signed or of any value. Which one is this one?"

"*Better World* from 1993. The title drew me and of course his artistry and use of color. Didn't even quibble about the price. Now cruise ships have art shows onboard, many from Peter Max, but his paintings have become less valuable because no one is one-hundred-percent sure if he painted them or just signed them. Either way, like you, I love his work."

Still reeling from the fact Roan owned a painting that was probably worth tens of thousands of dollars and by one of her favorite artists, Sammy noticed the bedroom was in the same minimalist, modern style as the rest of the house with earth tones dominating. Another set of French doors led out onto the same terrace like the one off the living room. The light-colored wood floor had continued into the bedroom and yet the bathroom which Sammy could see from where she stood had concrete floors and what looked like a long concrete counter topped with white sinks and chrome faucets. A large grey towel lay on the floor and shaving paraphernalia were scattered on the counter. The bed was unmade, but it looked like the taupe coverlet was made of soft linen and underneath the sheets of luxurious grey Egyptian cotton. It appeared the doctor had very good taste.

"Sorry the room is kind of a mess. I slept in this morning then after you called, I fell back asleep and never made the bed." He gazed into the bathroom. "Or it appears put away stuff from last night's shower." He pulled up the cover on the bed and walked over and picked up the towel in the bathroom.

She pointed to the bed. "Egyptian cotton?"

"Not sure." He smiled then said, "Want to try them out?"

She took a step towards him, reached out and touched his hand. "Try me."

That flustered him.

He took a step back and said, "Be careful. I told you that next time you try to seduce me I wouldn't be so gentlemanly."

She stepped closer and touched his chest, running her hands along the buttons of his shirt. "Then what happened last night. I was willing. You weren't."

"You'd had too much to drink. If I'm going to seduce you, I want you to remember everything." Her heart fluttered, her body reacted and somehow, she knew she needed him inside her now. Then he said, "I mean *everything*."

That was all it took.

She rose up to kiss him, instead of stopping her, with one arm he swept her up, carried her to the bed, ripped off the coverlet with the other and gently laid her on her back. He stood over her and slowly unbuttoned his shirt. She tried to sit up and he said, "No, stay there." He took off his shirt then his pants and she saw the obvious erection inside his tight black briefs so she began to unbutton her blouse. "No, not yet." He bent over and ran his hands under her dress, stopping just short of her inner thigh. Her desire for him escalated to the point she thought she might faint if he didn't get on with it. Again, she tried to sit up and reach for him to bring him on top of her. Again, he stopped her, this time as he leaned down, he ran his hands up her arms and over her breasts, then leaned over and kissed her, running his tongue around the inside of her mouth and gently tugging on her lower lip with his as he pulled away. She tried again to pull him on top of her, but again he stopped her and said, "No rushing this time. We take it slow."

And they did.

She gave in to the rhythm of his lovemaking and felt all the feelings he wanted her to feel and in return, she gave everything to him including her heart.

THEY'D FALLEN asleep and Sammy woke with an intense feeling of being home. Not in the sense that this was her house, it was his and would never be hers, but that she was home with Roan. Tucked in his arms still, her head buried under his arm, she quietly opened her eyes, raised her head, and saw that he, too, was awake.

"How are we doing?"

"I'm better than okay, doctor, I'm fantastic." She traced her finger around his nipple and then she turned her head and kissed his chest. Rolling to her back, she flopped her arms over her head. "But . . . I'm famished!" Jumping out of bed, grabbing his shirt off the floor and putting it on, she said, "I think we have some tapas to finish."

"Oh, you think so, do you?"

And he bounded up beside her, lifted her and laid her on the bed again. "I, myself, have some *other* unfinished business." She looked up at him from the bed as he stood over her and saw his 'business' was clearly unfinished.

HOURS LATER SITTING on a stool at the breakfast bar in the kitchen, Sammy in Roan's shirt with her feet on the last rung and Roan next to her, she playfully twirled around in circles.

Her heart full, her soul sated, her body satisfied more than she could ever remember, even more than her first time with Roan when her guilt had taken over. This time she felt no guilt, no remorse, she only felt good. He'd not only satisfied her sexual needs today, over these last few months he'd filled her need for intellectual and cultural stimulation in ways, that if she was honest, Peter never had.

They'd finished the vermouth, moved on to Rioja, munched on *Iberian* ham on rustic bread, olives, fried calamari, and just started on *patatas brava* with aioli, and the mussels. No longer hungry for food or drink she stopped the chair from turning, leaned into him and said, "Want another go?"

Eyebrows raised, he started to stand. "Will I have no peace?"

"I'm kidding, I'm kidding. Sit down."

"Thank, God. I'm good, but I'm just not sure I'm *that* good." He sat, downed his drink and said, "More food? Wine? There's still a bottle of Grappa waiting to be opened."

"Not for me, but you sure know how to give a woman a good time. Delirious sex and a full stomach . . . "

"Did you doubt it?"

"No, but then after all of this," she spread her arms and swept them so they included him and the contents of the table. "What more could a girl ask for?

"Dessert?"

"You—you are my dessert," she said and reached over and touched his face.

"Well, you can have me anytime you want." He took her hand from his face and touched his lips to her palm, and said, "I mean something sweet, something rich, and delicious."

"So, what did you have in mind?"

"Get dressed I'll show you."

She pouted. "But I don't want to get dressed."

"That figures, give a girl what she wants: sex, food and drink and now she's being difficult again," he said, then stood, stretched, looking quite pleased with himself in his sweatpants and no shirt, his chest thrust out, his ribs defined, his arms buff. "I worked hard for you—and if you're talking about another go-round later, I think I deserve a reward. And for that reward, I want *Torrijas*—chocolate ones from Seville."

"Wait. You're kidding, right? You don't mean *go* to Seville."

He leaned down and kissed her on the cheek. "Why not? I hear you flew to Paris on a whim."

She threw a napkin at him, indignant, she asked, "Who told you that?"

"You, did, silly." He moved behind her, rubbed her back and shoulders, kissed her neck and continued, "No, not go to Seville. There's a place around the corner that makes them. So," he turned her chair around to face him and stared at her, "are you coming with me or do you want to stay here and snoop through my apartment while I go and bring us back the most delicious *Torrijas* you will ever have?"

"I'll stay and snoop if you don't mind." She looked around the room. "Hmm, where should I look first? Where are your hidden secrets?"

"I'm an open book, my dear Samantha. Snoop all you want."

He dressed and as he started to walk out the door, she tugged at his sleeve. "When you get back and after we gorge ourselves on scrumptious *Torrijas* I might need to take a nap." She smiled coyly. "Or finish something else."

He grinned at her. "I was counting on that."

Later after dessert, they talked and talked until they were both exhausted, but not exhausted enough so late into the night they also 'finished' that something else. And for that night and the next three, Sammy stayed with Roan, waking to him beside her and going to bed at night with him next to her and they fell into a routine. During those lazy mornings Roan fixed breakfast, they'd have coffee on the terrace and talk about what to do that day. Those days filled with conversation, food and drink, walks in his neighborhood, coffee at his favorite place, tapas and sangria at his other favorite place. They made a trip back to the studio and also to her apartment to gather clothes. During those three days and nights, they got to know each other better—during the walks, during the food, during the drink, the only time they didn't talk was during those endless hours of lovemaking. It was during those three days that Sammy settled into this new relationship with deep affection for Roan. Ciara had been right. She couldn't go through her life not loving someone because she feared losing them.

CHAPTER NINETEEN

*I*t was Thanksgiving Day and for the past several days Sammy had been back in her own place. Roan was due to pick her up in fifteen minutes to go to Macy's. She'd agreed to make pumpkin pie for dinner, and now wondered why she'd done that. Sammy had proven cooking was not in her realm of skills. The pie was made and in the oven, but earlier each time she checked, it hadn't set. Sammy bent over again now, gave it a gentle jiggle and this time saw it was ready. She pulled it out, wrapped it—pie tin and all—in foil and kitchen towels as Roan knocked on her apartment door.

They hadn't seen each other for a few days and Sammy was especially eager to spend this day with him, but she just wasn't sure she wanted to share him *with* anyone else. She grabbed her coat, slipped the pie into a bag, making sure it stayed upright and opened the door ready to go to Macy's. Roan looking handsome and trim, young, and hip in black fitted dress pants, collarless white shirt with thin black stripes, open to mid-chest showing just a bit of chest hair bent down to kiss her. Not only were his clothes impeccable, he wore an expensive-looking fitted pale grey wool coat with off-center black buttons that hit him mid-calf. His ankles were bare and he wore trendy casual black loafers, and in his hands, he carried a bunch of flowers.

God, Sammy decided, he looks like a model.

He handed her the flowers and said, "There's some in the car for Macy, too. And a bottle of wine. Thought I should bring something." He ran his hand nervously through his hair and said, "Am I too casual? Wasn't sure how your group dresses for stuff like this."

"Nope you look great. But your hair is different and you have stubble," she said trying to squelch the desire to bag the dinner and take him to bed. His face: scruffy with bits of grey and she noticed for the first time it looked like grey also wove through in his sandy-colored hair perfectly—like he'd had it done professionally, like he'd just stepped out of men's fashion magazine.

"I needed a haircut; I told the barber to trim the sides and he suggested leaving the top longer. I wasn't sure—my wife always liked it short—but when I objected, the hairdresser told me longer hair is in trend and that I should just let him do his job. So, what do you think?"

"Very nice. I must say you clean up well. In fact, you look like I need to take you to my bed, right now."And she pulled him inside.

"In that case," he said as he stepped inside, set the flowers down, grabbed her around the waist, pulled her close, leaned down and playfully kissed her neck, then nibbled her earlobes, while pushing his hands down the back of her pants then up her blouse. She relaxed into him and felt her grip on the bag loosen and then it dropped.

"Oh crap."

"What was that?" Roan pulled back, searched around to see what happened.

"It's the pie. It's in the bag on the floor and I'll bet it's a mess right now."

Luckily, when she looked, it had only shifted a little. That distraction was enough for Roan, who said, "I think we better go, or I'm betting if we don't right now, we won't."

"You got that right. Now move out of the way and get your sexy ass out the door, before I change my mind."

* * *

THEY PULLED up to Macy's house with a line of cars trailing behind them and the street was filled with parked cars so they found a spot on the next block.

"Shit, this is going to be much bigger than I thought."

Roan patted her hand and said, "It'll be okay. I've got this."

"Glad you do, because I'm not sure I do."

"Look Sammy, really, if it gets crazy and you want to go, we go. Stop worrying. I've met some of your friends anyway. At least I'm not meeting parents. That always terrified me."

Now was as good a time as any to tell him. "Well, brace yourself because my parents called this morning and they are coming for Christmas, to see the new studio *and* stay for the open house. Which means they'll be here for weeks. How do you suggest we handle *that?*"

"Let's not worry about it now. We can talk about your parents' visit later. I'm sure we can figure it out," he said and smiled at her, squeezed her hand and held it for a second. "Is some of your trepidation about tonight because of our past?"

She nodded.

"Then we don't mention it. If it comes up, we'll change the subject or just say we literally bumped into each other one day, had a laugh, had a moment, I helped you with your packages—you being an obsessed shopper and all," he teased, "and the rest, as they say, is history. End of story. That's it, no lengthy explanation needed."

"Perfect, that is perfect."

THEY ALL LOVED him of course, but then why wouldn't they. He was a good man, funny, handsome, intelligent, and from the first moment she introduced him to someone, all her anxiety disappeared. The 'how did you meet' thing didn't come up at first and when it did a few times later, they were able to navigate without any issues.

It had been an easy fun evening, and miraculously the pie turned out. As they were leaving, Macy complimented her and said, "Now that we know you *can* cook, you'll have to start contributing."

"You should know, she makes a fantastic paella sauce," Roan said and nudged Sammy, "ask her about it sometime."

Macy, eyes questioning, said, "Do tell."

Sammy quickly pushed Roan towards the door and out they went.

On the way home, Sammy said, "Come over. And I want you to stay the night. I want good memories of you and me in my bedroom. Waking next to you will be that good memory."

He frowned at her and pulled over to the side of the road;

stared out the window and looked as if his mind was far away. He turned, put his arm across the back of the seat, his thumb rubbed the nape of her neck and shot her a sideways look and said, "Are we tempting fate? Things have been going so well."

"No," she said louder and with more fervor than she'd intended. "You leave Sunday and I'm sick of me and this ongoing struggle I've had. I like you, Roan. I like you a lot and there's no reason staying at my house rather yours should make any kind of difference. Nor why things between us shouldn't keep going well. Now move it bud. Get us back to my place so I can have my way with you while you are looking so hot."

"You'll get no argument for me," he said as he put the car in drive and pulled out onto the road back to Barceloneta.

CHAPTER TWENTY

*I*t was three days later; the Sunday after Thanksgiving and though they'd spent Thanksgiving night and the following two at Sammy's, last night Roan insisted on staying at his apartment alone.

"But you leave for three weeks. I'll miss you. I should come with you to your place so we can spend our last night together," she'd argued.

"I'll be up at five, then the next two hours showering, packing and making sure everything else is ready. It will be easier for me to do it alone "

In the end, she'd agreed.

But when she woke up last night at three, then again at four, and again at four-thirty she decided the heck with it, he couldn't tell her what to do.

Still rubbing the sleep out of his eyes, he'd answered the door in boxers. "Well, this is a nice surprise, but I thought we said goodbye last night?"

"Well, you thought wrong, bud." Feeling half-asleep

herself, Sammy pushed her way past him carrying a tray with two cappuccinos and four Xuxos.

Before she could set them down, he grabbed a cappuccino and said, "You're a godsend." Peering over her shoulder and pointing to one of the Xuxos, he continued, "And what is that delectable looking thing?" And he poked his finger into the sugar coating.

"Stop, dang it." With the tray held high above her head, she twirled away from him and darted into the kitchen dodging him as she went. He followed close behind, trying to tickle her. "Damn it, stop." She was laughing so hard she almost dropped the tray. "If you don't stop, I'll eat them all myself."

"Yeah, I'd like to see you give that a try. I'm bigger than you. And I can take you down in—"

He never got to finish his sentence because before he had a chance, Sammy had set the tray down and jumped in his arms, whispering after she kissed him, "If you're so damn sure you can take me down, do it."

So, he did.

AND NOW AN HOUR later Sammy sat on his bed staring around the room. In his room where the aroma of his after-shave still lingered, where a few of his clothes lay on the floor—flung there as he'd rummaged through his dresser trying to pack—where his towel still remained on the floor of the bathroom and where water trickled from the shower faucet, and where their unfinished cappuccinos and pastries were still on the kitchen counter. She tried with little success to will the emptiness away. A shred of disbelief she'd felt in the early days after Peter's death, trickled into her subconscious and disquieted her. The same unreality and hollowness of Peter's loss eked into her psyche, but she chastised herself, she wasn't this lovesick puppy, she was a confident, independent woman who hadn't really needed a man to fulfill her. Roan's gone for three weeks, she reminded herself, not forever. She needed get on with her day so she took one last look around Roan's apartment and walked out.

* * *

ON HER WAY HOME, she stopped by the studio and checked out the new bathroom. As she'd rounded the corner from Roan's she saw Ciara unlocking the front door of the school.

"Hey, what are you doing here?"

Startled, Ciara jumped then shaking her finger at Sammy said, "Finally. Where the hell have you been? You disappeared at Thanksgiving and I've been texting you. I was beginning to wonder if the doc kidnapped you."

"Geez, it's only been four days."

"Maybe this time, but you've been MIA a lot lately. I even went by your apartment a few weeks ago and that old guy, the one who is Peter's uncle, said he hadn't seen you for a few days."

"I've stayed at Roan's on and off."

Ciara looked surprised. "Is this serious now?"

Sammy shrugged. "Your guess is as good as mine. I know I like him a lot and it seems we are good together. And, most importantly, we seem to have gotten over our past."

"Hmm, if I remember he's not the one who had the problem with it, it was you. So, you're okay with it now?"

"I am. But he left this morning for three weeks and I'm going to miss him."

"You'll be fine."

"Of course, I will."

They settled in Ciara's office and Ciara offered her a bottle of water. She took a sip and said, "Say, I have some news of my own which is why I stopped by your place few weeks ago. Sean's getting a divorce."

"Really. I thought you didn't care."

Ciara shifted in her seat. "I don't. I mean not really."

But Sammy knew Ciara well enough to know she wasn't being completely honest. "What happened?"

"Sean found out his wife was having another affair. This time with some American actor that had come to Dublin to make a movie. Sean said he'd had enough, that was too much for him. Apparently, she loves this one."

"What happens if his wife moves to the US and wants to take the son?"

"Sean said he'd never let that happen; that he'd fight her all the way." Ciara straightened. "Enough of that. What brings you out so early in the morning?"

"I could ask you the same thing. You do know it's Sunday, don't you?"

"Had some paperwork to do. What about you?"

"I went by Roan's early this morning to say goodbye and decided on my way home to check out the bathroom in the studio. And I have to drop off some info at the marketing company I hired."

"By the way, did you remember Danele is having that Christmas Eve gathering? Will Roan be back?"

"Shit. Damn it. Yes, and my parents will be here. That should be a real disaster. Maybe we won't go."

"You have to."

"I know, but . . . my parents, Roan, and all my friends in the same place. It terrifies me just thinking about it. You know my parents drive me crazy. And they don't know about Roan and me . . . or our past. It could be awful."

Ciara just shook her head and said, "You're screwed."

Darn if she wasn't.

CHAPTER TWENTY-ONE

*A*fter she and Ciara caught up and before Sammy went into the studio to make sure things were going as planned, she checked to make sure the new bathroom for the studio was finished. At her request, the contractors made it into three individual stalls each with its own toilet, sink, and urinal rather than one big room with tiny stalls. It turned out perfect. In fact, all of her planning and the work the contractors had done for the studio seemed to be coming together better than she'd anticipated.

As always, she paused before opening the door to the studio and felt a shiver of anticipation. Would she love it as much as the last time? Would it be as grand? She entered and this time, she stopped just inside the door and rested her back against the door jam. She took it all in and pictured the room with eager young dancers, both girls and boys pushing and giggling as they lined up at the ballet barre at the end of the room. Around the rest of the studio, Sammy imagined hearing heels clicking on the wood floor as she envisioned older children and adults tap dancing, or couples flying through the room waltzing.

Her mind filled with possibilities. Down the road, jazz dance would be offered and eventually an introduction to music and dance for younger children for those kids who may not have been exposed to either at home. All lessons and offerings would be staggered throughout the late afternoon after school hours, in the evenings, and weekends. The complete winter schedule hadn't been finalized yet, but there would be a plethora of choices including in the summer a class called Dance-With-Me, so that children three and under could learn with a parent.

As she pondered the future of the studio, she grew more excited. To add an exclamation point to what she was feeling Sammy waltzed from one side of the room to the other where she stopped, turned, leaned against the ballet barre, and reflected on what she'd accomplished. It hit her hard and she was overcome by an overwhelming sense of pride and gratitude. Unable to push down her emotions she let herself feel all of them. Her eyes filled with tears and she couldn't stop them. She sunk to the floor suddenly feeling the weight of the last three years; especially these last few months. She quietly sobbed tears of loss, tears of joy, tears of anger, tears of pride. She cried for happy she cried for sad, for the loss of Peter, for the loss of her job, for her fight with Javier and conversation with Max, for her failed attempt at cooking, for her discarded clothes. She also cried for her wonderful new relationship with Roan and for his caring and kindness; for finding him. Finally, willing herself to stop, her eyes fell on the piano in the corner. She began laughing. She'd forgotten about the piano; she'd forgotten to have it tuned and how could she offer classes to couples when she also forgot to hire a pianist. The tears, the laughter, were what she needed and she stood up and after taking one last look around the studio, making a few notes about what else needed to be done, she left. On her way home, stopped at the marketing company to drop off information about the January open house and when she got back to her apartment, Roan called.

"How's my girl?"

"Excellent sir. But I thought you weren't calling me until tonight right before you sail."

"Should I hang up and call you tonight, instead."

"Not on your life bud, if you know what's good for you."

"Then I guess I won't. You sound like you are in a good mood. Here I thought you'd be sad because I'm not there."

"I was. Then I wasn't. Then I was again. Now I'm not." And she grinned waiting for his response, assured that he'd be a bit indignant as Peter always had when she pretended his presence was unimportant.

But as in everything else, Roan surprised her. "That makes me happy. I don't want you to be sad for any reason. How was your morning? Or did you go back home to bed?"

"No, I stayed at your place a bit, got sad, missed you then filled my morning with constructive things."

"What did you do?"

"I went by the studio." She told him about seeing Ciara, about how perfect the studio looked, and her stop at the marketing business, but she hesitated telling him about her breakdown—it would be too hard to explain.

"Good."

"Oh, Ciara reminded me that Danele is having a Christmas Eve gathering."

"Sounds like fun. If I'm invited, that is."

"Of course, you are. But so are my parents. Sorry. Looks like you'll be thrown to the wolves the minute you get back."

"I can handle it, Sammy. No worries."

"Not sure I can. They will ask lots of questions about my friends, the studio, and you." She sighed. "Maybe I should run away somewhere. Want to come with me?"

"Name the time and place and I'll blow off this pop stand of a job, and off we go." He laughed that deep throaty sexy laugh the one that right now made her want to jump through the phone or run down to the port and bring him back. "But, seriously, Sammy, it'll be fine. Take a moment." He paused. "Remember how anxious you were about Thanksgiving and that turned out okay. Right? I'm sure this will, too. But if you'd rather I didn't go, I'm okay with that"

"Absolutely not! You have to be there. You're my protection."

"Good, I'm your man then. Say, the reason I called now is because I might not be able to call tonight. There's always the safety drill right after we launch and now there's a pre-launch meeting for medical staff, so it might get too crazy."

She was disappointed but said, "It's fine. I'm glad you called now. I miss you already, you know."

"And I miss you already, Ms. Driscoll. I've grown accustomed to having you around."

"And me, you, Mr. Adair."

She hung up the phone feeling a bit of the emptiness and hollowness she'd felt in his apartment earlier; she let it be, then pushed it away. No sooner had she hung up from Roan than her phone rang.

"Hello, dear. It's Mom."

Well, talking to her parents wouldn't fill the emptiness but maybe she should face the inevitable and tell her mother about Roan.

"Hey, Mom, how's Ohio?"

"Oh, you know nothing changes much these days. How are you?"

Prepared to tell all, she said, "Now that you ask, I'm—"

Her mother cut her off. "Just wanted to let you know your brother is coming with us. He's over in the UK doing an international case for a few weeks before he comes back to Ohio. He wanted me to let you know he decided to take a quick trip to see how you are doing. Our flight is via London so we'll be on the same plane. He won't stay for your opening because he has to be back in the UK by the first, but he wanted to see you and your place. And your new adventure."

That threw her. She hadn't seen Jason, her youngest brother, since she left home ten years ago, and she wasn't sure she needed or wanted to see him now. They'd hardly spoken in the last ten years and they'd had a big fight before she left just like she'd with her father.

When Sammy decided not to finish law school, Jason became her father's focus. Jason, too had had other career and life aspirations and becoming a lawyer wasn't one of them. As the youngest, Jason had always been a little weak when it came to standing up to their parents' wishes, often capitulating whenever either parent objected to something he was doing or wasn't doing. His attachment to their parents was, in Sammy's opinion, the reason he was still single. In the end, Jason had given in to his father, finished college and joined the practice. But his resentment against Sammy had been palpable and worsened when she made plans to move to

Spain. She was still hurt by Jason's misplaced frustration and in the end, Jason was as angry with her, as her father had been.

"Mom, I don't think that's a good idea. We were hardly on speaking terms when I left and I'm not up for another confrontation, besides," she took a deep breath, "I'm seeing someone and I'm not ready to introduce him to the whole family."

"Samantha," she could hear the irritation in her mother's voice, "your brother is trying to make amends with you. Now, I don't want to hear another word." Her voice softened then. "And I'm thrilled that you have found someone. I know how hard it's been for you since Peter died. I've always regretted not knowing him and could never understand why you kept us out of your life once you left for Spain."

"It's history, Mom, but I need you to listen now." She plunged in. "Roan was the doctor that was there when Peter died. But that is a subject we won't discuss while you're here and under no circumstances do I want you to quiz Roan about it." And before her mother could respond or ask questions, Sammy said, "I've got to go, and I don't want to talk about it. So, I'll see you in three weeks." She hung up while her mother was still talking.

And it was done. They knew.

CHAPTER TWENTY-TWO

*T*hose three weeks flew by at breakneck speed. It was Thursday, a week and half before Christmas, two days before her parents would arrive, three before Roan. During the three weeks since Roan left, Sammy and Roan connected every day via text, talk, or video chat. He shared stories of his daily routine, often describing some of the places the ship docked. He told Sammy about Greece and how he'd love to take her there one day. How when the ship anchored just outside the port town of *Thira* and tendered its cruise passengers to the town center, he steered away and took the local bus to *Oia*, a beautiful village on the north-western tip of Santorini. He told her how tucked amongst the many whitewashed dwellings carved into rugged clifftops that hung over the Mediterranean in Oia, he found a tiny café and bar.

"It only has four tables, a well-stocked bar, and spectacular view. The owner and I got along well, so well that he insisted I try a red wine from *Santorini* called *Vin Santo*."

"Did you?" she'd asked.

"Try it? You bet I did. I wasn't on call that day so why not. The owner was quintessential Greek. Quite talkative, too. He spoke English and I know a bit of Greek so after two glasses, I guess I was pretty talkative, too, because as I was leaving, he said, 'hey doc, bring Sammy next time.'" Roan laughed. "I guess I must have talked about you quite a bit and you know what Sammy?" He paused. "You know I will."

Awash in the warmth of his voice, she said, "Will what?" Like she didn't already know what he meant.

"Bring you, Sammy. Bring you to this spectacular part of the world and hide you away, just for me."

His voice and words were like a sensual embrace and her body grew hot with longing for him. "You talked about me?"

His voice deepened as he said, "I talked about you a lot Sammy, to anyone that would listen."

She flushed; happy he couldn't see her reaction, she said, "Then I guess I'll give in this time and let you take me wherever you want."

He didn't answer for a time, then he said, "You have no choice."

During other conversations while he was gone Sammy shared her excitement and nervousness about the success of the studio. She told him about other parts of her life including book club meetings and visits with the girls.

"Do you talk about me?" he asked.

"Wouldn't you like to know?"

The truth was she'd talked about him so much to Ciara, Danele, and Sylvia, they finally told her to stop. "We're happy for you, but geez, enough already."

"But," she explained to them, "things are good. We've moved beyond our past. I'm letting my feelings take me and

I'm not as fearful that loving him means losing him. We've moved on beyond our past. I need you guys to respect that."

"We never had an issue, Sammy. You did." Ciara reminded her.

Now Sammy just hoped her family wouldn't have issues with Roan either. Family had always been hard for Sammy. Her feelings that she lived outside her family's inner circle made it difficult for her to be objective in normal family gatherings. It seemed she always found herself defending everything in her life and, whether she wanted to or not, she'd lash out in the most destructive ways. She hoped this visit would prove to be better.

Luckily though, she knew Jason would like Roan. His love of art equaled Roan's, so they would find common ground. In fact, an artist is what Jason had wanted to be. He was talented, passionate about abstract art, and even sold some pieces when he was younger. She loved her brother and hoped they'd have time to sort things out.

Her parents would be harder.

She walked into the kitchen tossed what was left of her coffee in the sink and set her cup on the counter then made her way into the guest room to take a quick look to see if it was presentable for Jason. She decided it was fine the way it was. The apartment was as ready as it would ever be and there was nothing else to be done before everyone's arrival except shop for Christmas gifts.

Her parents never let her get them anything, but this year she would surprise them with something unique to Spain—perhaps a Gaudi lizard or sculpture from another famous artist and an expensive bottle of vermouth. Since tasting it at Roan's she'd grown to love the flavor profile. Her brother would be satisfied with a bottle of expensive wine—the *Tinta de Toro* grape from the *Toro* regions of Spain—better known as *Tempranillo*. Her brother was a wine snob and would appreciate the local name for it.

The girls never exchanged gifts, instead they always took a trip together in summer. Last year they'd walked the Camino de Santiago, this year they'd talked about going to the southern coast of Ireland and staying in a castle. Ciara promised to do the research this time. It had been hard for Sammy to let go of that task—planning trips was her thing—but buying Christmas presents better be her thing today. It was after noon already. She'd put it off long enough.

* * *

SHE FOUND something right away for her parents and for Jason, now she was struggling with what to get Roan. Sammy ran into Macy coming out of Zara and asked for her help.

"You know all the shops around here better than I do. Where can I find something for Roan? Something a bit personal that tells him I consider him more than a friend, yet not too personal. You know, not like something you'd give a fiancé or husband."

Macy wrapped her arm through Sammy's as they walked and teased, "So now he's more than a friend? I love this. I told Tomas I was sure Roan was the man for you. Marriage is the best Sammy, you should . . . "

Sammy stared at the sidewalk as they walked, saying nothing. Finally, Macy did. "Sorry, Sammy. That was insensitive of me. I'm still new to this marriage thing and I love Tomas so

much. I wasn't trying to say you should marry, Roan, it's only .
. . "

"It's fine, Mace. I knew what you meant. And I love you for
it. Now let's get down to the task of finding something for
Roan before I lose my mind. Can you come with me or do you
have to go back to work?"

"Nope. I'm done. Let me call Tomas and let him know. And
Sammy?" She stopped walking and hugged Sammy. "How
about some dinner, too? Tomas can find something to eat. I'm
ready for some girl time, how about you?"

"I would love that." Finding something for Roan and a
dinner out with Macy made her deliriously happy. Macy took
her to an exclusive men's shop in an area of Barcelona Sammy
had not been to and gave her the perfect suggestion.

"Cashmere. Sammy, get him a cashmere sweater. That is
personal and yet not too much, I think. I got Tomas one the
first Christmas we were together. Unless he's not into clothes,
Sammy, or already has a lot of cashmere. If so, we can think of
something else."

"No, no, it's a great idea. It seems the last few months he's
taken an interest in what he wears. I know he has a cashmere
jacket, but I didn't see any cashmere sweaters at his place."
Sammy walked over and fingered the stack of sweaters. "But
what color?"

"Black, dark grey, navy blue are the best choices. It's
Europe Sammy. No fancy colors; go for sophisticated. And a
scarf! Does he have one?"

Sammy had only seen him with a scarf a few times, so that
seemed like a nice addition and maybe a book on the Camino
de Santiago trek.

"But, is that too much stuff?"

"Put the sweater and scarf in the same box. That way it looks like one gift and if you get the guide book, that will tone down any personal aspect and seem more friend-like."

Packages in hand, along with the guidebook they bought when they stopped in the local book store, Sammy linked arms with Macy and said, "Now, where should we eat?"

CHAPTER TWENTY-THREE

The Barcelona airport was packed with holiday travelers. A cacophony of languages echoed in the terminal's public area as people waited for passengers from inbound flights. The security line extended into the ticketing area; babies cried, toddlers whined, people complained, and Sammy had a headache. She should be sitting in her car in the express lot waiting for a call from her father to say they'd picked up their bags and were ready for her. But her father insisted she meet them *inside* the airport. "Dad, because of security I can't get to your gate. It's easier if I wait, pull up, and pick you up outside baggage claim when you are ready."

"Your mother brought her entire closet. We'll need a hand."

"Jason will be with you. He can help."

"Samantha, please don't argue. Just meet us in baggage claim after we've gone through customs. I'll text you."

So here she was, an hour after their flight was due, still waiting.

While she'd arrived on time, she discovered that the flight had been delayed in London. Neither the reader board nor customer service could give her a new estimated arrival time, so for the first thirty minutes she went back to her car and tried to catch up on sleep and the next thirty minutes she'd called both Ciara and Sylvia to complain about her parents. Finally, after an hour of waiting, both out of frustration and a strong need for coffee, she went back into the airport only to find the plane had in-fact landed ten minutes earlier. She'd heard nothing from her parents nor any notification to tell her which baggage claim area. So right now, she was in no man's land, between arrivals and departures trying to figure it out. She was grumpy and her head was killing her.

"Samantha. Samantha over here." Her mother's voice cascaded through the vast, sprawling terminal reverberating off walls so that it was hard for Sammy to pin down where they were. Then a whistle that she assumed was her father's made their location obvious—to her and everyone else within earshot. She followed the sound and watched as her mother and father, struggling with what looked like a hundred pieces of luggage, burst out of the doors from the customs area. Jason followed close behind pulling his one suitcase and carrying a briefcase over his shoulder. She could see from where she was that he was not happy—at least she and Jason had that in common. Just as she was about to walk over to them, someone grabbed her from behind.

"Shoot, I'll be darn. If it isn't my little filly friend from Pah-ree." As she turned to the voice, someone passing by shoved her into the arms of Jim Picard. Grinning down at her, he leaned in to give her air kisses just as her parents appeared; her mother fluffing her hair, her father clearing his throat, Jason lagging and all of them staring gleefully at Jim. It was her mother who was the first to pull herself together and held out a hand to Jim. "Hello doctor, I'm Sammy's mother Charlotte, so nice to meet you." Then before Sammy had a chance to correct them, her father chimed in, "Stuart Driscoll here, pleased to meet you doc."

Jim just stood there, stoic, said nothing but looked totally confused when a woman rushed up to them and gushed, "Darling, there you are. I thought you'd gone through security without me." Then she looked at them and said, "Hi, I'm Missy, Jim's wife."

* * *

THEY WERE in the parking lot, Sammy loading suitcases into the car as Jason said, "Jim seems like a nice guy. Where did you say you met him?" She'd managed to explain the situation with Jim to her parents, but Jason had missed it because he'd insisted on going off and grabbing a coffee at the airport. "Like I told mom and dad, I met him at Ian's wedding."

Who?" Jason said.

"Geez, Jason. Ian, our cousin. For God's sake, get in the car." This was not going to be a good visit; Sammy could tell already that this was going to be a disaster.

"Got it." Not moving, he continued, "He seemed—"

"I repeat, he's a friend of Ian's. Look, I don't want to talk about it. Period." Sammy closed the trunk, opened the back seat door, shoved the last of the luggage in between her parents and again told Jason to get in the car.

As soon as they were settled her father started in. "That Jim guy seems like a nice fellow and his wife seemed friendly."

"Friendly, Stuart? Ha, is that what you call it? She was all over you and Jason. That poor man better look out or he'll lose that friendly little wife to someone else," her mother added.

Sammy had had it. "That 'poor nice fellow' you all are talking about tried to seduce me while he was engaged to that 'friendly' wife. He's a jerk. Now can we stop talking about him?"

"Of course, dear," her mother said, "no need to get so angry."

For the next thirty minutes as they crawled through Barcelona traffic, no one said anything—Sammy feeling guilty about her outburst, her parents shifting luggage around behind her, Jason staring out the window. When they finally pulled into the hotel, her mother got out first and said, "We can't wait to meet Roan, dear, and see your place. Are you sure you're up for having us to dinner tomorrow night?"

No, she wasn't, but in her desperation to quell the chaos at the airport she'd invited them. Anything to get them all out of the airport and away from Jim and his wife. Now she was stuck.

"It's fine, Mom."

Her mother said a quick goodbye and immediately went into the hotel. Sammy popped the trunk for the luggage and got out to help her dad; he waved her away, and called for a bellman. Before she had a chance to talk to him about plans for later in the day or dinner the next night, he gave her a quick nod and disappeared inside. Jason exhaled, sniggered, and said, "That went well."

She pushed back on the response that had started to make its way to her lips and instead, grunted. Out of the corner of her eye, she could see he had turned and was staring at her. She ignored him and pulled around the circle drive. He continued to try to get her to look at him and when she finally did, his eyes crinkled with amusement then he started laughing. "Hey, sis, it'll be okay. They are just being parents."

She snorted a reply.

But that didn't dissuade him and he continued, while still laughing at her expense. "You should have seen your face as we all walked out of customs. You looked like you wanted to run."

"I did."

"Did, what?"

"Want to run. Didn't you?"

"Yup, you've got me there. I regretted ever mentioning to them that I wanted to see you." Then with emphasis, he said, "I regretted it every . . . single . . . second. . . minute . . . hour of that trip. At least the leg from London to Barcelona was short. Luckily, I won't be on the same flight going back. But I've got to hand it to ya, sis, having them to dinner is more than brave. You are my hero."

She sighed and said, "Your hero? I thought you were still mad at me for leaving home."

"Good, god, Sam, that was years ago."

"Years ago, or not, we haven't talked in a long time."

"Let's remedy that while I'm here. And I want to know all about this Roan guy and if it's serious."

"Later. We can talk later." They'd just pulled up to her apartment, she stopped the car and said, "Here's my key to the building and my apartment. It's on the top floor, number four twelve. Let yourself in. You're in the guest room. I need to park the car. I'll be right back."

She pulled away, needing space, and time to breathe. The catastrophe at the airport only exacerbated her anxiety and expectation that this was going to be a challenging if not disastrous month. A month! They'd be here nearly a month. Suddenly Sammy felt sick to her stomach; she needed air. She parked her car in the storage lot and walked the short distance to the beach. Calm was what she needed; calm and Roan. She punched in his number and quietly prayed that he would answer.

"Hello, my love."

She felt a swell of emotions, tears of frustration and joy at hearing his voice. In a moment of relief, Sammy raised her arms out to her side and twirled around until she was dizzy. Then out of breath, hoping her voice was steady, she said, "Hello to you."

"What are you up to?"

"Twirling in circles on the beach and calling you. What are you up to?"

"We're just off the coast, anchored. We'll dock first thing tomorrow morning."

"I can . . . not . . . wait. And my parents are excited to meet you."

"That's right. You picked them up this afternoon, right?"

"I did—and my brother." Then she re-experienced the chaos at the airport and as she was relaying it to Roan, she started laughing. "This is going to be the biggest cluster f . . . well, the biggest mess, Roan, I just know it. And I invited them to dinner. Tomorrow night, Roan. Tomorrow night! Your first night back and like an idiot, I invited them to meet you. And, Roan? I'm going to cook. What the hell was I thinking?"

As usual, Roan was calm and reassuring. "It'll be fine, Sammy. Order in. I'll bet Isa would make dinner for you."

"No," she said, and trying to convince herself, her voice

reached a higher octave. "I'm doing it, damn it. I know I can. I made the most amazing Bolognese sauce while you were gone and I froze it. We'll have that."

"There's my girl. I knew you were in there somewhere. It'll be fine, Sammy." With confidence and a bit of smugness in his voice, he said, "And how could they not love me."

If he only knew what he was getting into, he wouldn't be so optimistic. So, all she said was, "You'll see."

CHAPTER TWENTY-FOUR

*W*hen she got back to the apartment, Jason was already set up in the guest room and sound asleep. She checked in with her parents and found they were tired and happy to stay at the hotel for dinner. They made plans to have breakfast together the next morning and then Sammy crawled into her bed.

She woke hours later to dark skies, lots of noise coming from the kitchen, a missed call and voice mail from Danele.

"What's up?"

"Are you alive? The way Ciara and Sylvia talked, I figured you were somewhere curled in a fetal position."

"I was, but while I was feeling sorry for myself, I fell asleep." Sammy yawned and leaned back against the pillows. "My parents are already driving me crazy and they've only been here a few hours. What the hell am I going to do with them for the next month?"

"*Escucha* to me."

"Okay, I'm listening. Do you happen to have a miracle up your sleeve?"

"*Si.* I have a proposal for you?"

"Oh, crap, what's it going to cost me?"

"Nothing, *chica.* If my parents stayed with me for the holidays, I'd be *mucho loca,* so here's my plan."

"Tell me."

"Give them to me."

"Who? What?"

"Your parents, *chica.* I'll set them up with some tours while they're here to keep them busy and out of your hair. *Cómo es eso?*"

"How's that? Are you kidding? That's fantastic. You're a lifesaver; a Spanish princess—hell, you're the queen. That would be awesome, Danele. Thank you so much."

"*De nada.* Now spend that extra time with *Señor* Roan."

"Now if I could just figure out what to do with my brother."

"Your brother's your problem, I only fix one at a time. *Adiós,* see you here on Friday."

Sammy walked out of her bedroom feeling like a huge weight had been lifted. "I have the best friends."

"Who has the best friends?"

"I do, Jason. Now what the heck are you doing to my kitchen. It sounds like you're cooking something. Wait, it *smells* like you are cooking something, but that can't be right. You don't cook."

"Ah, but I do, sis. I've had to since living alone. Mom stopped bringing meals to me so I had no choice."

Sammy was incredulous. "Mom was cooking for you? How old are you anyway? I thought that kind of devotion went away when you graduated from college."

"I'm the baby, remember, sis. The baby always gets, um, babied."

While she was asleep, he'd apparently rummaged through her refrigerator, found some frozen cod and sautéed it in olive oil with fresh tomatoes and olives.

"I think that was really old, Jason."

"It has a bit of freezer burn but it tastes good. Come sit and eat with me. Do you have any wine around?"

They opened a bottle of *Verdejo* a popular Spanish white wine and settled into a friend, brother/sister routine.

"This is delicious," Sammy said and finally relaxed. Sitting here with what used to be her favorite brother she felt all warm and fuzzy inside. "I've missed you," she confessed.

"And I've missed you." He leaned back in his chair, patted his stomach and said, "I sure feel better." He took a sip of wine and continued, "Now tell me about this doctor guy."

Sammy told him everything. When they finished, they moved into the other room, Jason lay on the couch and set his drink on the floor while Sammy stretched out in the lounge chair. "God it's good to have you here. You know I didn't want you to come. I told Mom you shouldn't."

"I know, she told me."

"Sheesh, does she tell you everything, my little baby brother?"

"Pretty much."

"Is that why you're not married yet? You have a mother complex." She stretched, looked over at him and felt a rush of affection for her brother and thought he'd be a good catch. Maybe Danele? "I can introduce you to my friends."

"Are they men friends, because if so, then I'm interested."

Sammy shot up in her seat. "You're gay!"

235

"How could you not know that? Have I ever dated a woman?"

"You dated that little pep squad girl that was Danny's sister."

"Sammy. Look at me. Danny's sister. Danny, who I spent most of my high school and college days with."

"No way. I had no idea."

"You left before I was completely out. Our brothers knew. Mom and Dad weren't overjoyed when I told them. Mom was supportive, Dad not as much. As for you, well, you were just in your own world. A one-track mind to get out of there. You were oblivious to everything else."

"Are you happy?"

"Happy?" he questioned, staring up at the ceiling for a few moments before he continued, "I'm settled and happy being who I am without trying to hide it like I did for years." He rolled to his side, leaned over, picked up his glass of wine and took a sip, rolled back and said, "And, Sammy, like you, I have someone. Someone very special to me."

"Tell me! Spill, ole baby brother, spill."

"You can't tell Mom and Dad yet. I have to work up to that. I'm leaving the practice and moving to London."

"NO WAY!" Inside she was a bit giddy that finally her perfect little baby brother would not necessarily have the complete approval and devotion of her parents. Not that she wanted him to have a hard time, but maybe some of their disappointment and judgment would be taken off of her. But oh god, this was going to be one heck of a messy visit. They spent the rest of the evening catching up on the last ten years. Jason admitted he'd been harsh when she left law school and again when she ultimately left for Spain.

"I knew all that pressure that Dad put on you, would fall on me. I was a resentful young kid, only had two years of college under my belt and had already decided to change majors to Art History. You leaving threw a wrench into that dream—sorry I took it out on you." He yawned and said, "Let's talk more in the morning and I'll tell you more about Stephen. But now I'm beat. I'm heading back to bed." He rolled off the couch onto the floor, pushed himself up, walked over and pulled Sammy to her feet. "Sis, I'm sorry I was such a pain in the ass." He gave her a hug and headed to the guest room, turning back toward her he added, "And, Sammy, it's all good. If I hadn't gone into law, I wouldn't have gone to London for work and met Stephen. And Sammy, he owns an art gallery and we're opening another together in London. My life is good." And with that he went into the guest room and closed the door.

* * *

"Up, up, time to get up. We have to meet Mom and Dad in twenty minutes." Sammy nudged at the bundle of blankets that was Jason. "Come on, I'm not going by myself."

Jason poked his head out and said, "Afraid you'll have to. I'm not getting out of this bed. Besides I have a work call at eight. What time is it anyway?"

"Seven-forty. Dang it, Jason, I don't want to do this alone." She flopped down on her back next to him on the bed, sighed then rolled to her side and with her back to him curled up, knees to chin. "It's not that I don't love them, it's that they are so darn overbearing at times." She rolled to her back again and stared at the ceiling. "And judgmental."

"Tell me about it. They didn't necessarily totally embrace my gayness, just wait until I have to tell them, well, mostly Dad, that I'm leaving. But you'll be my buffer, right, sis?"

"Wait, what? Now I see. You didn't come to visit me and see the studio; you came because you had something to tell them and you wanted me around to defend you."

"No, no, Sammy. I'd already decided to visit you and the whole idea of moving in with Stephen came up two days ago." He sat up, looked at her. "You believe me, don't you?"

She thought about it for a minute, continuing to stare at the ceiling and decided it didn't really matter. "Yes, Jason, I believe you."

"Good, now let me up." He kicked the rest of the blankets off and when she didn't move. "Up, Sammy, I have to at least splash water on my face before my call."

"Fine, but you'd better not find some excuse to miss dinner tonight."

"What time does your friend come in?"

"Roan, his name is Roan. His ship is docking now, but he has to stay on-board until about noon. I'll pick him up, take him home then come back here and get ready for dinner. We'll eat around seven."

SAMMY LEFT the apartment and headed out to meet her parents. The hotel was only six blocks away and it was one of those days that Ciara, and the Irish, called a soft day—misty and shrouded in silence. Except for a few hardy boaters heading out, the marina was empty. Joggers slapped past her on the water-laden sidewalk running through puddles and splashing rainwater as they huffed along. In between the damp haze, an occasional raindrop plopped on Sammy's face and seeped through her hair layering it with droplets. No hat, didn't have a scarf, and no hood on her coat, she was sure she looked like a bedraggled vagrant; her mother wouldn't be happy.

Her parents were sitting in a corner window booth of the hotel restaurant. Her mother stood as soon as Sammy got close. "My god, you are soaked." She reached over and tried to fluff Sammy's hair with her hand then picked up a napkin and tried to dry it.

"I'm fine, Mom. Please stop. It will dry." Sammy took the napkin from her mom and did her own fluffing. "See, it's fine now. The advantage of short hair."

"Well, good. But I still can't get used to it. I loved your hair long."

"Charlotte. Sammy. Sit." Her dad was all business.

They did as they were told.

"Good," he said and picked up the menus, handed them to Sammy and her mother, perused his, gave them a few moments and said, "Ready?" They nodded. "Then let's order. I'm hungry. I hope breakfast is better. Dinner wasn't substantial. We won't be eating dinner here again."

Her father waved the waiter over. They ordered and while they waited, her father continued to complain about their dinner, their hotel room and the noise. Periodically her mother patted Sammy's hand while making small talk about what was going on at home. At one point she stopped mid-sentence as her attention was drawn to the port and a ship in dock. Sammy told her, "It's the one Roan is on."

"Your friend?"

"It is. His name is Roan. He's the doctor on board. He used to have a private practice . . . ," She stopped, realizing she didn't want to go into his history. "Both of you please listen to me. As I told you, Roan was the doctor that tried to save Peter. Our past is complicated because of that, but we moved past it and he's a truly wonderful man. I know you'll like him, but," and she stopped again until they were looking at her, "you cannot ask him any questions about that day nor quiz him about how he feels about our past. Do you both understand?"

"Of course, but since it's not an issue for the two of you, why does it matter what we talk about with him?" her mother asked.

"Because I asked you not to."

Her father reached over and squeezed Sammy's hand. "We will . . . " and he looked pointedly at Sammy's mother ". . . do what you've asked."

Relieved that that part of the conversation was done, she told them about Danele's offer. "Danele said the tour bus will pick you up tomorrow morning and take you around the city including a stop at La Sagrada Familia and then lunch. You'll have a full day."

They both seemed excited, even her father who normally hates sightseeing. Then her mother had to ruin it.

"Thank you dear and yes, we will keep mum about Peter around Roan, but I wish we'd met Peter." She shook her head and grumbled, "At the very least, I wish we'd known about him. Why didn't you tell us, Samantha? If he was important to you, then he would have been important to us," she took in a breath and with an exaggerated sigh, said, "Water under the bridge, I guess, at least we get to meet Roan."

Her father nodded in agreement, but said to his wife,

"Charlotte, I'm sure Sammy wasn't intentionally leaving us out." Then to Sammy, "It was a quick courtship, wasn't it Sammy? If I remember, you had barely met him before you decided to get married. Why was that by the way?"

This conversation was getting completely out of control so to take control back she gritted her teeth and said as politely as possible, "One of these days I will explain and tell you about him, but not today and not on this visit while we are with Roan. So, to change the subject," she clapped her hands together and made another stupid decision, "how about I show you my studio?"

A TAXI DROPPED them off at the international school's front entrance, but Sammy guided her parents over the side.

"Why aren't we going in the front," her father asked, half turning around to go back to the front of the school.

Feeling a sense of pride as she unlocked the side door she said, "I have my own entrance. It was part of the remodel." They climbed the stairs and Sammy pointed out every upgrade as they went along, but when they reached the landing in front of the studio door, she noticed her parents hadn't said a word. She stopped at the top of the stairs and looked at them. Both her mother and her father were frowning.

"So, what's the deal. You've not said a word, which I assume means you're either not impressed or something is bothering you."

"I can't speak for your mother," her father said, "but I'm a bit worried."

She was about ready to lose it but calmly asked, "Worried about what?"

"Your safety of course. Is this part of town safe? I'm sure that's what's on your mother's mind, too. Right Charlotte?" He turned, his eyes quizzing Sammy's mother.

Her mother's eyes opened wide and she nodded. "Yes Stuart. That's it."

Sammy wasn't sure she believed them, but opened the door to the studio and said, "Yes, it's safe."

Sammy showed them around the studio, telling them how it looked before she did her remodel, even showing them before photos. After what seemed like insincere compliments, Sammy endured another deluge of negative questions and gibes: How are you going to make it? Do you have enough students? Do you know enough about all dances to teach them? Who is going to play the piano? Not, you Sammy, you never did do well at that, did you? You never really liked piano, so why have one here? Clenching fists and gritting her teeth she calmly answered all of their objections, explained about the classes and yes, she knew enough about dance to teach and no, she wouldn't be playing the piano, she'd hire someone. They seemed satisfied, but it was the conversation she overheard her parents having when she'd gone off to use the bathroom that made her lose it.

Her father:"I hate that she's using all those years in law school just to teach dance. And here. Why here? Can she even speak Spanish well enough to teach?"

Her mother:"Now Stuart, it's not that I don't agree, but we need to keep our doubts to ourselves. She's spent all this money on this project, and on the bright side if it fails, she'll come home and join you after all."

Her father:"I doubt that. She's too pigheaded."

Her mother:"I guess that's true, she's always—"

With that she'd stormed back into the studio, shoving the swinging doors open so hard that one slammed against the wall and the doorknob poked a hole in the drywall.

"How would you know anything about me? And would you even care? You never saw me dance. Every damn recital I had as a kid, you always made excuses, usually to go to the boys' soccer, football, baseball, whatever games. And not only that, when you came to visit me here the first, and only time I might add, you made some lame excuse about not really liking flamenco music and dancing, and that mom had a headache. I don't know what I was thinking bringing you here." And with that she'd turned off the lights, guided them out the door, locked it behind her, and ran down the stairs as quickly as she could.

When they got outside, she shoved them into a taxi and walked back to her apartment trying to let the sun and surprising warmth of the day to calm her nerves. Of course, they'd apologized, kept saying they were only worried about her: about her safety, about making a success of this endeavor so far from the US without having family to lean on. It's not like she'd had family to lean on anyway for the last ten years—even before that if she was honest—so she was a bit dubious when they threw that concern at her. But she let them have their say because in a short time she was going to see Roan and that made everything okay.

By the time she got back to the apartment, she'd worked it out, knowing that her life was here and she had no regrets about it. The hardest part was letting go of her need to have her parents approve of her life. That was much of the reason she hadn't shared Peter with them. Today she shared her career and her dream and that hadn't gone well and now tonight she would have to share someone who had become very important to her and that was risky.

But she trusted Roan.

She trusted everything would be okay once she saw him.

CHAPTER TWENTY-FIVE

Sammy had never taken a cruise and had no idea how massive those ships were. Whenever she'd viewed them from the shore, even far in the distance she could tell they were large compared to pleasure craft boats, but standing there on the dock across from the ship's disembarkation doors looking up at the immense twenty-story ship she felt tiny and vulnerable.

Employees had already started to flow outside, carrying their luggage, personal belongings, and what looked like shopping bags full of purchases, but Roan had yet to appear. As she waited for Roan an entire realm of emotions played with her spirit with a range so contradictory that she nearly went back to the car to wait. She was anxious, nervous, and yet excited and at times giddy. Several times she thought she saw him and her heart jumped, and then she was disappointed when someone else came out. She knew her impatience was about her need to have his arms wrapped around her, to lean her head against his chest and feel that sense of solid ground, the foundation, that he gave her. They'd come a long way since they'd shared that tragic moment in the monastery when Peter died; they'd found a safe place that they could live within, a place that included just the two of them. That solid place would be tested tonight, and she prayed it would go well, but first she needed to get him back to his apartment where they could have some alone time.

Then she saw him.

Even with the sun shining in her eyes, she could still make out his silhouette against the dark background of the ship's exit portico. She knew it was him by how he greeted the person in front of him with a quick nod, how he laughed from his soul as someone must have said something funny, how he moved to one side to let a few of the women pass by, how he peered over their heads looking out, perusing the parking area to find her, until he saw her and waved. She resisted the nearly overwhelming urge to rush toward the ship, but she stayed where she was letting every physical sensation imbue her body, mind, and heart and she felt a rush of unexpected emotion, so intense that she could no longer stand still and instead walked toward him, taking in every bit of his being with her eyes, her soul, and her senses. After, saying a few words to another employee at the exit, he walked into the sunlight his arms full of bags looking every bit as handsome as when he left. He lumbered toward her with the biggest grin on his face, so wide she couldn't help but do the same. As he got closer to her, he dropped his bags, then gathered her in his arms and kissed her. In her mind it was the same as in any movie she'd ever seen when the warrior returns home from battle to the lovely arms of his beloved. And in his arms, she was home so she rested in that moment before pulling back, and looking into his eyes she realized with a start that she was falling in love with this man. This kind, gentle man who had all of the attributes of Peter and yet so much more.

* * *

"I HAVE TO LEAVE." She stared at his face lying next to her and saw he was having the same feeling she was having—disappointment.

"Why?"

"I'm doing dinner, remember? They'll be there in a few hours."

He stretched, yawned, and rolled to his side. "I should go with you and help."

"Stay. Rest. It seems you had a rough cruise this time." He'd just told her one of the passengers had died of a heart attack.

"Yes, someone dies in our care and we never get over it. It's never easy, Sammy," he said now, "like with Peter, when in spite of all the efforts a higher power makes the decision, we lose a patient. And we lose a part of ourselves every single time."

Even after such a glorious homecoming at the mention of Peter and death she unwillingly felt her mood shift a little.

Roan noticed and wrapped her in his arms and said, "I'm sorry. I know that my talking about Peter and death must bring back too many sad emotions."

But it wasn't that, it was the realization that this man beside her had come to mean as much to her as Peter had, and it frightened her because those feelings of love were too closely connected to death. She couldn't endure that kind of loss again. She felt tears push their way up from her heart. She quickly willed them away, got up, and said, "I'll dress and then

I'll come back and pick you up at around six-thirty." When he didn't say anything she turned to look at him and saw doubt and concern in his eyes. "I'm fine, Roan. Really."

Safe in the bathroom, she let the tears slip down her cheeks and allowed herself to feel the sadness, but not to let it overtake her nor negate the joy she'd felt the last few hours being with Roan. She splashed water on her face, dressed, and she walked back into the bedroom only to find Roan snoring softly. Once alone in her car on the drive back to her apartment that feeling of quiet despair returned. Common sense told her that love didn't always mean loss, but she was still edgy when she opened the door to her apartment and found Jason sitting on her lounge chair, flipping through TV channels.

Trying to still the disquiet and find a happy place, she smiled brightly and asked, "So what have you been doing today?"

"I went back to sleep after my phone meeting and for the last hour, I've been trying to find something to watch. Is there nothing that's not in Spanish?"

"Nope, you'll just have to talk to me instead," she said and walked into the kitchen to make some tea.

Jason turned off the TV and joined her and immediately started grumbling about having nothing to do. Then acting as if in his own home he opened the refrigerator and bent down, peered inside and rummaged, pulled out containers of food and randomly scattered them all over the counter. "What've you got to eat in here?"

Irritated she said, "Sure, Jason, just help yourself." She paused, tapped him on the arm and continued, "Please don't make a mess."

He straightened up, turned around so he was in front of her, crossed his arms across his chest and said, "Aren't we touchy? Breakfast didn't go well I take it."

It wasn't that, she wanted to tell him, but instead said, "Not even close." She filled the tea kettle with water, and put it on the stove and told him, "There's jamon and manchego in the back."

He took it out, put everything else back but started opening and slamming cupboards. She'd forgotten what it was like to have a man in the kitchen—like bulls in a china shop her mother used to say, and this kitchen was half the size of any china shop she'd ever been in.

She turned from the stove, frowned at him. "*Now* what are you looking for?"

"Bread. Where do you hide it?"

"The baguette is up there." She pointed to a bread box on top of the refrigerator. "What are you making?"

"Sandwich." He opened the refrigerator again and pulled out mayonnaise.

"Will you make me one, too?"

"Sure thing, sis. Now talk. What happened at breakfast?"

"The usual, but then I made the mistake of taking them to the studio which opened a new litany of things they're worried about. Or disappointed about. That list seems to grow every time I see them." She grabbed a jar of piquillo peppers, pulled a tomato off the counter, handed them to him and took the mayonnaise away.

"Hey," he said and tried to grab the mayonnaise from her.

She quickly turned her back to him and said, "Not in this house you don't. We are in Spain; we don't do mayonnaise on

249

ham and cheese." She laughed suddenly realizing she sounded just like Mateo.

Jason rolled his eyes at her and said, "I think maybe you're being a bit dramatic."

"Too bad that's the way of Spain."

"No, dork—not the sandwich, your reaction to the parents. I think they were probably genuinely concerned."

"Whatever. I don't want to talk about it now. Just finish with that," she said and flipped her hands at him to get on with it.

"Don't be so bossy. I'm doing it."

She made tea, sipped it as she leaned back against the counter across from him and sighed. "What was I thinking, Jason? Asking them to dinner to meet Roan. I'm just asking for trouble. I'm an idiot. Dang it, I need a Valium." As he was finishing making his sandwich, she inched closer to him, peered over his shoulder, nudged him out of the way, grabbed the sandwich, and left.

"Hey, that was mine!"

"Too bad; so sad." She giggled and went into the other room.

When he joined her, she filled him in on the studio visit and he agreed that their parents were out-of-line, but then he jumped to their defense. "I think they're nervous about this visit. They shared a bit on the flight. Dad was upset you never introduced them to Peter. He didn't understand why you didn't want your family involved in something so important in your life. He blamed himself for being too hard on you when you left."

"That had nothing to do with it. And I don't think I want to rehash it all over again, so I hope they don't bring it up at dinner." She finished the last bite of her sandwich, got up and started for the kitchen.

"Good luck with that," Jason said.

She knew he was right and she pointed a finger at him. "So, you're up; you need to help me. Promise if it gets too crazy, you'll step in. Either change the subject or make a joke or just tell them they're being awful." She turned around again to stare at him. "Well?"

"You got it, sis. Will do."

SAMMY HOPED Jason would remember because as she and Roan climbed the stairs to her apartment an almost debilitating trepidation had set in. Yes, thanks to Jason's help the table was set and the drinks were mixed. And, true, next to her, Roan was calm and looking smashing. But just up those stairs and through her door, her parents waited.

As they reached her apartment door, Sammy took in a deep breath, looked over to Roan as she was opening it and said, "Well, here we go. I hope you've got a good shield of armor around that heart of yours, because . . . "

They heard her mother first. "They should be here any minute, for God's sake Stuart, get out of there and put that—."

Jason cut her mother off and charged the front door, his hand outstretched. "You must be Roan. I'm Jason, Sammy's favorite brother." Roan put his arm around Sammy, pulled her close, whispered, "It's okay," while he was reaching for Jason's outstretched hand but somehow, he and Jason ended up embracing. Sammy wasn't sure if Jason pulled Roan in or if Roan did. They both looked a bit embarrassed but Jason winked at her over Roan's shoulder and said, "Welcome, bro."

They moved inside to a room that was stifling and Sammy wasn't sure if the heat had been turned up, which was something her mother always managed to do to the irritation of her father, or that the room felt like it was closing in on her. She stepped out of Roan's arms, slid around him and Jason while closing the door behind her just as her father sauntered forward, cleared his throat and said, "Pleased to meet you. Stuart Driscoll here, Samantha's father and this is my lovely wife, Charlotte." Then he turned to Charlotte and said, "Dear, this is Roan. Say hello."

Sammy's mother moved around from behind her husband with an amused look, then turned to Roan and said, "Yes, as Stuart felt it necessary to introduce me, I'm Samantha's mother." Then Sammy watched as her mother transformed into the other Charlotte: the one with social graces, the committee chairperson, the ever-accommodating hostess as she seemed to glide forward to kiss Roan on both cheeks, and said, "Pleased to meet you." Her face flushed and she continued, "That is how you Europeans greet each other, right?"

Roan hadn't moved from the doorway and stood awkwardly while all three of her family members blocked his way. He smiled, nodded, and said, "Yes that is true. Most Europeans do that." Then peering over their heads, he winked at Sammy and said, "But I also shake hands."

Exasperated Sammy said, "Geez mom, he's American. And could you guys move so he can get by?"

"Oh, goodness, so sorry, Roan," her mother twittered, as she moved to the side.

"And why is it so hot in here? Mom, did you turn up the heat?"

Her mother bristled, "It was too cold, Sammy. And where is your tree and all your Christmas decorations? Aren't you going to—"

Jason interrupted. "Drinks everyone? Sammy and I made a batch of GnTs but there is also some fantastic wine. Dad? Mom? Roan? What can I get you?"

Later in the kitchen, while Sammy reheated the thawed Bolognese sauce and boiled the pasta, she listened to the muted conversations going on in the other room. So far all seemed quite benign. No deep-digging questions for Roan about his life, only cursory questions from her parents with short, clipped answers from Roan. He was mainly doing the asking which was good, because her parents loved to talk about themselves and their life in Ohio. Several times though Sammy had to grit her teeth when her parents bragged about Sammy's own background in law and how well she had done in school, always countering that praise with their collective disappointment that she'd left Ohio and potentially lucrative law practice. Luckily true to his word, Jason jumped in to take the conversation down a different path.

"What's taking so dang long, sis? They're starting to ask about dinner." Sammy jumped, hadn't heard her brother come into the kitchen. "I can't do this for much longer. Give us bread or something to chew on so they keep their mouths busy. And shut."

She shook her head. "They'll have to wait." And she kept stirring the sauce.

He stood behind her, his chin on her shoulder, peering at

the stove then reached around her removing lids from pots. "C'mon. Anything?"

"Here." Irritated, she reached over to the counter where she had a basket of bread waiting to be taken out with the rest of the dinner. "We don't do that bread before dinner thing here. That's a very American thing, but here, take this anyway." She shoved the basket of bread in his hands along with a terracotta dish of *Mantequilla de Soria* a high-quality Spanish butter, and yelled out to the others, "Dinner in ten minutes. Jason's bringing in some bread and butter, if you're starving," she emphasized and drew out the word starving, "and can't wait."

She knew she sounded bitchy and regretted it when her mother decided it was necessary to call her out. "Sammy, if this is too much for you, we can all go out to a local restaurant."

Keeping her voice as even-keeled as possible and taking in lots of air, she calmly replied, "Everything's fine, Mom. I just know how you both love to have a bit of bread with dinner and thought you might like to try it with some very special Spanish butter while I finish up."

"A shot of bourbon might work better," Jason said under his breath.

Sammy kept her voice down, too, and replied, "Whatever works, because I have this awful feeling that this is eventually going to fall apart,"

"Don't worry I got your back, sis."

"Thank you. Now get back out there." She gave him a hug then a push and said, "I owe you.

"You bet you do."

· · ·

THEY LINGERED at the table after dinner; food had been eaten, drinks finished, bottles of wine opened, poured, and some were still being consumed. Everyone looked a little flushed and her mother almost giddy. Dinner had gone fairly well. Most of the dinner conversation revolved around her mother's excitement about the tours that Danele planned for them, but Sammy should have known it wouldn't last.

"Thank you Sammy, for setting us up," her mother said and took a hefty gulp of her wine. "Now wasn't Danele the one that also told you about . . . " she set her glass down, tapped her finger on the table and asked, "that job with that guy, what was his name? Your boss?"

"Max. Yes, Danele—,"

"Yes. Max. That's it. Now again why did you quit that job? It seemed you liked it, dear."

Sammy felt her anger rise and purposely didn't answer. She'd already had this conversation with them many times and they knew she'd been let go and she'd be damned if she'd give them the satisfaction of saying it again. And she was sure the question was just a segue into some other point her mother was going to try to make.

Her mother, sighed deeply, drank more wine and said, "You should have stayed. I fear this studio thing of yours is risky. Wouldn't you agree, Stuart?"

Her father cleared his throat, a habit he used when he was in a courtroom before he'd begin his defense, then he'd pause, stare down the prosecution so intensely that typically the prosecutor would drop their gaze which was when her dad would attack. Tonight, he set his stare on Sammy but before he could say anymore her mother jumped in again. "Never mind Stuart, I really want to ask Roan what he thinks Sammy should have done."

They all looked at Roan who picked up his glass of water to take a drink before answering. Yet apparently, he didn't answer quick enough for her mother's satisfaction because she pressed on, "Well, Roan?"

Roan set his glass down, looked over at Sammy, a smile subtly tugging at the corners of his mouth. "Oh, I think Sammy can make her own decisions." He paused. "Which she does, I might add, with exceptional success as I'm sure her business will be."

"Well, I'm not so sure," her mother interjected amidst her father's remark of, "My daughter would be successful at whatever she does" and her brother's suggestion they take their glasses of wine into the living room. Obeying her adored son, her mother stood and motioned for the rest of them to move. They all obeyed, grabbed their glasses, and while Sammy was still raging inside, Roan leaned over to her and whispered, "Relax. I have a plan."

If he did, his plan never had a chance to materialize because as they moved into the living room her father picked up the photo of Peter that he had obviously brought in from her bedroom then he handed it to Sammy. "Is this Peter?"

No one spoke as they all looked at her. Sammy held Peter's picture, stared into his smiling face, remembering that it was taken the day he'd proposed to her. Staring at the man she once loved, she was surprised at how hard it hit her—hard, like his death had just happened. It was too much and she felt light-headed and crumpled into the lounge chair hoping no one would see this shift in her emotions. Roan started toward her, but she put up her hand. Everyone else seemed unaware and she hoped her silence would stop any more questions, but as her father sat down next to her mother on the couch, he persisted, "Sammy, did you hear me?"

She set the photo face down on the table next to her chair to suppress the sudden sadness it brought. Roan and Jason stood over her, their faces concerned, until her father barked, "Jason, sit." Which Jason did—on the floor beside the couch. "Roan take a seat." Her father patted the cushion then said, "Sammy are you going to answer me?"

Sammy grabbed a blanket from the basket on the floor next to the chair wrapped it around her hoping it might protect her from all of them and finally said, "Yes, Dad, that's Peter."

Peter's presence loomed large in this room, in this conversation, and in her heart right now. She tried to focus, to let it go, but then her father said, "What a nice-looking guy. I wish we'd met him." Her father took a drink of his wine before glancing over at Roan and asked, "Roan, did you know him?"

Sammy couldn't believe her father would ask Roan such a question. Roan looked uncomfortable and tried to meet Sammy's eyes, but she stared at the floor fearing he might see the conflicting emotions she was having. Instead, she raised her eyes and glared at Jason, trying to get him to do something. But Jason seemed oblivious, and a little drunk, so Roan just said, "No, I never had the pleasure." And continued with, "I hear you've got quite the practice back in Ohio. What made you choose law as a profession?"

This question would normally set her father off into a lengthy dissertation about the law and how much he loved it, but before he could begin her mother chimed in. "Samantha has never talked to us much about Peter." Then she looked at

257

Roan and asked, "Has she with you? I mean since it appears that you two are serious, I'd imagine the topic of her short marriage would've come up."

Roan got off the couch and walked over, sat on the arm of the lounge chair next to Sammy and put an arm around her shoulders. She sunk into his side, resting her head under his arm, grateful for the support before he answered, "Well Charlotte, to tell you the truth, we've tried to concentrate on our relationship and not the past."

"But aren't you the doctor that was there when Sammy's husband died?"

Again, and little sterner this time, Roan reiterated, "The past is just that, Charlotte, the past."

Finally, Jason seemed to realize things had gotten tense because he got up from the floor, stood in front of his parents and said, "So Mom, Dad how about a little . . . ," he paused, turned to Sammy and asked, "Sammy how do you say it —*Carajillo*?

She was still frozen and could only nod.

"What is it dear?" her mother asked.

"A short cup of coffee with a shot of rum or whiskey. What do you say?" When they all nodded, Jason continued, "Sammy if you'll make the coffee, I'll dig out the whiskey."

She wasn't sure how she managed to move from the chair to the kitchen but Roan helped her up and when Jason came in to find the whiskey, she was in the kitchen boiling water to make coffee in the French press. She'd been pushing down her emotions while trying to concentrate on just making the coffee so she could get them out of there, but when Jason put his hand on her shoulder and pressed his cheek onto hers, she felt the tears coming. "I can't believe they did that. What the hell? Why are they so awful sometimes?"

Jason scoffed. "It's the role of parents, isn't it? To do whatever it takes to annoy, embarrass, criticize their kids.

"I guess, but I can't fathom how Roan must be feeling right now." Her own feelings about Peter under control, now she was worried about Roan and his.

"Well, right now they are insisting that he watch over you to make sure the studio is safe and successful."

She quickly wiped the tears from her cheeks and said, "Oh no! I have to get back out there to save him." She turned to leave, but asked Jason, "Do you know how to make coffee in a French press?"

"Just go. I'm gay remember. We don't do coffee any other way. Now get."

Sammy stepped into the room just in time to hear her father say, "But aren't you out on the ship most of the time? So, you really can't look out for her all the time."

"That is true, but I've known Sammy long enough to know she doesn't need anyone to look out for her. She's very self-reliant." He watched her walk into the room and said, "Plus Stuart and Charlotte, as I mentioned to Sammy a few weeks ago, I'm thinking of finding a job where I can stay on land here in Barcelona full time."

Had he? She didn't remember, but that seemed to shut her parents up.

CHAPTER TWENTY-SIX

Sammy also didn't remember how they'd gotten out of her apartment. All she did remember was telling Jason as she and Roan left. "I've had enough of them. Please get them a taxi and don't wait up, I won't be home tonight."

Now later that evening, Roan on his back and Sammy lying on her side tucked in next to him, her head resting on his shoulder, and her arm draped across his body and after a passionate, and sometimes fierce hour of lovemaking, so much so that Roan had asked her to slow down and relax, Sammy still couldn't stop lashing out at her parents and how they acted at dinner. "They were so awful. I'm sorry they brought up Peter, I know that must have been hard for you," she mumbled while tracing her fingers on his chest. She shook her head trying to erase the memory of Roan's puzzled frown and downturned eyes when her father had insisted on questioning him. She rolled to her back then sat up, twisted her head and looked down at Roan and said, "I'm really sorry."

He sat up next to her, stroked her arm, and said, "Not going to lie, Sammy. It threw me." He moved to get off the bed and as he started to stand up, he glanced back at her. "But I told myself they were only trying to understand." He bent down, picked up his pants, and pulled them on. "I think they were hurt you didn't tell them about Peter. Like I said, I understood. Not that I could tell them anything because I didn't know him."

"They were awful, Roan." She was a bit annoyed that he didn't see what she saw. Annoyed that he seemed to be defending them. "Then all that bullshit about my business. Asking you to protect me? Even after all these years, they have no idea who I am."

"Well, I have some news that might help alleviate their concern. Not that it was warranted. I know how strong and capable you are. How about a nightcap before we turn in for the night and I can tell you my news?"

She flopped back down onto the bed, pulled the covers up and over her head, trying to hide her annoyance. "You don't get it."

"C'mon. Up. Then tell me so I understand."

"No," she mumbled.

"Come on, let's talk. I have a nice bottle of Rioja that's calling my name." Then he leaned over, tugged at the covers until her face was visible; he kissed her and tweaked her nose. He picked his shirt off the floor and tossed it to her. "Slip that on."

When she didn't respond he uncovered her feet and tickled them. "Up you go." When she resisted, he continued, "Look I just got home from a long cruise and I've missed you. Don't let your parents ruin our reunion."

Begrudgingly she grabbed the shirt from him, pulled it over her head and stood. She wrapped her arms around his waist, rested her cheek against his chest and said, "Okay, but you better stop defending them or I'll help you pack and send you back out to sea."

"I'd like to see you try." He reached for her hand and they walked into the kitchen. He pulled out a bottle of wine, filled two glasses, and led her over to the couch.

She sat next to him and flopped her bare legs on top of his. "Now talk. What's this news you mentioned?"

"Well," he tilted his head to one side, ran his hand up and down her legs and said, "funny you should say you'd send me back to the boat because I don't think I'll be going out again. You might have to put up with me permanently."

"I don't understand. Are you leaving your job?"

"I am."

"But why?"

He took a sip of wine and leaned his head back against the couch cushion, eyes closed, his face pensive. He opened his eyes and said, "Remember I told you I'm sick of traveling."

She didn't remember so she shook her head.

"Ah, that's right, you were falling asleep when I mentioned it."

"Last night?"

"No on the way home from our Dali trip. Nevertheless, and, not to go into it again, when we lost that passenger, it affected me more than normal; I knew it was time to leave. Plus, I like it here. And I like spending time with you. Now we can do more of that."

He searched her face, waiting to see her reaction.

"Don't tell me you did this because my parents nagged about needing someone here to babysit me?"

He set his drink down, put his arm around her shoulders

and pulled her tight, kissed her forehead. "Not in the slightest. I let the cruise line know as I was leaving the other day, *before* I met your parents. Cruises are done until the spring anyway so this gives them plenty of time to reallocate the doctors they have."

"But what will you do for work?" She wasn't sure she entirely believed him. Residual feelings of annoyance at her parents lingered and she was still a little agitated at the possibility he had done this just to keep an eye on her.

"What I'd like," he continued, "is for my work to mean something. To give back." He took another sip of wine and frowned. "Though I'm not sure if or how I can. I'm not a Spanish citizen. I might have to volunteer and also work a regular non-medical job for pay. I've been looking into it for the last year anyway, so . . . " he lowered his head to make eye contact with her and said, "Look at me." When she raised her eyes to his he continued, "This has nothing to do with you. Okay?

She nodded.

"Good. It's rather exciting actually." His eyes seemed to sparkle, his face ebullient, and his voice animated, his enthusiasm for his new venture, obvious. "There are nonprofits that need the help of a medical doctor—and they pay. For instance, I saw a recent ad for one where I could serve as a liaison between medical professionals for a global non-profit or another query where I'd be conducting training for medical volunteers at international locations like Barcelona. See, I have options and I have money put away. I can take my time."

She wasn't sure what she was feeling now. It felt like a next step in this relationship, a shift, and she wasn't sure she was ready. But she reminded herself, this wasn't about her; this was his life; his decision for his career.

"There's something else, Sammy. I know you tried to hide it but I saw how upset you were when your father handed you that photo of Peter. I feel like maybe there's some unfinished stuff there. Like seeing me, you see his death. That makes me sad. And if I'm truthful, it worries me a little."

She grabbed one of the pillows from the couch and hugged it against her with both arms. "I'm not sure what that was about. I see that photo every day. It's next to my bed on the nightstand." She dropped one arm off the pillow and started playing with its cording trying to figure out what had happened to her earlier in the day. "I think I was really on edge." She hunched her body over the pillow, hugged it, looked back at him and stared until he looked at her. "I mean *really* on edge. I was a mess. I still am. They can get to me."

She could tell by his face that he wasn't sure he believed her.

"Truly, Roan, I think that's all it was. And no, I don't see Peter's death when I look at you. I see a good man whom I am very fond of. I don't want to talk about this anymore though. I just want you. And I want you right now."

Then she pulled him off the couch and led him back into the bedroom.

* * *

SAMMY WOKE before Roan the next morning. Lying on her side facing him, his face so close to hers that she heard him breathing sometimes with a subtle hum between exhales. Knowing that he'd had many nights of fitful sleep on this last

KATHLEEN MARY O'BRIEN

cruise she quietly slipped out of bed hoping not to wake him.
She rummaged through her clothes that she'd piled on the
chair next to the bed until she found her phone—seven-thirty.
She slipped on Roan's shirt again, stood and looked out onto
the terrace through the bedroom's French doors. Over the
tops of the tall bushes that insulated the patio from the
common complex courtyard beyond, she caught the slightest
glimmer of sun lightening the rose-colored sky making it the
perfect secluded place for morning coffee. A temperature
gauge that hung on the trellis that covered and protected the
patio from the hot summer sun showed it wasn't quite fifty
degrees and for a moment she wondered if coffee inside was a
better idea. And yet the brilliance of the purple agapanthus
bending a bit with a breeze that filtered across the patio as
well as the sun now creeping around pots of other vibrant fall
flowers beckoned her outside. It might be one of the only
mornings for the next week or so that she could indulge
herself because temperatures were supposed to drop to near
freezing tonight with a chance of snow in the next few days—
an extreme rarity for Barcelona.

She started for the bedroom door to head into the kitchen
to make coffee but looked back at Roan sleeping on his side
with one arm under his head and the other clutching a pillow,
his mouth slightly open, she felt something akin to what a
mother must feel when she looks at a sleeping child, and it
wrapped around her heart.

In the kitchen, she made coffee, grabbed the blanket from
the sofa, opened the French doors and walked out onto the
terrace. She wrapped up in the blanket and sat on the cush-
ioned lounge chair and let the hot coffee warm her hands as a
puff of the cool morning air ruffled her hair and sent a chill

through her. She took a sip of coffee and pulled the blanket tighter and higher up on her neck. Over in the corner a small water feature she had not noticed before bubbled in the silence of early morning; she was content and, with a start, realized that she could see herself living here.

With the warmth of the sun resting on her face, she felt her eyes start to close just as the French doors from the bedroom opened and Roan walked out looking sleepy. He blinked a few times, rubbed his eyes, ran a hand through his tousled hair, his cheeks were ruddy with morning scruff and he looked quite sexy in his black briefs, so much so that she was tempted to drag him back into the bedroom. Suddenly all of her worry about the last few days seemed to disappear.

His voice gravelly, he said, "There you are, I wondered where you'd gone." Again, he ran a hand through his hair then hunched over, and briskly rubbed his arms with his hands. "Brr, it's cold out here. Hold on, I'm going to get my shirt . . . ," he hesitated, squinted his eyes and said, "*another* shirt—I'll get another since I see mine has been taken over by some mysterious sea nymph lounging on my patio." He went in and when he came back out, he was wearing a sweatshirt and joggers and it looked like he's combed his hair. "Why didn't you tell me I looked like a character on that Gotham series."

"Who in the world are you talking about?"

"My hair." Then before she could answer, he said, "Never mind. I need coffee."

"I found a regular coffee pot so I made extra rather than use the French press. It should still be hot."

He went inside, poured a cup and when he came out said, "Boy, did I sleep well. How long have you been up?"

"Not long. Maybe a half hour. Come sit."

Before he sat, he leaned down and kissed her, "Good morning my dear Sammy. How did you sleep?"

"Very well thank you my dear Roan. You know Peter used to call me Sammy dear. It was his pet phrase for me."

He sat down on the lounge next to her and asked, "Does that bother you?"

"Strangely, it doesn't."

"Good because you are dear to me, Sammy dear," he said and winked. He pushed further back into his chair, leaned his head against the back of the cushion, relaxed, and closed his eyes.

"That makes me happy." She closed her eyes then and let the silence speak to her, let Roan sitting next to her be all that she needed this morning. No parent chatter, no Jason confessions, not even long conversations with Roan were needed. The sweet aroma of freesias blooming in the pots next to her drifted by and even the usually annoying chirp of the monk parakeet soothed her. The lovely tweets of the Spanish sparrow flitting from branch to branch above her head relaxed her even more and she opened her eyes and ventured, "This is lovely out here, Roan. It's a very special place."

Roan opened his eyes, set his coffee down on the table between them and looked around. "You know you're right. Now that the flowers don't look like they are on the brink of death, that is. If I actually can swing this job change maybe I'll spend more time out here this summer."

That reminder of his news last night caused a slight rumble inside her consciousness, but she ignored it and asked, "What are your plans for today?"

"I'm meeting your brother for a late lunch actually. We set it up yesterday. How about you?"

She groaned. "My parents, I guess."

"I thought they were going on some an excursion that Danele set up."

"That's right! Thank, God." Now she was giddy with thoughts of the day—an empty chasm waiting to be filled, or not filled. Maybe she'd just find a book and do nothing else. Then she had another idea and shared it with him. "Now that you won't be going back out on the ship, what will you do this week? We could take a couple of day trips. I'd love to visit that winery I told you about. What do you think?"

"Actually, my week will be pretty busy. I have some exploratory interviews with some nonprofits and a few regular interviews for positions that start after the first of the year. Sorry." He took a sip of coffee and continued. "And I'm taking Jason to see Dali. Want to go?

"No, you go ahead. I think I'd like to wait before seeing it again."

"Okay, but I hope you don't mind that I'll be tied up a lot this week."

"Not at all."

CHAPTER TWENTY-SEVEN

*B*ut it turned out she did mind.

It was just after noon on Christmas Eve and Sammy was a bit out of sorts. Everyone had had their own agenda this past week and for some reason, Sammy felt neglected. Roan had either been talking to people about a job or showing Jason around Barcelona, and her parents were busy with the trips Danele planned for them. And when they weren't busy with trips, they smothered Sammy with questions and concerns about everything: Roan, Peter, her job, her haircut, they even complained about Sammy's lack of Christmas decorations. Not that Sammy wanted to spend more time with them, but for God's sake at least they could show an interest. And Roan who had complained that he didn't want her parents to ruin their reunion after his long absence, didn't seem so concerned anymore. It was as if no one wanted to be around her, or so she thought, and then three days ago when she really did want to be alone to put up Christmas decorations, everyone showed up and the exchange of opinions ensued.

The entire day was fraught with frustration. Her parents couldn't understand why 'all of this hadn't been done already.' When she explained that in Spain decorations go up later than in the US and trees often weren't decorated until two weeks before Christmas. 'Well, that's just ridiculous' seemed to be the theme and constant mantra through the entire day and 'You're still late' was bantered about regularly, and when it wasn't shared out loud it was mumbled within earshot. Both parents were then stunned and appalled when she pulled her artificial Christmas tree out of the closet. They didn't let a minute pass without reminding her that picking out a fresh tree as a family when she was a child was the highlight of the Christmas season.

True, tree hunting had been Sammy's favorite part of Christmas so much so that she and Peter also bought a fresh tree, but after he died doing it alone brought back too many memories. The experience didn't bring the same joy it had in the past; so last year she bought an artificial one that, until you touched it, looked real. Still, her parents grumped about it and even Roan decided to put his two cents in with the 'I'm a fresh tree man myself' when her father questioned him, while Jason quietly sipping brandy laced eggnog the entire day seemed irritatingly amused. Even the little snippet of joy Sammy had reserved for decorating seemed to have been stripped away this year.

Right now, as she waited at the corner espresso café for cappuccinos for her and Jason, she looked out onto the mainly secluded streets and tried to push away her frustration with everyone. Free time had been her enemy; if she'd been busy instead of wasting time feeling like everyone had abandoned her, she'd have been content. Instead, she overthought—terrified the same thing that happened at her dinner gathering last week would happen again at Danele's tonight.

She took the drinks from the barista, carried them and two pastries back to the apartment noticing a sudden chill in the air. A drop of rain hit the sidewalk and as she pulled open the apartment entry door it began to snow. There had been a threat of snow all week but nothing ever materialized. The thought of a potential white Christmas gave her a glimmer of hope; maybe they'd get enough so her parents would be snowed in at their hotel, Jason with them, and she could have Roan all to herself.

"There you are." Roan greeted her as she walked into her apartment.

She didn't know why this annoyed her but her inside voice quipped 'what are you doing here so early.' Her outside voice only cooed, "Wonderful you're here." And she had to admit he looked darn good in black slacks, a dark grey zip-up cardigan sweater, a white dress shirt underneath and a red Christmas tie with reindeer.

He leaned down to kiss her and she raised her lips to meet his, cold but kissable and some of her annoyance at his early arrival seemed to vanish. "Sorry to show up so early, but I saw on the weather report it's supposed to snow and so I thought it'd be a good idea to get the car warmed up and head over. Found a spot on the street right away so we are set whenever we have to leave."

"Snow won't last. Never does. It's been sixty years since we had snow on Christmas. A fluke," Sammy said and handed Jason his drink as he walked out from the kitchen with a cup of coffee for Roan. She opened the box of pastries and said to both of them, "Have a little something before we go."

Jason handed the coffee to Roan and they both grabbed part of a pasty. Jason took a bite and said to Roan, "Sorry, bro, had I known you were coming over I'd have had Sammy get you a cap."

"No worries, mate."

Oh, good, they're bros now. She'd never heard Roan use the word mate for anyone. Nor Jason, but it bothered her. She loved her brother and the thought that he'd be friends with the man she cared about shouldn't be an issue. Now they were grinning at each other like Cheshire cats. Roan did know Jason was gay, didn't he?

"Jason, before mom and dad get here, tell me more about Stephen." Then she turned to Roan and explained, "Jason is gay and Stephen is his boyfriend."

Roan grinned at her; eyebrows raised. "Sammy, I know Jason's gay and I know all about Stephen."

"Yeah, sis, what's the deal?"

"Never mind," she bristled, as her phone rang. "Hey, dad, what's up?"

Her stomach tightened as she listened to her dad talk about her mother having a headache then ask if they could take her car to the party. "No." She paused. "I said no. It's going to snow, Dad. Dad. Dad?" Exasperated she looked at Roan and Jason, and said, "He hung up on me."

"What's up, sis?"

"They want to take my car. Apparently, Mom has a migraine and they want to be able to leave early if they have to."

"Why did you tell them no?" Roan asked.

And of course, Jason jumped in. "Yeah, the ride will be peaceful without them. Give them the car."

"There's a threat of snow. I don't think it's a good idea for them to drive in snow in an unfamiliar place and I don't want them wrecking my car."

"Oh, for God's sake, Samantha, they live in Ohio. We drive in snow all the time. Has your memory disappeared?"

Today was getting worse by the minute, even Roan's handsome face grinning at her didn't help. She grabbed her phone and punched in her father's number. "I've been overruled. You can have the damn car."

SAMMY DROVE her car to her parents' hotel with a whipped cream-topped pumpkin pie trembling on the passenger seat next to her. Danele had asked her to make another pumpkin pie and it turned out better this time. Sammy's confidence in cooking had grown while Roan was on the ship so much so that she made two pies and left one at home for Christmas dinner which Roan and Jason decided they would make and give her a break. But apparently, the bromance prevented either from telling her what they intended to cook.

Sammy braked quickly at the hotel as another car pulled out in front of her and she held her breath hoping the pie wouldn't slide off the seat. It stayed. She pulled up next to the front door where her parents were waiting. She got out, gave them the keys, and instructed her mother to hold the pie on her lap while they drove so the whipped cream wouldn't slide any more than it had. Then as Roan and Jason pulled up, she put Danele's address into her parents' phones in case they got lost.

"Aren't you coming with us?" her mother asked.

"No, Roan doesn't know where to go either. I need to show him."

"Samantha, your father doesn't know this area. You need to come with us."

Her father opened the passenger door for her mother and said, "Charlotte, get in. I'm perfectly capable—"

"Nonsense Stuart. She needs to show more concern for our welfare instead of only worrying about Roan."

"Charlotte," her father yelled, "I said get in."

Her mother shoved the pie back at Sammy and said, "You take it." She started to get into the car before turning back, looked at Sammy and said, "You're being inconsiderate you know. I just hope we make it okay without getting lost."

With her heart beating fast, trying to control her anger, and juggling the pie and her purse, Sammy got into the back seat of Roan's car. She set the pie down, slammed the door shut and sputtered, "They are driving me crazy. I'm not sure I'll survive being around them today."

Jason turned around in the passenger seat and asked, "Why, what happened. I noticed mom didn't look too pleased."

She didn't have the energy to go into it with him, so she just said, "Just them being them." She could see Roan looking at her through the rearview mirror, his eyes questioning. She shrugged and said, "It's fine, Roan. Here's Danele's address." And she handed him her phone.

They rode to Danele's with Sammy sitting quietly in the backseat and Roan and Jason chatting in the front. Roan occasionally checked on her through the rearview mirror, the last time he did it she got annoyed and said, "You better keep your eyes on the road, it's starting to snow again."

They pulled into Danele's street and parked. As Jason

walked over to help her parents, Roan pulled her aside and asked, his voice unusually agitated. "So, what's going on? You've been edgy this entire week."

Irritation nipped at the back of her head but she forced herself to smile at him, tucked her arm through his, rested her head on his shoulder and said, "I'm sorry. It's not you, it's them."

He reached over, pulled her tightly against him, he kissed the top of her head and said, "They'll be gone soon and it will be just us again." He tilted her chin up so she couldn't help but look into his eyes. "And that, Sammy, is enough for me."

And it was for her, too, she just wished time would fly.

"Just be patient, Sammy."

Jason and her parents walked toward them and Roan whispered, "Let's have a nice evening. I'll intercede if your parents get too overbearing. Deal?"

She nodded and for a second, she yielded and leaned into him. Maybe everything would be okay.

CHAPTER TWENTY-EIGHT

*A*nd it was for a while.

Danele's house was beautiful. A festive nod to Spanish Christmas with the traditional feast of roasted lamb, roasted pig, various seafood soups, salad, and tapas. Traditional sweets included *Turrón* (almond nougat), marzipan, glacé fruits, and *mantecados* (traditional powdery sweets). Guests drank a plethora of Cava; Roan drank his fair share of mulled wine and as he relaxed, he became more talkative. Jason had too much to drink and was entertaining, and captivated both men and women with his enthusiasm about his new love and venture in London. She rarely saw her parents which was fine, but she kept wondering what were they saying about her, about Roan, about Peter.

During the evening she made small talk with some of Danele's employees all the while perusing the room to see if she could locate Roan or her parents. She was telling one woman about her new studio when the woman's face got very serious and said, "I was so sorry to hear about your . . . " The woman hesitated as if she didn't know what to call Peter. To save her the embarrassment and get the conversation moving Sammy said, "Peter, his name was Peter. And thank you. I—"

"Yes, that's right, Peter, but . . ." the women's face lit up and she continued, "but I'm so happy to hear you are in love again. Roan seems like a great guy." The women playfully nudged Sammy. "Do I see a wedding in your future?"

Another couple joined the conversation and the man joked. "Your mom's already planning the wedding." The other women contributed. "Yes, we hear you might be getting married again. I felt so bad when I heard about Peter. I'm so happy you've found happiness."

Sammy felt the room close around her and it felt as if everyone in the house had gathered around her, listening. She panicked and demanded, "Where did you hear that? I'm not getting married again."

The woman frowned; her face confused."Oh, I'm sorry. I overheard someone say it in the other room. I must have misunderstood."

Sammy left them then, apologizing, "It's fine. Do you know where Roan is?"

They all shook their heads.

On her way to find Roan, another couple pulled her aside and said, "We are so happy for you."

She just nodded and nearly bumped into Ciara. Frustrated, she asked, "Why do people think I'm getting married?"

Ciara took her arm and pulled her over to the side of the room. "I hate to tell you, but I think your mom is saying things. I don't know exactly what she is saying, but that's what I keep hearing as I walk through the house."

"Where is she?"

Then from behind her, Sammy heard her mother talking

softly to Macy and her husband. "Well, it's clear they are in love." Her mother's voice dropped, so Sammy had to take a step back and strain to hear. "I see a wedding in their future. You know we weren't invited to the first one, in fact we never knew about Peter."

Sammy felt the fury rise, she looked at Ciara. Ciara reached over and touched Sammy's arm. "Breathe Sammy. It's okay. She means well. She's a mom; aren't all moms built to give their daughters grief. I know mine is."

Sammy was trying, trying not to get angry, trying to stay calm and not snap back at Ciara. What she wanted to say was, no, all mothers weren't like that—just hers. Instead, she said, "I need to stop this. What can Roan be thinking? I don't even know how he truly feels about me let alone how I feel about him. Now . . . "Sammy's fury returned. "She's telling people we're getting married. It needs to stop. Where did she go? Did you see?"

"Just now, it looked like Roan was steering her and your father into the kitchen."

Sammy turned to leave but Ciara stopped her. "Be kind. It's Christmas and they're family and Roan is such a dear, he'll understand."

She forced a smile and thanked Ciara then made her way through the crowded room and headed toward the kitchen. As she got closer, she heard their voices and Sammy tucked herself against a wall in the hallway and listened.

Roan, firmly, but gently: "People I don't know are coming up to me to congratulate me. You need to stop talking about us to other people, stop telling people Sammy and I are getting married. We are still trying to maneuver through our relationship and this isn't helping—especially if Sammy hears of this."

Her mother, apologetic, yet defensive: "Oh, that's silly. You two are obviously heading that way."

Roan, steadfast: "Charlotte, you don't know that. We don't even know that."

Her mother, firm, not gently: "What gives you the right to criticize me anyway, I have eyes you know. I can see you're in love."

Then Roan, obviously frustrated: "Charlotte, I care deeply for her, but again, Charlotte, if we are that is for us to figure out. And I'm sorry, it is not for you to be talking about this to people you don't know. Sammy would not be happy."

Sammy started toward the door then stopped when her father joined in.

Her father: "Charlotte, I agree with Roan. You need to stop or we'll go home." A pause, then her father again: "But Roan, why didn't she tell us about Peter?"

Her mother: "Yes, Roan, please tell us what you know of him. If he was dear to Sammy then he would have been dear to us. Was he a doctor, too?"

Sammy could hear Roan clearing his throat and she prayed that he wouldn't answer; that he'd distract them by changing the subject or walkaway.

But instead, she heard him say, "No, he wasn't a doctor. I understand he had his own business and was quite successful, but traveled a lot for work."

Her father: "But what kind of man was he?"

Roan: "Stuart, you have to understand I didn't know him and it's been somewhat difficult given how Sammy and I met.

I can tell you based on what I know of your daughter, he must have been a pretty special guy."

Her mother: "She sure didn't care enough about us or him for that matter to bring him into our lives. Why, Roan?"

Roan: "I think—"

At that point, Sammy had had enough and stormed into the room.

"He can't tell you anything, Mom, because as he told you and I've told you he didn't know him nor do we talk about Peter. It's none of any of your business. None of you." And she glared at all of them including Roan. She was annoyed at her parents, but that Roan contributed information about Peter to her parents was hurtful.

Her father said, "It's obvious we have upset you, Samantha." He turned to his wife. "Charlotte, I think it's time we go."

"Sure, go out there and slide around in that mess. Don't wait for us in case you can't find your way back?" The snow had been coming down fast and it looked like there were a few inches already.

"We will be fine," her father said with an edge to his voice. "Come on dear, get your coat. Sammy, we'll see you tomorrow for Christmas. I hope you cheer up. You've not been yourself since we got to Barcelona."

Roan walked over and put his hand on Sammy's shoulder and his other to shake Stuart's hand. "She'll be fine, Stuart. She's had a stressful couple of months with the development of her business and remodel of the studio. Right, Sammy?" He turned, his eyes on hers.

She couldn't even look at him, brushed his hand off her shoulder, and sniped, "I'm fine."

* * *

SAMMY, Roan, and Jason left the party about an hour after her parents, telling Danele she needed to get home before the snow got too bad. Outside a couple inches of snow had already accumulated, everything was quiet, the scene serene, and it should have brought a sense of peace and joy to Sammy, but she was still furious and didn't understand why. When Roan tried to help her into the front seat, she shook her head and got into the back and watched while both he and Jason brushed snow off the car. When Jason got in the front seat he glanced at her and made a gesture to ask why she was back there. "What's wrong?"

"Nothing, please, just get in." She could hear the tremble in her own voice and was so afraid of losing control of either her anger or . . . what was it? Was it grief still? Did Roan's conversation with her parents make her sad? Make her remember Peter and his death? She didn't think so, but she didn't know why she was so upset.

On the ride home, Sammy was quiet, still trying to figure out why that conversation had irritated her so much. She did have strong feelings for Roan, so her mother's telling people shouldn't have bothered her. She didn't like Roan talking about Peter, but even that wasn't the reason. Just as she was about to lean her head back and close her eyes to forget about the last several hours, they saw yellow lights flashing up ahead. As they got closer, Sammy made out the silhouette of her father helping a tow truck driver hook up her car to pull it out of a ditch.

Anger surged again from somewhere deep. "Damn it, damn it. I knew this would happen. If you two hadn't—" She let the angry tears come then, but brusquely brushed them away.

"Whoa there, sis. How about let's make sure they're okay before you start blaming people," Jason said turning around in his seat, trying to catch her eye. She quickly lowered hers and looked down at her gloved hands so he couldn't see her face, see her fury.

They pulled up behind the tow truck. The tire tracks in the snow clearly showed Sammy's car had slid off the road into a shallow ditch. Her mother huddled on side of the road wrapped in a blanket, her father visibly shaken as he followed the tow truck driver to the cab of the truck talking animatedly. When her parents saw Roan's car drive up, her mother struggled to get up off the curb. Her father reached down to help her mother up, then raised his arms and dropped them to his side, as if to say he didn't know what happened. Sammy got out of the car and walked toward them.

Her mother's voice broke as she limped toward Sammy and said, "We slid off the road."

Jason, pushed by Sammy and hugged his mother. "Are you okay?"

"I think I twisted my ankle when I got out of the car, but yes, we're fine dear." She pulled her arm out of the blanket to pat his cheek.

"Good, now let's get you in Roan's car to warm up," Jason said, took her mother's elbow, and guided her around Sammy and toward Roan's car.

Her mother pulled away. "No, no, I'll go with your father. The car is fine. The tow truck driver said there was no damage. We just couldn't get it out of the ditch. I'm sorry dear. We're not sure what happened. I think he hit some ice."

"Yes, that's probably it," Sammy said and reached out to hug her mom. "I'm just glad you're both okay." Not letting Sammy hug her, her mother turned away. Wind bit at Sammy's face and she felt the sting of her mother's apparent rejection. She just stood there letting the snow that had turned to ice pellets beat at her body—maybe, she reasoned, this is one of those times when the punishment did fit the crime. Of which crime she wasn't sure, but she did know her anger had not made anyone happy lately.

Sammy moved cautiously on the icy road toward her car to see if there was any damage. She watched as the tow truck pulled it out and was relieved to see everything was intact. Roan come up behind her and said, "It looks like there's no damage, Sammy, and everyone is okay. Why don't you go back and sit in the car to keep warm?"

She wanted to be calm, to be the Sammy Roan 'cared deeply for' but right now that Sammy was nowhere to be found. No matter how hard she tried, she couldn't bring that Sammy back in that moment, so she attempted to be someone who was nothing to him, not angry friend nor loving girl-friend, so she said, her voice flat, emotionless. "Please, just go help them. I'm fine."

"Are you sure?"

She nodded, too annoyed to trust herself to say more. But then ventured, "Just give me the keys. I'm cold. I'll start it up and get warm." She knew she still had an edge to her voice, so when Roan looked at her, his lips were tight and his eyes dull, like all emotion had fled. And in apparent frustration ,he just tossed the keys to her and went over to where her father was now talking to the tow truck driver. Before she went over to the car, Sammy watched as her mother tried to maneuver her way through the snow to get to her father. "Mom, take it easy, you'll fall," Sammy shouted.

Jason yelled, "Mom, stop! Come back here. You're not getting back in the car with Dad. I'll drive Sammy's car and take you both back to the hotel then I'll bring the car back."

"I can drive, Jason." Her father yelled back, "I'm not an idiot. We just hit ice."

"I know you're not an idiot, Dad," Jason said as he got closer to him. "You're shook, I can see that. Just let me drive the damn car back." When her father turned away from Jason and started back toward Sammy's car, ready to get in it again, Jason pleaded, "Please, Dad. It's Christmas Eve. Let's not argue about it."

"Fine," her father said with emphasis, obviously frustrated. Then he handed over the keys.

And that's how they drove back to Sammy's: her parents captive in a car driven by her brother and Sammy captive in the car of the man she had thought she was falling in love with, but now wasn't sure how she felt. She tried to swallow all of it, every emotion that she'd had for Roan just to figure out what was going on in her head. Not her head—her heart.

When he stopped to drop her off at her place, he turned off the engine and said, "Okay so obviously I have done something to upset you." He turned to look at her and his eyes flat, emotionless which should have told her something.

She knew hers were cold when she looked back at him and all the anger and tears that she had suppressed came out in the most horrible way. "Why the hell did you think it was okay to talk about Peter to my parents?"

He looked pained like he'd been punched in his heart. He shook his head, stared at her and said, "You know, Sammy,

I've been trying to be patient because I know you've been under a lot of stress with the new studio and having your parents here, but I can't keep letting you—"

"He was my husband. You don't know anything about him yet you felt it was okay to share information about him with my parents. What gives you the right?" She'd hurt him. She could see and she knew she was going too far yet she couldn't stop herself. Sammy choked on the words as she repeated, "He was my husband, Roan. Not yours."

"I think you've said enough and before I get angrier, you should go inside."

Sammy opened the door and turned back briefly to look at Roan. He stared straight ahead, his hand tightly gripping the steering wheel, his jaw tight, not looking at her at all.

Her heart raced and, in her soul, she knew she might have ruined everything, so she panicked as she closed the car door, opened it back up and said, "I'll see you tomorrow?"

Then he turned and looked at her, his face expressionless, his eyes behind his glasses, completely empty. "Maybe, I don't know yet."

After she closed the door, he pulled away, not glancing back once.

"What is going on with you?" Jason said when he got back to her apartment after dropping her parents at the hotel. "You were rude to mom and dad, and I get that you were pissed about the car, but for Pete's sake Sammy they had an accident. Mom was a mess when I drove her back to the hotel. She confided in me that Dad has been having some memory issues. Can't you see they're old and we don't know how long they'll be with us."

"It wasn't them." She paused, thought for a moment. "Okay, yes, they're driving me crazy, but it was something else."

"Well, you were rude to Roan, too. And on the drive home I could see you in the rearview mirror, you looked furious."

Sammy flopped on the couch, covered her eyes with her hands and said, "Mom was telling everyone we were in love and getting married."

Jason said, "So."

"Then I overheard Mom and Dad talking to Roan and they asked about Peter."

"So. Why be mad at Roan?"

"He shouldn't have answered them. He should have left or changed the subject. It wasn't his place to talk about Peter, so I got angry and," she sighed and got off the couch and walked into the kitchen, yelling over her shoulder, "I told him he had no right to talk about Peter."

He followed her into the kitchen. "Geez, Sammy. I don't understand you. He's a great guy and ever since I've been here, you've done nothing, that I can see, but give him a bad time. I'm surprised he hasn't gotten angry."

"He did. He left just now and wouldn't even look at me."

"You'll lose him, sis, unless that's what you're hoping for."

She grabbed a glass and filled it with water, took a big gulp, leaned back against the counter and said, "I think . . . oh god, I don't know what I think; I think I screwed up, Jason." Was she self-sabotaging their relationship? She didn't think so but she couldn't get his conversation with her parents out of her head and each time she thought about it, it pissed her off.

CHAPTER TWENTY-NINE

*S*he'd just gotten out of the shower Christmas morning and was in the bedroom dressing when she heard her father's voice, then her mother's. They were here. All ready. She felt deflated; like all the joy about this day, this time of the year was gone. And there was no way to get it back.

She'd woken in the night after nightmares of Roan and her parents driving off a cliff and falling into an abyss filled with cotton candy. It terrified her, but this morning when she first opened her eyes, she laughed at the absurdity. Then reality hit and she remembered everything about the night before. She tried to breathe through the uncertainty of what today might bring and find a place where she could be at peace with both her parents and Roan. She told herself that she was lucky to have her family and a man who cared about her during the holidays but hearing their voices just now took all that potential joy away.

She grappled for her phone to see the time. It was only eight-thirty. She took a breath, tried to sound happy, and yelled, "You guys are early. I haven't even made coffee yet." She finished dressing, stopped to put a smile on her face, and walked out.

"Jason made us coffee and we brought some almond croissants," her dad said.

She gave him a hug, then her mother, and then as she headed toward the kitchen over her shoulder she said, "Nothing's open on Christmas Day in Barcelona. Where did you get them?"

"At the hotel and they're not bad."

Sammy nearly bumped into Jason as she walked into the kitchen. "What smells so good?"

Jason grinned. "Christmas dinner."

"Really? I never thought you guys would really pull it off. I'm impressed." But in the kitchen, she was greeted by an ungodly mess: counters strewn with open cans and containers, dishes filled the sink, on top of the stove something bubbled, and her French press was nowhere in sight. She felt her irritation rise in her chest but she tried to keep it under control as she joked, "Did a cyclone make its way to Spain? What have you done with my kitchen? And where's my coffee?"

Jason shrugged. "Sorry, sis. That's how I cook. Don't worry. I'll clean up."

"I guess that will have to do. But where's my coffee?"

"Over here." Jason pushed aside some of the clutter and tucked in the corner was her French press with only a bit of coffee left. "No worries, sis. I'll make you more."

She raised an eyebrow and said, "I'll believe that when I see it. What are you making us for dinner?" And she tried to nudge him out of the way to look into the oven and lift the lid off the pot on the stove.

"Lasagna. It's done and in the fridge already to be put in the oven when we're ready." And as he left the kitchen he added, "Roan's bringing a ham—some Spanish specialty ham."

"Why lasagna?"

"Because I know how to make it. And it's spectacular if I do say so myself."

From the other room her mom's voice lifted over the Christmas music her father had just asked Alexa to play. "Where *is* Roan?"

"Lovers' quarrel," Jason said louder than necessary.

Sammy poked her head out of the kitchen and glared at him. "Not a lovers' quarrel. We're fine," she said as the sound of God Rest Ye Merry Gentlemen filled the room.

Since it didn't seem like her brother was going to make her coffee, Sammy stayed in the kitchen to make it herself and clean up the mess Jason had made. Clanging dishes, slamming cupboards, and trying to keep her annoyance down while grumbling to the refrigerator as she returned warm milk and other open containers. Squishing the irritation that kept rising inside, she poked her head out into the other room and asked, "Anyone want more coffee? I'll make extra."

Water boiled, beans crushed, she made coffee, waited the four minutes, plugged the stopper then sat in the kitchen avoiding going out there amongst her family. Slowly she sipped coffee and tore pieces off the croissant Jason left for her. Letting each delicious morsel rest in her mouth before swallowing, thinking maybe if she took enough time by herself her mood would soften before Roan arrived.

* * *

WHEN IT WAS noon and Roan hadn't shown up yet, nor had he called or text her, she struggled. Should she reach out? No, she decided, if he wanted to see her, he'd be here. And yet when he knocked on the door around one, she had Jason let him in and she made herself busy rearranging presents under the tree. When she stood up trying to look and feel as if everything was normal, she saw he was juggling multiple packages and a couple bottles of wine.

"Well, there he is." Her mother gushed and rushed over to him. "Sammy wouldn't tell us when you were coming."

He smiled wryly, nodding to all of them. "I have more stuff in the car." He turned to Jason. "Can you give me a hand? I have part of dinner down there."

"I can help, Roan," Sammy said, trying to keep her voice light and cheerful.

He turned away from her, headed out the door, and said, "I think we've got it."

TENSION between them filled the day even as they opened presents and though Roan loved his sweater, he avoided looking at her. He got her a lovely scarf along with a bottle of perfume that she'd mentioned she liked. Her parents got her a very expensive Coach bag. Her father ruined it by adding, "It can double as a briefcase if you do ever decide to go back into law."

She let it slide and later felt as if everything was back on track when Jason opened his bottle of wine from her and she said without thinking, "Does Stephen like wine, too?"

Her mom looked at Jason and asked, "Who is Stephen dear?"

"A friend."

Sammy teased, "Oh, he's more than a friend. Right, Jason?" Then she turned to her parents and said, "You know. He's Jason's new love." Sammy glanced at Jason and saw his jaw tight and he was glaring at her. Confused, she said to him, "I thought they knew." She looked over at Roan, who wouldn't meet her eyes.

"Know what, Jason? What is Sammy talking about?" her mother asked.

"Yes, Jason, who is Stephen and what is all the secrecy about?" her father interjected.

She could tell Jason was furious at her, so she grappled for an apology. "You were telling everyone at the party about him and London, so I was sure mom and dad knew. I'm sorry."

"London?" her parents said at the same time. "Jason," her father yelled, "what is going on?"

The next hour was a blur. Everyone was so angry. No one spoke during dinner and by the time they were all finished, Jason had shut himself up in the guest room and her parents had gone back to the hotel saying they'd discuss Jason's plans once he came to his senses. Sammy and Roan were alone. A heavy silence hovered. Roan was the first to talk. "Sammy, I know you feel bad about what you did, but why, . . . why would you bring up Stephen to your parents when you knew Jason wanted to wait until they got back to Ohio to tell them?"

She got defensive. "Well, he was telling everyone at the

party. Didn't it make sense that they already knew?" She'd ruined Christmas and she knew it. She hadn't meant to do that; hadn't meant to get mad at Roan for talking about Peter; hadn't meant to be angry at her parents, for, well, just being parents. Hadn't meant to out her brother and leave him at the mercy of their parents without warning or protection. Like a dark fog, a cocoon of sadness crept around her and she let it, cosseting her against criticism or accusation from Roan. She closed her eyes, felt her heart empty, her breath hollowed out. She was tired. Tired of feeling; of loving, of hating, just tired.

"Sammy?" Roan's voice, gentle and questioning. She opened her eyes and saw he was staring at her. He reached over and brushed something off her face.

Instinctively she turned away and touched her own cheek wondering why it was wet. Where had that tear come from? Then another, then tears were rolling down her face.

"Oh Sammy, come here." His voice soft in her ear and she wondered how did he get there. How was he wrapping his arms around her, kissing her cheek, wiping the tears away? And she wondered why he was doing it after she'd been so awful. She wanted him in her life but also wondered what happened to that girl who didn't need love? When had she become dependent on his attention? His support? Frustration and angst at her own neediness pushed their way through her weakened state and she felt her defenses rise. She pulled away, it was agonizing because she wanted to lean on him, needed a foundation that he gave her.

He misunderstood her response, stroked her head and, his voice raspy with emotion, whispered, "It's okay Sammy, I love you. Everything will be okay. Jason knows that . . . "

His words took her breath. She wanted desperately to fall

into it, but instead felt panic and fear set in. It was too soon. It was too soon for him to quit his job to stay here, to be with her; too soon for him to love her; too soon for her to have those feelings about him. She had to close off these emotions. Shut them down. It was all happening too fast.

She needed to tell him; tell him to stop. Stop loving me, stop quitting your job, stop being you. Then the voice whispered louder than any other. You can't love him, if you love him, you will lose him. You could lose everything. She could feel herself closing down those feelings of love for her own protection.

Peter had loved her and she'd love Peter and look what happened. She'd done that once and that love had come with so much pain and sadness after Peter died. She wasn't sure she could endure that again.

Irrationality took over and she lashed out. "Just go I can't do this. You and me. This is too much."

He sat back like he'd been shot. "I don't understand. This isn't about us, is it?"

She moved farther away from him and said, "Everything has changed. I don't know what I feel about anything anymore! I just know you need to go."

His brows creased; his face confused, he stood and said, "About me? You don't know how you feel about me?"

"No, I don't, Roan." Fury and panic rose inside her; she stood and handed him his coat.

He looked down at her, his eyes a slow burn. He took his coat from her and putting it on said, "I just said I loved you and you looked at me like I'd told you, you were the worst person in the world." His body slumped, his face showed her he had given up, that he had had enough. With hurt and anger in his voice, he said, "You hold me responsible for his death."

She wanted to tell him he was wrong, that it wasn't about Peter anymore. Maybe it was in the beginning, but not anymore. She needed to tell him, but she wouldn't. Now she just needed him to go. "Just go," she nearly screamed.

As soon as the door closed behind Roan, Jason opened his bedroom door and said, "Well I hope you're happy. It looks like you're by yourself again. Now that you've driven everyone away you can pat yourself on the back." And he slammed the door.

She wanted all of them gone; every last one: her parents, her brother, and Roan. She wanted her life back the way it was before the studio, before love, before complications confused her about what she wanted in her life. No more love. She loved and now she'd lost. Again. She wouldn't look at the reality that it was she who pushed them all away. In her mind, it was them. Love meant loss, so good riddance. She was better with her parents in Ohio, Jason in London, and Roan wherever he wound up. Her friends were her family, her studio was her new love.

She didn't need anyone, least of all Roan.

CHAPTER THIRTY

*B*ut that mindset slipped away in the days that followed Christmas and she wondered what she'd done. She missed Roan and was sorry she'd behaved like a child, but pride kept her from picking up the phone to call him.

"Too late," Jason told her numerous times. "You pushed him away, what did you expect." Jason had forgiven her for telling her parents about Stephen, but her parents hadn't and they went back to Ohio.

"We're not staying for your opening, Sammy. This trip has been too stressful for your mother and now that Jason is leaving the practice, I have some management and employee issues to solve," her father had told her. She could hear the disappointment in his voice, not because of Jason, but because of her. So much so she hadn't even tried to convince them to stay.

Jason and their parents had a long talk the day after Christmas and once Jason told them all about Stephen and the gallery and how much he loved both, they capitulated and were even happy for him.

"Of course they were, you're the baby after all." She said to Jason as they were walking along the beachfront of La Barceloneta. Remnants of holiday bonfires many with embers still glowing rested along the shoreline, every once in a while sparks flew up as an ember popped. Sammy kicked at the sand, bundled her coat tighter and turned around to walk backward and face Jason as they walked. "And yet," she added, "they still beat that annoying drum of 'why didn't you tell us about Peter' bullshit, and yet they forgive you,"

"Why didn't you, Sammy?"

"Why didn't I what?"

"Tell them about Peter? If you loved him unconditionally as you've said numerous times, why? I mean you introduced us to Roan. Is your love for Roan stronger than for Peter because it would seem that way?"

"I didn't have much of a choice, did I?"

"A choice of what?"

"Letting you meet Roan. You guys were here, he's here, I'm seeing him. Case closed."

"Not really, Sammy. You could have easily kept him out of our lives. Knowing him this short time I know he would have understood if you didn't bring him around, yet you nearly shoved him in our faces. Then got mad when we liked him."

She knew he had a point.

"He's special, Sammy. And I can tell you think he is. You've made a mistake by pushing him away. You made those ridiculous analogies about him not saving Peter. I'm pretty sure you know there is no way he or anyone else could have. So, what's up?"

"I'm afraid."

* * *

IT WAS JANUARY 4, the day before her studio open house, classes would start on the fifteenth and she was frantic trying to get everything ready. She and Roan were still at a pause in their relationship. Sammy wasn't happy about it, but Roan had insisted when, after many missed calls and cryptic messages on both their parts, they finally connected a few days ago. She was on her way back from dropping Jason at the airport to go back to London when she decided to try Roan again and he answered.

"I'm sorry."

"Who is this?" he joked.

"Your illogical, grumpy female friend." She'd wanted to say girlfriend, but it stuck in her throat and came out friend with the girl part lost in no man's land with some unknown emotion.

"Are you still grumpy?"

"Not as much. I'm so sorry. I was in such a state with my parents here and they, well, . . ." She barely took a breath and rambled on so fast her words jumbled so much so that he started laughing while she said, "Wait, why are you laughing?"

"Because it's okay. I'm not mad at you, Sammy, but I do think a break is a good idea."

"I don't."

His voice was gentle, but firm and a bit detached when he continued. "We need time to let the last few weeks settle, Sammy. Like I said I'm not mad, a bit bruised maybe for lack of a better word. Telling someone I love them doesn't come easy for me. Then you discarded it and shoved me out the door."

She wanted to be conciliatory, wanted him back in her life, but something in his tone and the word love put her off, and she shut down. When she didn't say anything, he sighed, cleared his throat and said, "Plus I have several interviews coming up in the next few weeks so it's a good time for us to look at our relationship and get some perspective. I think you might need that time."

"Well, fine then. Let me know when you can fit me into your schedule," she bristled.

His voice rigid, he continued, "Sammy, let's not. Your studio open house is in a few days. I'm sure you're busy with that." When she didn't say anything, he sighed, obviously frustrated. "Look, let's talk again after the open house."

He was rejecting her. Just like she thought. Love brings loss. She pushed down the tears and anger that had marched their way into her eyes and her heart. Then more gently, he said, "I'll be there for you. I'll come to support you. After all," he chuckled, "it was my idea."

"Well, that's just grand isn't it, Roan. Goodbye." And she hung up on him.

Since that conversation, she poured herself into preparations for the open house and wouldn't let herself think about him. Now, just a day before her opening she was frantic trying to get ahold of Isabella to add some new food items to the buffet list because there had been some last-minute additions to the guest list.

"*Hola.* Talk to me."

"Isabella, it's Sammy. I need to add more tapas. I don't care which kind, but I need another dozen or two. Can you do that?"

"What! You think I am superwoman or something."

"Please, please. I'm a mess."

"Not to worry. Of course, I can. I can do anything. Now," her voice lowers, "tell me is your lover going to be there. Ooh la la—*mucho caliente*"

Her heart sank at the mention of Roan, and she admitted, "Oh Isa. I messed up. I don't know if he'll be there or even if I'll ever see him again."

"Oh, now, it will be fine, *mi dulce chica*. He adores you. I see with my own two eyes."

"No more, Isa. Sadly, no more. I have to go, thank you. See you at the studio tomorrow at two to set up?"

"*Si, si. adiós.*"

She got off the phone and pushed away any thoughts of Roan. It made her sad to think she might have lost him, but her focus had to be on the studio. If it was a failure, she'd lose that too and that disappointment she couldn't sustain.

CHAPTER THIRTY-ONE

*S*ammy's trepidation about the open house was unnecessary. The afternoon and evening turned out to be magical.

She'd opened up the studio at one o'clock to make sure all was in order. Isa showed up as planned at two and everything was ready when they opened at four o'clock. It had all gone smoothly and right now the studio pulsed with activity.

Music played and kids freeform danced. A table was set up for sign-ups and food and drink were plentiful. Isa had created many different types of tapas and she and her staff were diligent about making sure the food table was never empty. There was punch for the kids and nondrinkers, and wine and sangria for adults. The studio vibrated with joy and Sammy's soul filled with pride and optimism. Even Mateo showed up with his family and brother-in-law. Sister Mercedes made an appearance with Father Thomas. Everyone in fact was there to support her except her own family and Roan.

As the celebration continued and afternoon transitioned

into evening, she was ready to close it down when the door opened and Roan walked in holding a bouquet of flowers. He immediately walked over to her, kissed both cheeks and apologized, "My interview went longer than I thought." He looked around the room. "But I can see this is a smashing success." He turned back and beamed at her. "I'm so happy for you, Sammy. How are the sign-ups going? And by the way, what did you name this place?"

She tried to catch her breath. Her mind raced between the speech she had to give in a few minutes, how handsome he looked in his black suit, the flowers in her hand, and her conflicting emotions about his tardiness countered by just being happy he was there. Her mind a muddle, she barely croaked out, "Heartbeat Dance Studio, dancing the world."

Again, he grinned broadly at her. "That's fantastic."

But there was something wrong. Not a coolness, not really aloofness, but like a brother would talk to his sister or a stranger might talk to an acquaintance. Not like a lover talks to his girlfriend. There was no intimacy in his exchange, in his eyes or movements. None. His eyes wouldn't meet hers. He just kept perusing the room then lightly touched her hand and said, "I think I'll get something to drink. What can I get you?" And he seemed nervous. Not at all like the Roan she knew. Then it hit her. He was making sure to keep within the friendship boundaries. And making sure she knew it.

She gathered herself and shook her head. "Nothing thanks. I have to give a little talk soon. But you go ahead and get something." She turned away from him to talk to Macy and her husband who had just walked up.

Roan greeted them as well. "Tomas, great job with the studio. Sammy had been telling me your company did a bang-up job and she wasn't kidding. I didn't see it in its before state, but from what she said it wasn't an easy job."

"It was a challenge and . . . "

Sammy let the three of them continue to talk and she slowly eased away to ask the pianist to stop playing in ten minutes so she could give her speech. It was seven-thirty, already well past the end time for the open house and kids were getting more rambunctious and parents testy. She wanted everyone out while it was still a positive experience. More importantly, she wanted everyone gone so she could talk to Roan alone. She would ask him to walk with her. Isa and her friends had already offered to clean up, so she was free to see if she could explain things to Roan and try to set things right.

Ciara came over to Sammy and touched her arm, her eyes searching Sammy's face. "Are you happy with everything? It is magical. It's going to be a success, I know. But are *you* satisfied?"

"I am." And Sammy let the joy fill her. This was her baby and it turned out better than she imagined. At least if things didn't work out with Roan, she had this and that was enough. She'd have her friends, who always sustained her, she'd have this business in a city she adored and she'd have dance in her life just as she always wanted. It would have to be enough. She'd persevered after Peter died; she could do it again if she lost Roan.

The pianist stopped playing and Sammy took the mic from her. She tapped lightly on the mic and said, "Welcome every-one. Please let me . . . " at that point, everyone turned and looked at her; kids quieted, dancers became motionless, and Roan smiled at her and nodded. She faltered, took a breath, smiled and continued, "Welcome to Heartbeat Dance Studio. Thank you so much for supporting my dream." She paused. "A dream I didn't even know I had until someone," she locked eyes with Roan, "a very special friend, suggested the idea when I was struggling with what to do with the rest of my life. You see, dance is in my soul in every fiber of my being and when it became clear that I wasn't going to be doing it for much longer, for a variety of reasons, this studio was my lifesaver. It . . . " she faltered again and felt a rush of emotion. Tears rested at the precipice of the corners of her eyes and she knew if she didn't push those emotions down, she would start to cry and wouldn't be able to stop so she willed them away, and continued, ". . . has been the best three months of my life getting this dream ready to share with all of you. Thanks to Macy's husband Tomas for creating this beautiful space, to Roan for the idea, for Isa for the delicious food and," she turned to the pianist, "to Greta for her beautiful music. I look forward to seeing many of you in ten days. Thank you." And she blew kisses to the crowd. Then yelled, "Be safe as you journey home."

The crowd began to disperse and she quickly walked over to Roan. "Would you walk with me? I didn't drive and I really need to talk to you."

"Of course."

"I don't need to stay to clean up."

"I'll wait outside. Just meet me when you are finished." He took her hand. "Your talk," he paused, "very heartfelt."

* * *

SAMMY FOUND him around the corner leaning against a building with his back to her. Above his head, a light on the building shone down, haloing his body against the darkness of the night. His face—pensive and serious as he looked towards the spires of La Sagrada Familia. He'd taken off his suit coat, loosened his tie, and looked every bit the sexy handsome man that she loved. Her heart broke as she remembered how she'd treated him. Yes, she loved him, and had reconciled her fears about that, but perhaps it was too late. She resisted the urge to run at him and wrap her arms around him. As she took a step forward, he sighed and as he turned, caught her watching him. "There you are," he said and gave a short little half-laugh.

"Yes, here I am. Let's walk." She didn't take his arm or his hand, not that he had offered, but she didn't want to walk too close. She knew if they inadvertently touched, she would lose all composure and beg him to reconsider their split. She only wanted to talk, to see if she could fix what she'd apparently ruined.

"Jason left. My parents, too. I guess I pushed them away, well not Jason. He was always going to leave before the open house." She fiddled with her purse and drew it further up onto her shoulder because it kept falling down her arm. Each time it did, Roan slipped it back on her shoulder. Even that tiniest of touches when his hand brushed her shoulder was too much so she moved her purse to her other side. No touches, no temptation. "Jason really likes you a lot, Roan. He told me I'm an idiot. But then I knew that. You must know that, too." She looked up at him as the moon peeked out of the clouds behind his head, resting light on his face, serious now, intent as he listened to her. He stayed silent so she added, "He says I should make you come back to me."

"But what do you say, Sammy? You need to want that. You need to want me to come back for your own reasons, not because your brothers said so."

"But it is for me, Roan. I made a mistake. I conflated too many things. I let too many things cloud my mind. Too many people confuse me as to what I truly want. "

"What *do* you want Sammy because I remember from our conversation on Christmas you said you don't know how you feel about me anymore. I'm happy to give you that time to figure it out. I'm not going anywhere Sammy, but it can't be like it was. And we can't continue right now anyway. I've got too much going on. I've still not found work, and . . . " His voice trailed off and he took her hand. "Look Sammy, this break is for you to figure things out. You are still edgy and I think you're still confused about your feelings for me. I know how I feel about you; I already told you. I love you, but you have to figure it out. When you're ready call me, text me, heck show up at my place. I'll still be here. But not now. You, . . . both of us actually, need time apart." They'd reached the corner where she would turn off to her house, where he would leave and go to his.

"My parents," she said as the tears ran down her face, "my parents ruined everything, ruined us."

"There is no us right now. Please don't make this any harder than it has to be and no, Sammy, it wasn't your parents. You know it's been hard for you since the beginning, since I ran into you on the train. Our past is complicated. It's not easy. You see me, you see Peter's death."

Now she got angry. "That is NOT it."

"Then," he asked, his voice quiet and tender, "what is it?"

"I'd . . . I'd." She was crying now. "What if I love you and you die. If I lose you like I did Peter?"

At that moment the emotion was too much and she turned from him and ran. Ran as fast as she could, hearing him call her name. "Sammy. Wait." But when she kept running, he yelled, "I love you, Sammy. Remember that."

CHAPTER THIRTY-TWO

*H*e tried to reach out to her only once after that, but she ignored his call and his text. When he didn't try again, she accepted he was gone from her and she occupied her time with the studio and classes to make it easier to forget him. It had been six weeks since she ran from him and she and Ciara were having coffee at Ciara's place.

"You're being foolish." Ciara insisted. "You love him. You just told me that. People die, Sammy, it's life. You can't let Peter's death dictate the rest of *your* life."

"It was just fine. My life. Before Roan. It will be fine after. I have you guys, I have my studio, the classes, the kids, I have Barcelona. I don't need anything else. I don't even know if he is in Barcelona anyway; he could be anywhere."

Ciara frowned, obviously dubious about what Sammy just said. "So, then you're not even going to try to see him? You're going to go through the rest of your life alone?"

"But, I have you guys and—"

"Yes, Sammy, you have us, but eventually we are all going to be with someone other than each other. Sylvia is already talking about moving back to California, Macy wants kids. Unless she's working, Danele's locked up with her new guy from Australia and she's planning on going with him back to Australia for his summer. And who knows how long I can hold on before I have to go back to Ireland and help out. My dad is not well and no one seems to be willing or capable of helping him."

"You can't leave. I need you here."

"See what I mean; the four of us have other people and things in our lives. Right now all you have is your studio."

"But all of you have been my rock when things got bad, we've always been able to support each other."

"Yes, and we'll always do that, but as I just told you we will all be going our own separate ways eventually. Sammy, you really don't need any of us anyway, truly. You're strong, you always have been. You never really needed any of us except when Peter died. Why would now be any different? Is your split from Roan worse than when Peter died? If it is, that should tell you something."

"Of course, it's not the same. Of course, it's not worse. Why would you say that, damn it? Peter died. Roan is just, well, being stubborn."

Ciara laughed at that and said, "That is the most ridiculous thing you've said today. *Roan is being stubborn?* I do believe it might be you."

No, she wasn't being stubborn, but Ciara was right; she didn't need anyone least of all Roan Adair. "I need to go; I have a class at one. But before I go what's this about your father? Is he ill?"

Ciara stood to walk Sammy to the door and said, "He's not well. He had a minor heart attack and is having a hard time getting back to his normal self. My mom is terribly worried and she told me Dad is depressed. Barely gets out of bed in time to open the pub by eleven."

"Can't anyone help him? Your mom, your siblings?"

"Most of them are married with kids of their own and the youngest ones are off at university. Sean has been helping out, but he has his own business to take care of. I may have to go back, but if I do, there is one thing that can't change."

"What?"

"All of you will still visit this summer even if I drag all of you there."

"Of course, but Sean again? So, you've been in touch?" Sammy chided.

"Time for you to, go. Now scoot." And Ciara helped her out the door.

* * *

THIS WAS one of Sammy's favorite classes— her pre-ballet class for three- and four-year-olds. It took the most patience and at times it was frustrating, but the joy she got out of it far outweighed any issues. She loved the enthusiasm and conversations she had with the three-year-old kids too much to change it now. There were six in the class; four girls and two boys. The boys, who were four, surprisingly were the most attentive. Two of the girls were three and two were four. During class they spent most of the time working on positions, stretching, and then just free dancing to music.

"Megan loves it so much. Thanks for letting her join. I know she's barely three, but I can't tell you how much better she is when she comes home. She doesn't even argue about nap time anymore."

Sammy was having a conversation with Megan's mom, Julie, who was the wife of the American doctor that took Roan's place at the cruise line. Sammy wasn't sure how Julie found out about her classes and she didn't want to ask. She suspected it might have been from Roan, but the only information Julie shared about her husband's new job was that he was replacing a doctor who decided to leave for another job. And Sammy didn't ask her any more questions; she didn't want to know.

"I'm happy Megan enjoys it," Sammy said. "She is delightful and really pays attention. She wants to get it right and always helps the other kids."

Sammy said goodbye to Julie and the other parents and kids, turned off the lights and made sure the room was ready for tomorrow's tap class with the older kids. She'd decided to do some shopping today after class. She hadn't done any since the time she ran into Roan and she needed clothes for spring now that the weather had begun to warm. The first day of March was this coming week and the cruise season would begin again; Barcelona would be busy.

She left the studio and, as always, unconsciously glanced down the street where Roan lived just a few blocks away. It hurt that it was something she did without realizing it until she was in the midst of doing it. It hurt even more to know all she had to do was walk down there and let herself be vulnerable.

His presence loomed even larger as she neared the Bridge of Sighs where they'd bumped into each other on her last shopping trip. For that reason, she cut over along a more residential lane. Denial was her protection against the pain of losing him. She shut down those memories and walked into a store that was new to her.

"Hello, welcome. We are still sorting things out, but you are welcome to browse. Let me know if you have any questions," a faceless female voice with a very British accent shouted from the back of the store. The store looked like it was newly opened and not quite ready for customers. Boxes were being unpacked and clothes were brought out from the back storage area and put on racks.

"Thank you."As Sammy rummaged through a few racks at the front of the store, she glanced out the large storefront window as a group of people walked by talking loudly. Tourists, Sammy thought. Pre-cruise season had begun. At the back of the crowd, Sammy caught a glimpse of a man that looked like Roan and her heart clenched. The man turned and it wasn't. Relieved she wandered back to the end of the store where the owner was pulling out a rack of summer dresses.

Hands on her hips, the woman walked over to Sammy, obviously exasperated. "My apologizes for the mess. We planned on opening today, then all of my stock was late in arriving and it was too late to change the ads. Please if you see anything you'd like that isn't priced let me know or why don't you come back later this afternoon. I have help coming and should be in better shape then."

There were several things Sammy had seen that she might like to try on later so she thanked the store owner, told her she'd be back, and headed out in the opposite direction of the group. As she rounded the corner, she caught a glimpse of the Roan look-alike this time sitting at an outside table at a café talking with another man. And yet Sammy knew this time it couldn't be the same man she had just seen. This time she heard the man laugh, a deep rumbling, hearty laugh from his soul, and she saw his profile, watched as he set his glasses down and ran his hand over his face as he always did when he was nervous. She watched him because she had to, because, he was still in her heart, still had her soul.

Roan and the man rose to leave the café. Sammy turned to go the other way, but as she did, Roan saw her and raised his hand in greeting. She was stuck so she put on her brightest smile, like his presence hadn't taken her breath, hadn't made her want to run *to* him and not away this time; hadn't made her wish that the last two months hadn't happened so she could be back in his arms again.

"Roan, how good to see you."

His eyes searched hers, his smile tentative, his approach wary, he said, "Hi, Sammy." He seemed to struggle to gain his composure which was so unlike Roan, but it gave her the confidence to lightly kiss his cheek then step back. The man with him stepped forward and Roan introduced him. "Sammy, this is Rodger Jones." Roan cleared his throat and said, "I'm talking to him about a job. Rodger runs a nonprofit out of the states and needs to hire a team of qualified doctors. We were talking about where I can fit in. Rodger, this is Samantha Driscoll. Sammy and I are," he ran his hand over his face again and scratched his ear, "ah, old friends."

That hurt. But then what could he call her? Past girlfriend? Past love? Past pain in his ass? She needed to get out of there without falling apart, so she looked at her phone and said, "Goodness, I'm sorry I have to run, I had no idea it was so late. Roan, it was good to see you; Rodger good to meet you." She looked at Roan then and said, "I hope the job works out for you." Then to Rodger, she said, "Roan is a wonderful doctor. You'd be lucky to have him."

And though her instinct was to run again, she turned and walked away at a pace that she hoped showed him how unaffected she was at seeing him. She rounded the corner and as she did, glanced back at him. His eyes on her, his face beleaguered, his body stance suggested he had reconciled to losing her as she had to losing him. But she hadn't, not really, not in her heart of hearts. She wouldn't admit to anyone that she'd ached for him every minute, every second of the last six weeks, that every path she went down in Barcelona, every place they'd ever been screamed of his presence so much so that she often had to leave the places she had loved because of the memories. If she went to Isa restaurant all Isa wanted to know about was Roan. If she went to the deli, Mateo asked her what new dish she'd made for Roan. She'd told both of them countless times they were no longer together. They both shook their heads and said, "He will come back." Even when she explained to them it was her fault, they had the same answer: 'You will go to him.' But she couldn't. She'd be awful and she knew it. And yet seeing him again she felt the agony of losing him. The truth was, she hadn't felt this broken since Peter died. Like Ciara had said, 'What did that tell her?'

Maybe it told her that she needed to try one more time.

She walked aimlessly trying to focus, telling herself it was useless to think they could be together again. Then suddenly she was under the Bridge of Sighs. All those memories and emotions of running into him here flooded back. It was here under this bridge and the moment they shared here and later at the restaurant that cemented her future, not the moments at the monastery when Peter died. Her relationship with

Roan, her new career all started here first— by him, by the man she loved. Yet now he was gone.

She looked up at the bridge fighting back tears, she remembered what the folklore had said about the skull with the dagger on the bridge: '. . . if you make a wish while walking backward under the bridge and looking directly at the skull then that wish will come true.' She wiped her eyes, strode out to the center, stared up at the skull, walked backward under the bridge and whispered, "I wish," she stuttered then, "my wish," she choked back the tears, "my only wish, is for him to forgive me and come back to me."

Then she turned and ran as fast as she could to find him. The café and surrounding areas were empty. She panicked and began running without any idea of where she was going, without direction—randomly, erratically, indiscriminately, blindly because she had to find him. She looked everywhere and tried to quell the rising fear that he was gone and maybe that moment was gone too. But if she truly wanted him back, she'd find him no matter. She hailed a taxi and gave him Roan's address.

Feeling hopeful again, she nearly skipped up to his front door. She had a plan: she'd rush at him when he opened the door, she'd wrap her arms around him, apologize, let him know for the umpteenth time that she had temporarily lost her mind when her parents were there, that now that she had her mind back, she loved him. She rang the bell, she knocked, she banged on the door and hollered, but he didn't answer. She peered into the side windows and even walked around to the terrace to peek in the windows to see if he might be asleep or something. What she saw when she looked in the bedroom window was an open box filled with papers and a suitcase laid out on the bed, full of clothes, but no Roan.

Disheartened she left him a note tucked into the crack between the doorframes of the French doors asking him to call or text her. She walked back to her apartment wondering as she walked if his not being there was a sign: they weren't supposed to be together.

But the folklore . . . she believed it. She had to.

CHAPTER THIRTY-THREE

*a*nd yet as the days went on, she was less and less convinced and by the fifth day after no response from Roan, she'd again rejected the idea of them ever being together. As she'd told Jim Picard at Ian's wedding, she didn't need the love of her life anyway. She'd had one once, she didn't need another.

Her ballet class for the three-and four-year-olds had ended and Julie, Megan's mom rushed in to pick up Megan. "Sorry, I'm late. Traffic was awful and then I had a message to call my husband which by the way—I forgot to tell you—we met Roan Adair a few days ago, the doctor my husband replaced, and he mentioned he knew you. Such a dear man. In fact, I was just at the airport and saw him. It looked like he was catching a plane to the states. The guy he was with was arguing with the TSA person about what they could take into the US. I asked my husband about it just now and he said he thought Roan had taken a job in New York with a nonprofit and was heading out for that."

Sammy's heart dropped. Leaving? Moving? No, he

couldn't. And she realized at that moment she'd just been kidding herself. She needed him to be the love of her life and if that wasn't to be she needed him to tell her face-to-face.

"Do you know what flight they were taking?"

"I don't but they did announce that the flight to New York was delayed two hours. That must be the one." Julie looked at her phone. "That was about thirty minutes ago."

"I'm sorry, but I need to get out of here now." She ushered Julie and Megan out the door, closed up, walked outside and hailed a cab.

THE TAXI WAS STILL ROLLING when she paid the driver and jumped out at the drop-off area of the airport. Frantic, she scanned the terminal trying to find a display board with flight notices. She ran from one end of the terminal to another looking for information. When she finally found one, it said that the flight was in the final boarding stages. She rushed up to the TSA person to see if he would let her beyond the checkpoint.

"My husband forgot his medication. It's imperative I get this to him," she begged.

The TSA agent looked her up and down with apparent mistrust. "No. You need to go, ma'am."

"But, please, you don't understand."

"Ma'am if you don't step back I'll have to call security."

Then she heard over the intercom that the doors of his flight had closed.

She was too late. He was gone.

She backed away not paying attention to the people she bumped, or those who shoved her.

He was gone. She'd lost him.

She staggered. Her legs felt weak. Her mind fogged; everything around her morphed into a bleary mass, a haze that made her head spin. In a daze, she searched for a secure place to rest her body, her mind, her emotions. She moved to a wall next to the information board, leaned against it, then slid down until she was crouching, tears running down her face.

"Ma'am, are you okay?" A woman stood next to her.

"No," Sammy nearly shouted at her, and the woman backed away. Sammy stood, wobbled, wiped her eyes, and still reeling, she blindly headed back outside to go home. To home, where there was no one, where no one cared about her, where she'd made a life with Peter, then started a life with Roan, then lost both of them. She was tired, resigned about what she'd done, about what she'd lost. Her fault, she only had herself to blame. She hadn't been brave, hadn't taken that step that would have made her happy again.

Outside, travelers walked around her, taxis whizzed by, voices swirled. She needed to get a grip; she needed to leave here. She raised her arm to hail a taxi but when the taxi pulled up to the curb and she reached to open the door to get in, a man's hand reached in front of her and said, "I'm sorry miss but this cab is taken."

She looked into his eyes and life surged back into her body. She crumpled then. Crumpled as he caught her. Other people stopped to make sure she was okay and Roan let them know he would take care of her. He waved the taxi on and, with his arm around her, they walked back inside the terminal where Roan found a quiet spot for them to talk.

"You didn't call," she sniffled.

"You sent me away," he answered.

"I didn't want to."

He wiped the tears from her face. "I know."

"I didn't realize it," she tried to explain, "but after Peter died, I'd quietly begun to hope for nothing in the way of love again."

"I thought that every time you saw me, you saw Peter, you saw his death."

She shook her head. "I did, but only in the beginning, Roan before I knew you. Because, my dear Roan, when I look at you now, all I see is you. A wonderful man whom I love with all my heart. And that's all I want to see."

"Good because I can't give him back to you, all I can give you is the future if you want it."

"I," her voice caught, filled with emotion as she said, "I may have lost Peter, but I found you Roan, and that's all I need."

"No, Sammy, we found each other.

"Can we start again?" she pleaded.

He touched her face and whispered, "I don't want to start again. I want to carry on. I want forever. "

And with a terminal full of people Roan grabbed her and kissed her like it would be forever.

EPILOUGE

The scene that lay below her took her breath. She'd never seen water as blue nor felt air so fresh, nor wind so delicious. A breeze took a wisp of Sammy's long hair and swept it across her eyes. She brushed it away and let the scene imbue her soul. The sky, azure against the perfect backdrop of white and pastel-colored buildings many with blue-domed roofs perched on the cliffs of the Caldera, changed as the sun began to set. The whitewashed walls of Oia, Santorini, Greece turned to soft aubergine, the sky out on the horizon to fire.

She felt Roan's arms wrap around her then as he nuzzled her neck and kissed her cheek he said, "Come back inside. Nicholas just brought our wine."

"But it's so lovely out there. I could stay here forever."

"Maybe we should chuck it all in and move. Just you and me to a little white bungalow overlooking the sea. We could live like hermits, just loving each other. We wouldn't need clothes or shoes—or anyone else. No parents, no brother, no past, just the future and us."

"That's," a voice much deeper than Roan's said behind

them from the open door of the café, "a fair enough dream, but the winters hereabouts get pretty cold and the wind can bring a mighty bite."

Sammy and Roan backed off the café's Juliet balcony, went inside, and sat while Nicholas, the owner of the tiny bistro above the Aegean, set their drinks down.

"Thank you, Nicholas," Sammy said.

They were on their unofficial honeymoon in the café Roan had told her about when he visited Greece last year on his last cruise. They sipped their wine while Nicholas hovered, waiting to see if they approved.

"Excellent Nicholas. Thank you."

Nicholas turned to Sammy. "You, miss?"

"Superb."

Roan winked at her and said to Nicolas, "See I told you how lovely she is."

"*Nαί*. She is."

Nicholas left them to help another couple who had just walked in. Sammy sighed, looked across at her husband and marveled that it had all fallen in place once she let her fears go and let Roan capture her again so completely and without reservation. In the last six-months she learned to live again, to love again, unconditionally. To embrace Roan's love, she'd had to let go of old fears. Today, love didn't mean loss. Love meant Roan, love meant a place to anchor her heart, a place where her soul would be nurtured and treasured, and where she could treasure his.

The wind whispered through the open window next to their table, it caught her hair again and she felt the delicious tickle that happened more often now. It was a sensation she'd missed, a forgotten sensation from the past, but oh so perfect for now, for the future. Her hair was long again; her eyes bright, no dark circles anymore and love had filled her body, her soul.

So much had happened in the six months since she found Roan at the Barcelona airport.

"I wasn't leaving, Sammy," he'd explained to her that day. "Just dropping Rodger at the airport. He offered me a job here in Barcelona. So," he'd peered into her eyes, "I'll be here permanently now."

She'd stopped crying, but started again when he told her that. "I," she said and hiccuped, "can't think of anything I'd love more, except to marry you one day, my dear Roan."

And now that had happened, they were married, just like she'd wanted; just like the Bridge of Sighs promised. A week ago today, Father Thomas married them in the Chapel at Santa Cova on the side of Monserrat with Sister Mercedes as a witness. A moment she and Roan shared only for each other.

Her parents were initially angry when she told them they were going to marry, just the two of them, but she explained that she and Roan would go back to Ohio for another ceremony and reception. "A big wedding, Mom, so you can invite everyone. A full-on wedding with wedding gown, tuxes, bridesmaids, and flower girls." Her mother was delighted. It would be in September so she could still take her trip to Ireland with the girls in August. A wedding with all the people who cared about her and Roan—Ciara, Sylvia, Danele, Macy and Tomas, Roan's sisters, and Sammy had even bought tickets for Mateo and Isabella and their families.

Sammy and Roan finished their glasses of wine, said goodbye to Nicholas, and walked down the narrow, cobbled streets, with the setting sun laying cotton candy shadows on the path. They made their way back to their room in a spec-tacular inn ensconced in the cliffs of the Calderon. Sammy pulled Roan out to their balcony to watch the sunset. She leaned against the railing and Roan put his chin on her shoul-der, and said, "Do you know how much I love you, my dear Sammy?"

"I do."

As a puff of air, chilled by the sea, funneled upwards onto the balcony, they both turned and walked inside. Sammy paused to look over her shoulder one last time and, as the sun dipped into the sea, it was Peter's voice, his chuckle, his Sammy dear that she heard and she knew he was telling her everything was going to be okay.

ABOUT THE AUTHOR

Kathleen Mary O'Brien's career in journalism began as a columnist for a regional newspaper in the PNW, and encompassed travel writing, interviews, and news articles for many major publications. Her novels have received critical acclaim and she is an active member of the PNW writing community. Kathleen lives with her family on an island in Puget Sound, where she is working on her next novel in the World of Love Series, as well as an epic World War II novel. The Moment We Shared is her third novel.

ALSO BY KATHLEEN MARY O'BRIEN

If you liked book two of the World of Love Series, The Moment We Shared, then you will love Where We've Been—book one. Book three, Finding Our Way Back, set in Ireland with Ciara O'Rourke will be out in 2023—or sooner. To be the first to lean news about my other books before anyone else you can reach me at: kathleenmobrienbooks@gmail.com and I'll add you to my newsletter list. Please put Future Books in the Subject header.

Book one in the World of Love Series:

Where We've Been

Other stories:

A Light in the Heart